THE SEASIDE BOOK CLUB

HELEN ROLFE

Boldwood

First published in Great Britain in 2026 by Boldwood Books Ltd.

Cover Design by Alexandra Allden

Cover Images: Shutterstock

Paperback ISBN 978-1-80657-850-4

Large Print ISBN 978-1-80657-852-8

Hardback ISBN 978-1-80657-849-8

Trade Paperback ISBN 978-1-80657-851-1

Ebook ISBN 978-1-80657-853-5

Kindle ISBN 978-1-80657-854-2

Audio CD ISBN 978-1-80657-844-3

MP3 CD ISBN 978-1-80657-845-0

Digital audio download ISBN 978-1-80657-847-4

This book is printed on certified sustainable paper. Boldwood Books is dedicated to putting sustainability at the heart of our business. For more information please visit https://www.boldwoodbooks.com/about-us/sustainability/

Boldwood Books Ltd, 23 Bowerdean Street, London, SW6 3TN

www.boldwoodbooks.com

To all my readers,
Thank you from the bottom of my heart
for your continued support,
Much love, Helen x

PROLOGUE

DRIFTWICK BAY –
JURASSIC COAST – DORSET

Two weeks ago

Howard switched on the classic bronze table lamp at his desk. Darkness surrounded the cottage in Driftwick Bay, and silence – apart from the low hum of the laptop when he pressed the power button – cloaked the room.

Five minutes to go.

As the laptop warmed itself up, Howard went into the kitchen to fetch his mug of tea, and clutching it between both hands, he managed to get it back to the rear room of the cottage without spilling a drop.

He found the link for tonight's book club session in his emails and clicked, as usual almost taken by surprise by his face on camera. Sometimes he genuinely forgot that he was in his seventies, with grey hair and lines on his face that showed a life well lived, because when he disappeared into books he felt like a different person. With books he got to inhabit a whole range of worlds, meet a cast of different characters, some likeable, others not so much. He loved nothing more than absorbing himself in a story and becoming a part of it. And it wasn't only the books on his shelves at home that gave him pleasure, it was the many hundreds lining the shelves of Driftwick Bay Books, the bookshop he'd taken over soon after they moved down this way. He'd saved Driftwick Bay Books from being bought by a developer and turned into more holiday accommodation and it had not only warmed his heart to do so, it had also earned him kudos in the town with locals, who still thanked him to this day that they'd got to keep their beloved bookshop.

Howard's love of reading had been his companion ever since he was a little boy. He had always found bookshops and libraries magical and enticing. But owning a bookshop wasn't something he'd ever put on his wish list until he came here and heard on the local grapevine that the bookshop was about to be bought up and subsequently got rid of. He'd told the other members of the book club about the locals' plight, and he'd found himself saying out loud that he wanted to save it. He wanted to learn the ropes. He'd retired but he'd missed having a focus and this shop could make him and Bonnie a real part of this town where they wanted to spend the rest of their days. And so, with the encouragement of the members of the book club, he'd made a counter-offer to the bookshop's owner and while it wasn't as high as the money offered by the developer they agreed to sell it to him at the last minute. He'd signed on the dotted line and taken it on. And now, he couldn't imagine it any other way.

He caught sight of his copy of *The Railway Children* by E. Nesbit slotted in at the end of one of the shelves behind his desk. When it had been his turn to choose a title for book club he'd wanted the others to experience this one because it was a particular favourite. A couple of attendees had turned their noses up at the choice, as was their right – they'd get their own back soon he was sure. But his favourite people at the book club, Faye and Margot, had both been excited. Faye, in her late twenties, had never read it! Margot had but not for years and couldn't wait to leap into the story again. He imagined they'd found a more up-to-date version of the book than his rather battered paperback he'd had since his dad gave it to him in the late 1960s. His copy had yellowing well-thumbed pages, but diving into it again had been special. Set in the early 1900s, the story was a joy to read, full of charm with its English countryside and characters who were brave and kind.

As he'd reread it he'd gone back to his childhood. He'd been the boy on the steam train with his grandad during one of England's humid summers, the boy who loved the playground and making friends and being brave at the smallest of things. But mostly it had been an escape for him to lose himself in the story, which reminded him that he'd had a good life. He'd had seventy-one years and more experiences than many and he was grateful, but he needed to keep being brave just like those characters in *The Railway Children* were and stand his ground because he was being pressured by the developer who had wanted the bookshop originally and was still after it.

The screen in front of him changed as Faye, the young woman who ran the book club, came into view. When he'd joined up a year ago the book club had gone by its original name, The Seaside Book Club, and had been run by its founder, Clare. Clare was an insomniac who had sought solace in reading, but after she passed away Faye, her niece, took over her legacy. She was doing a fine job with it too. And soon after Howard joined, given the time of the book club was always at the midnight hour, he'd suggested they change its name to The Midnight Book Club. He'd been joking, he'd thought Faye would want to keep the original name, but Faye decided they could try it out. He'd felt bad, suggested The Midnight Seaside Book Club instead, to incorporate the original name, but she'd dismissed his worry and announced to everyone that from now on they would go by the name of The Midnight Book Club. The fact that plenty of members lived by the seaside or had strong ties to the coast made it a seaside book club anyway, she'd assured him with a smile.

Next to appear was Margot. The three of them were different generations but that didn't matter. They were the regulars, the ones who were always there, the constants while other members dipped in and out. Howard didn't mind in the slightest though because they seemed to have an easy rapport and usually had a bit of a natter before anyone else joined.

And as the town of Driftwick Bay settled down in their beds, Howard felt some of his weariness fall away when the carriage clock on the bookshelf ticked so that its hands met on the hour.

It was time. Time for the Midnight Book Club.

1

MARGOT

Fifteen minutes before midnight, Margot leaned across the bed to check that her husband was asleep. She didn't really need to. Perry had always been a heavy sleeper, a snorer, and once he was out for the count nothing would wake him. It had been the same throughout their entire marriage and she doubted it would ever change.

She slipped out of bed and crept downstairs, along the hallway, and down another flight of stairs into the basement of their country house near Ascot, Berkshire. The house was old and a bit creaky but they'd modernised a lot of the interior, and down here there was a gym to one side and on the other a walk-in cellar that could hold one thousand bottles of wine. It was a showpiece Perry liked to impress all their visitors with. She'd already been down here twice tonight – once with a business client of Perry's following a dinner she'd hosted, to give them the 'grand tour' of the house. And the second time was when Perry was cleaning his teeth. She'd smuggled her laptop down here so she'd be ready to go. Thanks to Perry and his job in technology, not to mention his drive to have the very best of everything, the Wi-Fi in the basement was excellent and it meant that every Wednesday she could be a part of the Midnight Book Club, a lifeline Margot hadn't quite realised she'd needed until she got involved almost a year ago.

She turned her laptop on. Most book clubs met at a reasonable hour but not this one. Run by Faye, a young woman who lived in Australia, the online book club was always held at midnight in England which was currently 9 a.m. local time in Queensland for Faye – moving to 10 a.m. for the host when England's clocks fell back at the end of British summertime. The original club had apparently been called the Seaside Book Club and had been run by Faye's Auntie Clare, who by coincidence had lived in Dorset, Margot's favourite county in the entire country. Clare, who had suffered from terrible insomnia according to Faye, had set up the club for others who might not be able to sleep and would want to chat books at the midnight hour. Margot had never met Clare, who had sadly passed away, but according to Faye her auntie had desperately wanted the club to continue after she'd gone and so she'd taken on her legacy.

The Midnight Book Club, as it was known these days, was something just for Margot, and for her, the time worked out perfectly. She'd joined up saying that she too struggled to sleep but really it was because this was the one thing she could do without Perry questioning it, or interrupting her, because he was rarely awake at midnight. Being a part of the club made her feel like the woman she'd been before she became a wife who had no life outside her marriage, and maybe that woman was still in there somewhere.

Members of the club couldn't always attend but every week herself, Faye and an older man called Howard, were always there. And each of them was connected to Dorset in some way. Howard had retired to Driftwick Bay on Dorset's Jurassic Coast, Faye was born in Poole and raised in West Lulworth, the town adjacent to Driftwick Bay, and Margot had grown up in Bournemouth. They loved to talk about all things Dorset and one evening, Margot floated back to one of her fondest memories. She usually kept her private life close to her chest. She was so used to not being able to share what went on at home, but over time she'd begun to like and trust these people, these friends. She'd recalled how her mother told her that Driftwick Bay was one of the most beautiful towns in the area. She'd shared how she and her mother had stayed in the bay for a short break, the sun shining down on them the first day as they admired the striking scenery of the coast, the rock formations of Durdle Door and Old Harry Rocks, the landscapes that stretched for miles in their beauty. Wind and rain had come after the first two days, flattening the grass on the undulating hills, adding a ferocity to the sea that made them both feel incredibly alive.

Something Perry had never questioned was Margot going to see her mother. He knew where she was and who she was with when she visited, but her mother had gone now. Margot no longer had that escape. Her mother had, however, in her wisdom, passed down the money from the sale of her house after she died, to her grandsons, Margot's boys, Sebastian and Alistair. She told Margot when she rewrote her will that she'd done it so that her money couldn't be something else that Perry could control.

Margot's sons now both had healthy bank accounts with the inheritance that had bypassed Margot, and although she had been in tears when she realised that Perry's controlling behaviour bothered her mother to such an extent she'd seen a solicitor to alter her will, Margot would be forever grateful that her sons had the freedom she herself lacked and craved.

She clicked on the Zoom link for the online book club. Occasionally she joined the session early so she was ready to go, and a few months previously Howard had, by coincidence, done the same. It was during their chat that first day and a few further conversations when nobody else was there that Margot had begun to open up. She'd not done that with anyone else, but Howard had been there for her, much like a father figure or a parent, neither of which she'd had for a very long time, and she'd felt listened to.

She pulled her hooded cardigan a bit closer around her. It might be July with its warm sunny days but down here in the still of the night it was chilly without the soft furnishings and deep carpeting of the rooms above. Sometimes she was tempted to do this in the lounge given she could clash cymbals right next to Perry's head and it still wouldn't rouse him – his body was programmed to wake to his 5 a.m. alarm and not much else – but she didn't want to risk having him find out and take something that she loved away from her. He'd taken enough already.

Was it crazy to wonder whether she felt the chill more now that the boys had left home and the house felt so ridiculously big? Sometimes she longed for the little student flat she'd shared with three others during her first and only year at Middlesex university, with its haphazard layout of non-matching furniture in the lounge, the bathroom with the grotty tiles but at least fully functioning shower, and the small bedroom she'd taken and made into her own space with twinkly lights around her pinboard and a beautiful purple duvet for a pop of colour. That year, embarking on a degree in English and American Studies, she'd felt as if the world was stretching out in front of her ready to grab with both hands. Everything had changed when she met Perry, got pregnant, and the life she'd had planned had been upended.

What on earth had happened to the last thirty years?

Margot had met Perry on a night out in a pub. They'd both been there with friends. His group had just taken part in the yard of ale challenge, which he won by a mile. He'd left the rowdy bunch he was with and headed for the door but with her standing in front of it he'd had to squeeze past and they'd got talking.

'You didn't want to try to win a second time?' she asked as another group lined up to attempt it.

Dressed in a deep-blue button-down shirt and jeans, with a jacket gripped in his hand, ready to face the cold January night, he was red-cheeked from either the alcohol or her attention. 'Work tomorrow,' he said. 'I need to keep my head clear.' And then he smiled. 'Clearer than *two* yards of ale anyway.'

She melted beneath his gaze and his smile. 'You finished way ahead of the others.'

'I've done it before, but I know when to stop.'

The way he said it endeared him to her. He was much more mature than any of the boys she'd met at university. He sounded in control, like he knew what he wanted.

They talked about her studies and his, the fact that he'd finished university and had already started a graduate job working for a tech company.

'Off they go again...' She watched his friends gearing up for the next challenge.

'They don't like to lose. Neither do I.' When she felt his hands on her waist it sent a shudder of pleasure right through her. He whispered in her ear, 'Let's get out of here.'

What had happened to that guy she'd met at the pub, the one who was mature and charming rather than controlling and manipulative? Or had he always been like that and she just hadn't seen it? He'd told her that night that he didn't like to lose, and that was Perry all over. He liked to win. At everything. The guy from the pub had gone and in his place was a man she recognised less and less as the years went on.

Margot's coping mechanisms to deal with Perry's behaviour varied. She kept a nice house, she was a dutiful wife, she kept everything and everyone organised. And that was the way it had been ever since they got married. But over time she'd given up friendships and her independence with every questioning glance and phrase he threw her way. Sometimes losing herself in the pages of a book was the biggest and best escape of all. She fell for heroes in a novel and became a part of the characters' lives, relationships and situations, instead of facing her own dismal reality that she didn't know how to get out of.

Margot had hoped Howard might be early on the Zoom session again tonight, but it was Faye, their host, who appeared first in a little rectangle with her name at the bottom corner. Her gaze was upwards as if she might be moving her computer mouse around to do something on her screen as she waited for the connection, but she waved at Margot and Margot waved back. She might not see friends in person any more, but book club was a weekly salvation that somehow kept her going.

'Hey!' Faye had the most interesting backdrop. It looked like she was sitting in a grass area, perhaps a garden, and the sun was definitely shining on the other side of the world.

Another rectangle on the Zoom session appeared, this time with Howard's face filling it.

'Howard, we can't hear you.' Faye's lips exaggerated each word for the man you couldn't help but adore. Her gaze went down and presumably she was sending him a message on the platform. He did this often. Sometimes he forgot the video, but usually he was on mute.

'Better?' he asked moments later, his voice now loud and clear.

'Perfect!' Faye, all Aussie-tanned and bright-eyed made Margot feel every bit of her forty-nine years. She'd never really felt that flourish of youth she should have had at university and in the years afterwards.

Faye looked confident, in control, happy when she asked, 'How are we this week?'

Another two members – Sarah and then Joel – appeared, eighty-one-year-old Sarah doing the same as Howard, and Faye repeating her prompts to switch on the microphone. Joel, fifty-two, always looked so serious but as soon as he spoke his face transformed and it was obvious he was as friendly as the rest of them.

They were still waiting for Winston to join if he was coming this week, so with a few minutes to go, just like on other weeks, they had a brief catch-up. When it was her turn Margot talked about her recent FaceTime with her youngest son, Alistair, who was doing a teaching degree apprenticeship. She gave them the latest on her eldest son, Sebastian, who was a ski instructor and went wherever the job took him. She didn't let on to any of the other book club attendees that both boys clashed with their dad so much that they put themselves at a physical distance she hated. Neither of her boys liked being in the family home any more and who could blame them? Margot could only blame herself.

She wished she'd been able to make things different for her sons. She'd thought about leaving her marriage over the years and Perry knew it, because more than once he'd dropped snarky comments about her being reliant on him and unemployable with no skills. He'd told her that she wouldn't be able to afford anything like their lifestyle on her own, that if she left she'd soon come crawling back. Margot had found it easier to stay than it was to ever try to walk out. But she was going to turn fifty on her next birthday. Was she really going to accept that this was it for the rest of her life?

Howard told them all about the walk he'd done at the weekend with his wife, Bonnie, on a short section of the coastal path near where they lived, with its spectacular views along the Jurassic Coast. What Margot would give to be there now. Her house and its proximity to London was great in some ways – close to airports for their holidays, good schools when the boys had needed them – but lately it felt more stifling than ever to be so close to the capital.

'How's the bookshop?' Joel asked Howard.

'Are you still being badgered into selling?' Sarah asked before Howard had a chance to respond to Joel.

Howard gave a slight nod. 'I've had another visit from a suit. They weren't successful with their bid to buy the shop. I was, so you'd think they would move on to something else. I can't say I enjoy them coming in so often. I feel like they see me as an old man who will give up eventually.'

'You could threaten to call the police,' said Margot, worried about Howard. He was in his seventies and she had visions of heavies going into his beloved bookshop and continuing to up the financial incentive for him to get out until he got so sick of it he had no choice. And that would be incredibly sad. He was a cheery soul as it was but since he'd taken on the bookshop he'd got even more of a metaphoric spring in his step and seemed to have found his calling in retirement.

'They're not doing anything wrong,' said Howard. 'I just hope they get tired of it. I know I've had enough.'

Faye frowned. 'Don't be pushed into something you don't want to do, Howard.'

'I promise I won't.'

'And keep us updated,' said Margot.

'I promise to do that too.'

'How are sales going?' Faye asked. She was always good at jollying the conversation along, whether it was a personal chat like this or about a specific book.

'It's going like gangbusters.' His remark brought a smile to everyone's faces. He clearly had no regrets about taking the shop on six months ago. Margot only wished she had his courage and could make such a major change in her own life.

Talk moved on to Faye when Howard asked, 'How is your dad finding it back here in Dorset?' Her dad had apparently swapped the Sunshine Coast of Queensland, Australia to come to England to be closer to his brother in West Lulworth two months ago.

'He's enjoying it, and spending time with his brother has been good for the both of them. Dad told me he can't wait for his first British winter in years.'

Margot's rectangle on the screen illuminated around the edges when she said, 'He'll soon lose that desire when he can't feel his fingers or his toes.'

Faye admitted, 'I miss it too sometimes. I have good memories of winters, rugging up in coats and hats and big woolly scarves.' Her family had emigrated when she was a teenager.

'Rugging up?' Howard interrupted.

'It's what you say as an Aussie,' said Faye.

'Bundled up,' Howard put in.

'Wrapped up,' said Joel.

Faye's smile grew as she noticed what Howard was wearing. 'May I just say, very nice PJs this evening, Howard. Are they new?'

He chuckled. 'Quite the opposite. These are my

oldest pair. You don't want to see the bottoms, but the top passes as acceptable – otherwise my Bonnie wouldn't let me be on camera.'

'You should get your wife to join in with us.'

'We'd all love to meet her,' said Sarah, squinting from behind a pair of glasses. She'd been coming to the book club intermittently for five years.

'Bonnie doesn't particularly like late nights. And she's not into books, remember.'

'I'll never understand how anyone isn't *into* books?' said Faye with a shake of her head.

They all felt that way, and it was easy to forget that not everyone in the world did. Ever since Margot was a young girl and got her first library card, she'd read whatever she could get her hands on. She couldn't even remember a time when she hadn't had a book next to her bed. Whether she'd had an exhausting day in pregnancy, or after the boys were born, or with the demands of catering work functions for Perry, doing all the laundry and keeping the house clean, she always found time to read at the end of the day. Even if it was just for five minutes. It was always worth it. It was a step back from the real world, after all.

'Bonnie really doesn't understand what the fuss is all about,' Howard went on. 'But then I don't understand her love of splashing colours all over a piece of paper.'

He'd told them before that Bonnie was a painter. 'What's she working on at the moment?' Margot indulged his desire to talk about his beloved. Part of what she loved about the Midnight Book Club was that it was as much about friendship as it was about the books. And she needed that desperately.

Howard momentarily disappeared from camera and came back into view with a picture resting on an easel.

'That's the bay!' said Faye. 'I recognise it. Oh, it's beautiful. I do miss Dorset.'

'With all that Queensland beauty?' Margot doubted. 'Surely not.'

'Oh, I do. There's something about the Jurassic Coast especially.'

'I wholeheartedly agree,' said Joel who lived in Scotland but had grown up in Devon. He was another member who had found the book club because he struggled to sleep most nights.

Margot admired the painting some more while Howard pointed out that the bottom of the picture was the foot of their garden and everything else was the view beyond – the road winding down towards the bookshop and then on to the sea, Lulworth Cove in the distance.

With no sign of Winston this week Faye announced that they should make a start.

'Whatever has happened to the Australian contingent?' Howard asked before they could get going. 'Are they all away on their summer holidays?'

Faye shook her head. 'It's winter here, remember.'

'That does not look like any winter to me.' Margot twirled her index finger. 'Turn the camera a bit.'

Amused, Faye turned her laptop, and into shot came the ocean, curved, with golden sands and white-tipped waves. It was stunning. And the vast expanse of blue sky didn't speak of winter in the slightest.

'Do you honestly miss winter here?' Howard asked.

'Sometimes I go down to Melbourne to get some proper cold,' said Faye and to a few doubtful faces added, 'You'd be surprised. We get snow in some parts of the country.'

Margot knew. Sebastian had skied over there last month.

'So what did everyone think of the book?' Faye took control, otherwise they were in danger of chatting way into the night before they even mentioned books.

Their latest read was *Where the Crawdads Sing* and this time everyone had finished it. They didn't always – Margot usually did, so did Howard and Sarah, but Faye was sometimes too busy with her job and Joel rarely got to the end of a book before the discussion. They'd pondered doing this only once a fortnight so everyone had a chance to read a full book, but to Margot's relief even those who didn't make it every week wanted it to continue the way it was. 'More chance of me making it then,' Sarah had said.

'I galloped through this one,' Howard enthused.

'I finished but it was a heavy read,' said Margot.

Sarah hadn't warmed to the story at all, and Joel had only liked it in parts.

Another Midnight Book Club had begun, and Margot had an hour of escape before she would have to slip back into bed, alongside the man she'd met one chilly January night, the man who had subtly changed over time. He wasn't abusive. He provided and then some, but emotionally he was closed off.

And perhaps worst of all, he didn't see her as anything other than his wife.

And he probably never would.

2

FAYE

Hosting the Midnight Book Club gave Faye a sense of normality and calm. It was as much of an escape as reading books and she'd needed it more than ever since the scandal broke and its subsequent fallout caused her whole world to fall apart.

Howard was right that the Aussie contingent of the book club had fallen away. She'd had one member (who she'd thought a friend) email to tell her that she didn't want to be linked with the Gunnersons – Faye's family – online, because you never knew who was watching these days. Another member had messaged to say, 'You're her, from the news!' She'd replied to point out that no, she wasn't. She'd been forced to add that the 'her' in question was her identical twin sister, Steph, also twenty-nine years old, also with bobbed blonde hair and a side part, as well as blue eyes and golden-kissed skin.

It seemed whatever her sister did still had the power to ruin things for Faye even after all these years.

Faye hadn't known anything about the scandal until the day she returned home to her apartment block after a long shift at the hairdressing salon where she worked. She'd bumped smack into a photographer who shoved his camera in her face to get the best shot, and badgered her all the way into her building. He'd called out enough questions that she got the gist of what had unfolded and once inside all she'd had to do was open up the internet on her phone to see exactly what was going on. It was all over the news. All over social media.

The scandal had been following her around ever since and she was only glad that her mother was far away and her dad was on the other side of the world. Both of them were aware of what was happening but at least neither of them were in the firing line – her dad because it would break his heart to see his daughters suffering, her mum because Faye wasn't sure she would be much help at all. Daria Gunnerson had always been selfish, didn't give much thought to other people's feelings when she decided to do something, and it seemed that with Steph, it was a case of like mother, like daughter.

Three weeks after the news that her sister was having an affair with a married politician more than twice her age broke, Faye hoped the gossip might have fizzled out, that people would move on to something else, but she'd been kidding herself. And what was worse was that Brad, the man she'd committed to spending the rest of her life with had left her to deal with it all on her own. He'd buggered off when the news hit, hiding away at his family's holiday house in Tasmania for the last few weeks, away from the glare of the media and the gossips. Then again, she supposed it was hard for him too. The young woman in the scandal was her sister, but the man embroiled in the affair was Brad's father.

As well as working as a hairdresser, Faye often helped out at her dad's water-sports business on an ad hoc basis. With her dad out of the country for the foreseeable future to be with his brother, his friend, Hugo, had stepped in to look after things and Faye had agreed to put more hours in for lessons with customers. Last week, however, she wished she hadn't been quite so helpful. She'd been booked in to take a beginner kayaker out on the Noosa River. The man had been clever. He hadn't asked her any questions before they got on the water – he was clearly a beginner and had no clue – and he'd waited until they were well away from their launching spot before he revealed he was a journalist wanting to get a different take on her sister's affair with a key politician.

That journalist had been lucky she'd led him back to dry land and not left him out there on the river to make his own way back. She'd been sorely tempted.

She felt her shoulders drop now as the current members of the Midnight Book Club got to talking about their latest read.

Faye had taken on this book club to continue her auntie, Clare's legacy. Auntie Clare had been a dreadful insomniac and during those wee small hours when she couldn't sleep Clare had found herself on book forums and threads, desperately grasping for something to take the edge off. She'd told Faye once that insomnia was dreadful but that at least she'd had books, and when she founded the book club which she ran at the midnight hour and realised other people had the same problem as she did it was as though everything had come together. She'd run the club for five years and had told Faye more than once that she would never ever give it up.

When she knew she was sick she'd been so determined that it carry on after she was gone that she'd instructed Faye's Uncle Frank to give Faye the money to cover an upgrade on Zoom. That way the sessions could run as far into the night as members needed.

Members were now all Northern Hemisphere people apart from Faye, but perhaps she should be glad about that. Without other Australian members the club had become a safe haven away from the news at home and any gossipmongers. She could lose herself in book discussions with Sarah, who was an unlikely thriller addict given she looked like a sweet old lady who would go for something cosy; she could hear about historical fiction from Winston, the classics from Howard, true crime from Joel, or women's fiction and romance from Margot.

Faye could do book talk. It gave her a different focus, allowed her to forget everything else. Stories helped her distance herself, regroup, get some perspective. She could pretend she was in a different world, not her real world, which at the moment was pretty grim.

At this morning's book club there had been five of them in the end, including her two favourite members, Howard and Margot, who never missed a week. It was worrying to hear that Howard was still getting visits from a developer who had set their sights on the bookshop. But knowing Howard, he would be polite but firm. She only hoped they were nice to him. He didn't deserve to be hassled.

'I was engrossed from start to finish,' Howard had said after they'd discussed characters, the setting, the underlying messages in the book. 'It was a powerful story.'

'It's been made into a movie too,' Margot announced.

'I've seen it,' Faye admitted. 'I watched it before I started reading the book.'

'You know the movie is never as good as the book,' Howard insisted. Sarah was inclined to agree with him.

'The book was powerful,' said Faye. 'But actually, I think I got to grips with the book more after seeing it on screen. I don't feel like it ruined the story for me.'

'Each to their own,' Howard replied with a nod from Sarah. Faye loved that they all had different opinions; it was what made their book club interesting.

'Not a moviegoer?' Margot asked Howard.

'Not really, are you?'

'I enjoy movies and from what Faye's said, I think

I need to watch the adaptation for this one.' She pulled a face as she admitted, 'I struggled with the story. Maybe it was just me.'

Faye wondered whether Margot was a bit like her – with other things going on in her life that made it hard to focus? Perhaps, also like her, Margot needed some escapism.

'Definitely watch the movie,' Faye urged Margot. 'I really enjoyed it. Ignore Howard.' She laughed at his expression. Sometimes he looked like he disapproved, but he never really did, he was quietly taking in everything that was going on around him.

'So what are we reading next?' Sarah asked. 'Can we avoid crime? The news is depressing enough.'

'And thrillers are uplifting?' Howard asked, earning a quiet chuckle from the eighty-one-year-old thriller fan.

'We haven't had a romance for a while,' said Sarah. 'I like those too.'

The word 'romance' must have been what made Howard peer closer to the screen. 'Faye, you're not wearing your engagement ring.'

She'd showed off her ring when Brad proposed; they'd all known how happy she was.

She had to think quickly. 'I often take it off for work. You know, chemicals and all that.'

The explanation seemed to suffice and after further talk of the next book they'd tackle, Howard yawned a third time and Faye suggested she let everyone go to bed.

Howard smiled. 'It's a real adventure doing this at midnight.' His face, illuminated by the desk lamp, was full of joy despite his tiredness.

'You have to get up and run a bookshop,' said Joel. 'I don't know how you do it.'

'It's a pleasure, that's why.' His smile, warm and friendly, spoke about the man he was.

'Sleep well, everyone. Or as well as you can,' she said for those she knew struggled to do this simplest of things, the same way Auntie Clare had. 'And I'll see you all next week.'

She'd closed down her laptop and sat for a while with nothing but herself and an incredible view for company.

Sod all those people who had fallen away from the book club because of the scandal – the real reason behind what had happened in her life to make her remove her platinum engagement ring with the emerald-cut diamond.

Eventually she stood up to get some feeling back in her legs. It was peaceful here with nature, the ocean, the lack of prying eyes. It was one of the best lookout spots on the Sunshine Coast.

Would she admit to her book club friends that she was no longer engaged? Maybe next week. Either that or put on a fake ring along with a fake smile and pretend everything was right with her world when really it was a hell she felt no more ready to face up to today than she had been yesterday.

She could almost imagine what someone like Howard would say when he heard how Brad had broken it off with her. She got the impression that Howard's marriage was one of those rock-solid partnerships, like her grandparents had had, there at each other's side through thick and thin.

Brad hadn't even broken it off with her in person, he'd done it over a FaceTime call when the miles separated her in Queensland from him in Tasmania where he was showing solidarity with his dad and the rest of the family. However, it soon became apparent over their messages that the running away had been as much for Brad's benefit as it had been for anyone else's. Phrases like *I* can't cope with all the attention, *I* hate what this is doing to my family, *I* have to focus on my big work project and don't need anything else on my plate, wore thin very quickly when she'd had no choice but to stay here. She didn't have the luxury of some place to run to miles away. She didn't have the ability to work from home, because she rented a chair at the local hairdressing salon for her clients and taught water sports or worked behind the hire desk at her dad's business. She'd had no other option but to stay in the firing line.

Their last call had been the one that ended it. She'd called Brad using FaceTime for a change as she wanted to see him rather than guessing at how he must be feeling or what he was thinking. It had been three long weeks and she was stressed, upset, lonely and had no idea when her fiancé was coming back. Her dad wasn't here either, and she couldn't bear to talk to her sister. She felt so alone.

On that last call with Brad it had been obvious that this was taking a toll on both of them and at first Faye had thought they could console each other, get through it together.

'How can we ever come back from this?' he'd asked. His dark hair had the same flick at the front that he hated and she thought looked cute. 'This is a complete nightmare, Faye.'

'I know, I'm living in it. Every single day.'

'Don't get pissed off that I left and came to Tasmania. I would never have been able to keep working at the office with this going on. My boss said the press were camped outside for a week to get my take on it.'

'I've had people showing up here too – you know I have.' She'd texted him enough times when calls didn't connect.

'I just can't believe this is happening.' He could barely look her in the eye.

'It's horrible.' Her voice wobbled.

'Dad isn't enjoying it much either.'

She cringed. Any mention of his father made her feel nauseous. And the man had brought this on himself. What did he expect, doing something so untoward when he was in the public eye? Faye had tried to imagine what Steph could've possibly seen in the slightly balding man with a beer belly and an uptight demeanour that he thought made him sound superior. She'd never told Brad that was what she thought of his dad, but every time Mark appeared on the television Faye saw him as one of those politicians you should never trust.

'My parents are doing their best to make things work,' he said. 'You always told me that your sister liked attention and was as selfish as they come.'

'She's still my sister.'

'I can't believe you feel sorry for her now.'

And she couldn't believe he was defending his father. He wasn't wrong about Steph, or about her feelings towards her sister, but hearing him place all the blame at Steph's feet hit her hard. 'No matter Steph's part in all of this, your dad is the one who's married, older, and in the public eye.'

'What's that supposed to mean? Are you trying to imply he pressured her?'

'No, I wasn't saying that.' She suspected Steph would've been in control all the way. She and her sister might look the same but their personalities couldn't be more different. 'All I'm saying is that she doesn't have a voice with the press; your dad does.'

'He's not spinning the story. All he's said publicly is that he regrets what he's done to his family.'

She tried to land on something neutral for them both. 'Do you know how they even got together?'

'No, but I'm guessing she went after him.'

'Because that's always the answer, isn't it,' she snapped. 'The woman's fault. The low-cut dress, the short skirt, the—'

'Stop it, Faye.' Irritated, he asked, 'Have you seen her?'

'No. And I don't want to.'

'My dad is sorry, you know. For what he's done. He hates that he has hurt those he loves.'

Faye couldn't bring herself to have any respect for the man. And with him saying his piece on the nightly news and current affairs programs and Steph staying quiet, Steph was just the other woman and the one in the wrong. She was condemned for her part and what was he? Lauded for standing together with his family? It was so wrong. No matter her clashes with Steph, her sister didn't deserve for this man to not show any remorse at the repercussions for her. By the sounds of it, Brad's father was only sorry for the effect his affair had on him and his life, and Faye had no doubt that a part of that was the regret at having been found out.

'My sister was supposed to be our bridesmaid,' she said in a small voice, her thoughts on her own life for a moment. Her dad would give her away. He'd said he'd fly back for the wedding. It was supposed to be their big day, the start of her life with Brad.

'When are you coming back?' she asked him when he said nothing in response to her comment about her sister.

He dragged a hand down his weary face and she knew there was something going on even before he confessed, 'I've had a job offer. Here. In Tasmania.'

She sat upright and rather than her legs tucked

beneath her they were fixed at a right angle. 'What are you talking about?'

'A week ago, I met with a recruiter. He mentioned a company who might be interested. I spoke to them, and it turns out they're offering a really good package.'

'Wait a minute,' she stammered. Was she shaking? Could he tell? 'You met with him a week ago?' The truth set in like an enormous rock pinning her down. 'You've been planning this?'

'I can't do it, Faye. I can't be a part of the fucking nightmare over there.'

'But you are a part of it! I'm a part of it. You can't just run away.' She shook her head, stood up, paced. 'I don't want to live in Tasmania.'

It took her a moment to realise that he didn't respond to her plea and a moment more to deduce that with his lack of response he'd told her everything else she needed to know.

A tear spilled traitorously onto her cheek. 'We're not getting married, are we?'

She'd expected Brad to call her back the second she hung up, or at least send a message, but nothing. He'd sent a text a few hours later, assuring her that he would cancel the wedding arrangements. She hadn't responded.

Who ended a relationship like that? Who ran away and left their fiancée to deal with an absolute shitstorm? What sort of man was he?

Not one she knew as well as she'd thought. That much was evident. And perhaps the truth had always been there, she'd just been swept up in the excitement of it all, a future, the family they might have.

That evening she'd removed the ring from the fourth finger of her left hand, the ring she'd watched catch the light the day he slid it on there and asked her to be his wife.

Now, with her laptop stowed in her rucksack, she left the ocean behind. She left the safe haven of the lookout point and the Midnight Book Club for another week, and with a baseball cap pulled down over her ponytail, she kept her head down with no desire to be recognised at all.

Her sister had fallen into bed with a married politician and along the way they'd used taxpayer money to fund their dalliance – flights, hotels, fancy dinners, a spa escape.

And the whole country knew about it.

3

BONNIE

Bonnie ran a duster across the cherrywood classic English desk. Howard had just come home from the bookshop, which he'd left in the capable hands of his assistant, Iris, and in about eight hours he would sit here, just like he had last week, open up the laptop and join in with the Midnight Book Club.

She moved on to dust the windowsills next to the double doors she'd left flung open to bring the July air inside. This room had the best natural light out of all the rooms in the cottage with its enormous windows on three sides, one of which had the doors that led out to the garden. It was a perfect space to have their reading room and art room combined.

She paused. She closed her eyes briefly and inhaled the sea breeze before she opened them again to admire the view. How could anyone resist doing so? From this quiet elevated spot in the town of Driftwick Bay nestled snugly near West Lulworth in Dorset, the rear garden of their cottage was bordered with low stone walls and hedges. They were also blessed with a beautiful view of the countryside sprawled on either side of the meandering road that led down towards Lulworth Cove.

After Howard's parents – her in-laws – had passed, this cottage, his parents' own retirement property, had become a holiday house, Bonnie and Howard's way to escape work and the busyness of their lives in Reading. But it had turned into so much more than that. Relocating to Driftwick Bay had been done swiftly and with no regrets as soon as Bonnie had taken retirement from her job as a district nurse. And after she and Howard went travelling together – conscious of having more days behind them than there were ahead, travel was something she wanted them to do before they ran out of time – they had settled in and made the town their home. Now they said hello to people in the street and in the shops, and they got to see this magnificent town and the stunning coastline whenever they liked. Being here on a permanent basis was the best thing they had done – she knew that already. Driftwick Bay was beautiful. They were a stone's throw away from the 95-mile stretch of Jurassic coastline in Dorset and had incredible scenery and walks at their fingertips. And even more importantly she and Howard had time together.

The cottage had needed work, but they hadn't done anything much until they moved here permanently – before that they were never here in the bay for long enough. Instead they'd carefully and considerately gone through Maureen and Brian's belongings each time they came, and for a while everything else stayed the same apart from the garden, which they either tended to if they had time on one of their visits or hired someone to come in and keep on top of things. They were especially aware of the hedges and keeping those healthy, as well as the wisteria around the front door that in the spring produced purple, pendulous sweet-smelling flowers that lifted the cottage's beauty even more.

A couple of summers ago they'd repainted the white picket fence surrounding the cottage and given the front door a fresh coat of ocean blue paint. Soon after that the bathroom had needed urgent repairs, which had turned into a remodel, and then they'd made the decision to enhance the kitchen ready for the day this would become the place they called home. They'd gone on to repaint all the rooms last summer.

Bonnie sighed and adjusted the clip that kept her curly hair piled on top of her head out of the way. Taking in the view wasn't going to get the housework done, was it? She'd always liked a clean house and coming to Dorset was no different in that respect to the Victorian two-up two-down terrace in Reading they'd lived in since they were married. Cleaning was at least far easier to fit in now that she was retired. There were a lot more hours in the day.

She should've done some housework earlier to get it over with but as usual, painting had grabbed her attention and before she knew it Howard's working day had come to a close and he was back at the cottage. He'd had a great day of trading at the shop he'd said. They'd both wondered whether he'd be able to hack going back to work again, but he was full of joy and enthusiasm, at least for now, and he had part-time help with Iris who knew the bookshop well, having worked there for the previous owner. The only irritating and slightly tricky-to-manage part of his new role was the developer who had been after the bookshop in the first place. The man or one of his minions kept visiting Howard at the shop and offering him more money. Howard said he didn't know how many more ways he could tell them that the bookshop simply wasn't for sale and never would be.

She turned away from the view to finish dusting the windowsill. Howard was in the kitchen staying out of the way at her insistence, even though he'd tried to pitch in like he always did. But he had a working life again so in her mind it was only fair that she did the bulk of the cleaning.

She dusted the back of Howard's leather reading chair, a chair so big and comfy it almost swallowed you up when you sunk into it. She cleaned the top of the tall set of drawers she used for her art supplies, plus the top of the table pushed into one corner where she could do some of her work. She moved on to dusting the vast collection of books Howard had built up over the years. He had a few of the classics, some he'd embraced, others not so much. He loved *Little Women* by Louisa May Alcott – she remembered him reading it for the Midnight Book Club and she'd heard all about it on one of the few times she'd woken up and wandered closer to the back room. He didn't know but occasionally she'd sat on the tiled floor in her nightie outside the room, a blanket beneath her bottom and pulled around her, and listened to her husband of more than four decades laugh and chat away about his love of reading. The way he talked about characters was the way he spoke to and about people in real life, with respect and understanding.

These books on the shelves were Howard's treasures: a copy of Kenneth Grahame's *The Wind in the Willows* that he'd found at a second-hand shop and looked like it had been loved for many years; a signed copy of *The Da Vinci Code* by Dan Brown: a special edition of an Agatha Christie murder mystery she'd gifted him last Christmas. He had a whole variety of genres, many titles collected since boyhood including The Secret Seven books by Enid Blyton as well as the entire collection of The Famous Five books, all a little bit tired and worn, but Howard had told her that was what made them so special.

For years Howard had attended book clubs in person. Some of them were questionable: one seemed to focus more on the alcohol content of a meeting than the word content; another was too wishy-washy, he said, with nobody really wanting to read anything that challenged their minds; another was single genre and that wasn't for him as he liked to read widely; and the last one had simple fizzled out as people dropped away for alternative commitments.

Howard had found the book club a year ago and, being a night owl, attending at midnight wasn't a problem for him. When he took on the bookshop Bonnie had suggested he start his own club instead, perhaps run it at a more sociable hour, but he'd insisted that the club that met at the midnight hour was still the best thing for him – he didn't have to host, he could do it from home, and he could wear his pyjamas if he liked. Howard never missed a session, even if he was feeling under the weather and should be tucked up in bed letting her fuss over him. Books to him were the best type of medicine and they made him happy.

As she carried on with the dusting her mind reflected on the last nine months. They'd gone by in a bit of a whirlwind since she retired. She and Howard had gone travelling a fortnight after she wrapped up her working life, much further afield than either of them had ever been. Of course asking Howard not to read for two months would've been like asking him to chop one of his legs off and so he'd bought himself his first Kindle especially for their trip. The Kindle had gone with them on safari to Africa, on a boat trip along the Norwegian fjords; it had accompanied him on the many rail journeys connecting them from one European country to another, and amid all of that he'd kept up with the Midnight Book Club online – no matter what time zone they were in.

Bonnie couldn't understand the allure of books, but then again Howard couldn't understand her passion for painting. She'd taken a sketch pad with her on her travels, along with a set of pencils, and many a time she'd disappeared into her own little world, mostly while Howard was reading. She and Howard were different in enough ways that it made their relationship interesting, and yet totally on the same wavelength with other parts of their lives.

Her chores complete, she went into the kitchen where she found Howard eating a biscuit and of course reading a book.

'I'm going to nip out for a walk.' She loved the lengthy days that came with summer. She washed her hands at the sink. 'I want to get to the post office before it closes.'

She turned to look at her husband as she dried her hands and pumped a little of the cream from the ceramic dispenser next to the sink into her palms. 'Howard, did you hear what I said?'

He looked up.

'I'm going for a walk,' she reiterated, the cream all rubbed in now.

He refocused on his book. 'I'll come with you.' And still reading, he popped the last bit of his biscuit into his mouth.

'You've only just walked up the hill.'

'It's good for me,' he said. 'And don't worry, I won't be nipping into work. Iris is closing up. She'll tell me off if I go back in.'

Iris was lovely and firm for which Bonnie was grateful. She liked that Howard didn't do ridiculous hours now he'd taken on the bookshop. He came home to her at a reasonable time. 'I'm leaving now,' she told him. She wasn't, she still had to find some sandals and get her bag, but if she told him that he'd snatch another few pages before he even thought about getting ready.

He didn't take his eyes off the book. 'No, you're not – you haven't even got your shoes on.'

She started to walk away. 'Getting them on now,' she called back over her shoulder.

Howard didn't take long to get himself together and ready to leave. And as usual they'd only just locked up when he took her hand.

They headed down the hill towards the shops. The only thing Bonnie didn't like about Driftwick

Bay, and the reason they'd rarely spent summers down here previously, was the crowds drawn to the Jurassic Coast, especially Lulworth Cove and Durdle Door, and all the other hidden treasures. She could see why of course. But selfishly she couldn't wait for September when the busyness would fade. She was a people person – she'd had to be with her job – but she also liked solitude and already she was thinking about the kids returning to school, adult groups heading back to their own homes and jobs, and the town once again becoming a little quieter. This morning's painting session had been wonderful though, because she'd purposely got outside nice and early. There'd been a light breeze, birdsong in the background, the crashing of the waves in the distance and the odd screech of a gull overhead, rather than any traffic noise or tourist chatter as holiday-makers made their way past the cottage and down the hill.

First stop in the small town was the post office where she posted a letter to Beverly. They communicated by WhatsApp most of the time but Beverly had said when Bonnie retired that she loved to write and receive letters, so Bonnie would surprise her with this one. The pair had worked alongside each other for more than a decade and Bonnie missed their friendship. She got a little thrill sending the letter on its way and tutted to herself that she was far too late to stop at the bakery as she'd hoped and chat with Cathy the owner or pick up their favourite farmhouse whole-meal loaf. They'd had supermarket-bought loaves for years until they were within walking distance of this bakery and now they were converted, favouring the most delicious breads, free of all the additives and preservatives that had become so commonplace.

Time to head back up the hill again, the hill that should help keep them fit as they cruised into old age. *Cruised* – Howard had started using the word when they were on safari and it had stuck. They'd both worked for so many years – she as a district nurse for Berkshire Healthcare, he as a civil servant in public administration, that she supposed this sort of life did feel like cruising. But, as she was sixty-six and younger than his seventy-one years, she'd told him that while he could use the term *cruising*, there'd be no talk of old age just yet.

'I just want to nip down to the telephone box li-brary,' said Howard.

'You could've done that after work,' she said with a fond roll of her eyes, because it shouldn't surprise her. It was in sight after all and no matter he'd spent all day with books, he loved looking inside this community initiative that saw people taking paperbacks out and leaving one in their place. He'd never been one to resist anywhere that had books, whether for free or for sale. At the airport terminal during their travels she'd known she could get through several cups of tea while he perused the books in whatever shop he came across. He'd found a gem of a bookshop in Amsterdam, and in Venice as they'd relaxed in a gondola she'd half expected him to jump in the canal and swim to the open door of the bookshop he'd spotted.

While Howard went down to the telephone box library Bonnie paused. This spot was perfect. She'd not thought about it before. Three-quarters of the way up the hill, it took in the best of the main street in Driftwick Bay, its small collection of shops, the mouths of the cobbled walkways, the lovely red of the postbox, the surviving phone box that Howard had now opened the door to. There was a sneak peek of Lulworth Cove way beyond but, best of all, Howard's bookshop to the left had a commanding presence with its beauty. This view would be a joy to paint.

She took a few photographs with her phone so

she could pin one or two to her easel while she worked.

When Howard emerged from the telephone box library they started the walk up the hill back to the cottage.

'You didn't grab a book.' She hooked her arm through his, glad he was steady on his feet. He wasn't always, another thing that came with old age she supposed, and when things like that happened she knew he worried about developing Parkinson's like his brother had before he passed away. It was one of the reasons she'd retired sooner than she'd really been ready for, so that if either of them were faced with a life-altering illness or disease, they would have at least done the things they wanted to do, and they wouldn't have any regrets.

'Not this time.' He pulled her arm in a little tighter against his torso. 'I might donate a couple more though. I thought you'd appreciate me getting rid of some. I did promise I wouldn't bring home too many more books when I bought the bookshop after all.'

She laughed. 'Can I have that in writing?'

The rest of the evening passed with dinner, a Pimm's in the garden to make the most of the weather, and when bedtime rolled around Howard climbed into bed beside her to read for a while before he would get up again and disappear into the back room quietly for another Midnight Book Club.

She switched off her bedside lamp when she grew sleepy. 'You know, a lot of wives might be upset if their husband had a weekly midnight rendezvous with at least two other women, let alone if he still had his pyjamas on.'

His laughter rumbled in his belly and she felt him put a kiss to her cheek. 'Good job you're not a lot of wives then isn't it.'

'Goodnight, Howard.'

'Goodnight, my love.'

She fell asleep, content. Time together was a precious thing and one that should never be taken for granted.

4

___

MARGOT

Margot was making a shopping list and planning the meals for the week. She liked to be organised before going to the supermarket, otherwise she'd wander aimlessly up and down the aisles and have Perry ask why she'd been out for so long. It was amazing how a businessman as busy as he was had the time to keep tabs on his wife using text messages, the app on his phone, and the doorbell security camera as well as the never-ending questions.

She caught sight of the calendar on the fridge door flipped over to the month of August. She didn't need reminding that it was Wednesday, the Midnight Book Club was tonight and it had been three weeks since she last attended. Perry had booked them to go out to dinner with clients two weeks in a row, both dinners on a Wednesday night, the very night she appreciated his strict, and somewhat anal, bedtime of 11 p.m. so she could sneak off once he was asleep. Those nights out could've got them home in plenty of time, but instead they'd led to drinks after the meal, then it was on to cigars, and they'd ended up getting home at just gone midnight on each occasion so she'd missed the only thing she looked forward to every week.

It sounded ridiculous that she didn't have a life outside this house apart from an online club. It wasn't as if the housework, the shopping, the admin tasks and what remained of her parenting duties now the boys were adults took up every hour of every day. But, Perry had made sure she'd been kept so busy with all of those things over the years that the very few friends she'd had fallen away one by one. Trinny, her closest friend from mother's group when Sebastian and her son, Marty, were a couple of months old was the only one she was still in touch with, but even then Trinny was busy running a bridal gown business in Edinburgh and they barely got time to catch up on the phone let alone meet up. Bethany, the mum she'd hit it off with the most after Alistair was born – the boys were born so far apart

that the first group had already disintegrated and
Trinny had returned to work five mornings a week –
called now and again and they'd met up once a fortnight for a long time. But that had faded away too
with Bethany's mother needing care and Bethany
relocating to North Wales.

Tonight, Margot was determined not to miss
book club. She was desperate to see her friends again
and feel that little bit less alone, and she especially
looked forward to seeing Howard, who had been so
kind to her.

The first time she and Howard had talked about
her marriage, she hadn't intended to share her secrets with him. They'd been chatting normally,
mostly about his bookshop, when she'd suddenly
jumped up and disappeared off the screen. She'd
thought she heard a noise upstairs but it must have
been the trees outside in the wind or the washing
machine on its spin cycle because there was no sign
of Perry when she checked. She'd gone back down to
the basement but trying to act nonchalant hadn't
fooled Howard.

'You look like you've seen a ghost,' he'd said
to her.

She was still shaking. It wasn't like she was
doing anything wrong, but Perry liked to keep her

close. He didn't like her doing things without him or away from the house, and if he knew she was in an online world with people he hadn't vetted, he definitely wouldn't approve. He would put a stop to it like he had her tennis and any shopping spree that was solo and too far away from home. He often went out with her, suddenly able to be away from the office, or he invented something that desperately needed seeing to at the house when she'd still been at the stage of inviting friends over, which felt like forever ago now.

'The wind here is terrible,' she told Howard that night. 'The trees are bashing the windows. And the washing machine is on late. There's not normally any sound when I'm down here for book club.' She'd been reading and lost track of time, which was why the washing was on, because Perry wouldn't be happy if he didn't have the appropriate shirt to go with the right suit in the morning.

Howard wasn't fooled, however, and asked her what was really going on. 'Are you okay, Margot?'

Despite her best efforts her face betrayed her and all of the stress, the build-up of her feelings of failure, the misery inside her marriage, came to a head. 'Actually, no. I'm very much not okay, Howard. And I haven't been okay for a really long time.'

'I'm a good listener,' he'd said to her kindly. 'And it's just the two of us at the moment.'

The invitation was like an open door to a whole new part of her, being able to tell someone how she felt.

'This is your time, Margot,' Howard had said after she told him everything. 'This book club is an adventure for me, but it sounds like it's an escape for you. And we are friends, all of us. We are here when you need us. Never forget that your life is your own, nobody else's. Nobody has the right to take from you the way your husband seems to.' She knew all of this of course, but hearing a friend say it felt different. 'Don't lose yourself because of someone else,' he'd finished. He hadn't made her feel silly for not leaving, or told her to simply walk out. Somehow he'd understood just how hard it was for her.

They'd been interrupted then by Faye appearing on the screen, and another book club had got underway.

Perry came into the kitchen now while she was still making her shopping list. He had a late start at the office after an early morning meeting in his study. He spotted the postcard from Sebastian on the kitchen bench and picked it up, but he put it down without reading what it said. 'Nice to see Sebastian is still bumming around in New Zealand.'

She didn't contradict him, or remind him that their eldest son was working hard over there. It just wasn't worth it.

When Perry went into the hallway, she picked up the postcard and read it again. The wording on the back was short and to the point, as it had to be with the limited space – a quick update of things he'd seen that week. Sebastian's phone calls were few and far between, but she loved that he sent a postcard every couple of weeks from wherever he was. This wasn't the first from New Zealand, but it was a different picture – the first had been a photograph taken at dusk showing the lights of a small town with water nearby and mountains in the background whereas this one was of Lake Wakatipu, which was stunning. The image had her wanting to pack her bags and travel, something she'd never done solo because she'd never had the chance. And not for the first time she yearned for that degree she'd missed out on, the year in America she would have experienced as part of it.

She fixed the postcard beneath a drawing pin on the pinboard so it was on display with the others.

Seeing them all warmed her heart every time she looked at them.

'There are too many bloody cards on that board.' Perry was back and now and frantically searching the kitchen, moving on to checking the windowsill behind the curtains.

She ignored his remark about the postcards because she knew what he was looking for. 'Your laptop is in the butler's pantry. On the shelf behind the sink,' she said. 'I had to move it while I cleaned the inside of the windows.' And the table, the floor, the backs of the chairs. She was nothing if not thorough.

He disappeared into the pantry but the next thing she heard was him roar a swear word that made her jump.

He came out, red in the face. He snatched up the tea towel she'd just changed and hung on the handle of the oven. 'What happened to the bloody plumber?' He wiped the front of his shirt vigorously. She could only assume he'd not leaned over the sink carefully enough to reach the shelf behind. The issue with the tap hadn't been sorted yet so water kept pooling around the sink.

'This is a priority!' His arm shot out beside him, his fingers splayed, indicating the direction of the problem in the pantry as if she didn't already know.

'He's due at midday today.' She wanted to point out that plumbers were busy, and sometimes other people were a bigger priority, but Perry would never understand. He liked things to be done his way, right away.

His temper was another thing that had ramped up since they got together. He shouted often, whether in frustration at something that had happened, something he had done, or something she had or hadn't done. He was never violent towards her, but he didn't have to be. The way he behaved made her world smaller by the day and slowly she'd shrunk into the background.

He put the strap of his laptop case over his shoulder while still swearing about his shirt and the 'bloody water' and the 'incompetent plumber'. He gestured to the pinboard she was standing beside. 'Time to thin that out.'

She said nothing, just stepped away as he muttered, 'The boy could've had a proper career.' The age-old argument reared its ugly head again. 'They both could.'

Sebastian *had* a career. It just wasn't the one Perry had wanted for his eldest son. And so did Alistair, but Perry didn't like his choice either.

'They're both happy,' she said without looking at

him. She didn't usually argue the point, but when her sons rather than her were being criticised, she couldn't stay silent for long.

'Yeah, well, happy doesn't pay the bills, does it.'

He'd probably heard that sort of thing as a boy from his own father. Had it really encouraged him or had it ever made him feel so down about himself that he wanted to run away? Just like their sons had done. They both lived far away from home and Sebastian had put as many miles between them as possible. She was just glad that her boys had each other. They got on well and always had done, despite the age gap of nine years. She never wanted them to lose that connection. Perry had accused her many a time of mollycoddling them and babying them rather than turning them into proper men. But parenting was the one thing she did her way and she'd kept strong on that.

Perry took his keys from the hook on the wall next to the butler's pantry before reaching for the coffee she'd pre-made him in his thermal cup with the lid and left next to the shiny new Ninja coffee machine. He'd bought the machine last year desperate for barista-quality coffees at home but he'd never bothered learning how to use it. Instead she'd been the one to read the manual and had added barista to her housewife résumé alongside house-keeper, washer-upper, picker-up of random ties and shirts left on the backs of chairs dotted around the house, entertainer of sinfully boring businesspeople, trophy wife when required on important nights out, and generally a person who was close to invisible. She felt like a foreign maid who came in, didn't speak the language so kept quiet, did the job while the person who'd hired her carried on as if she wasn't even there at all.

When had she become this woman, at someone else's beck and call?

She knew when. It was the moment the home pregnancy test was positive and she'd given up her dreams to support Perry in his.

She sometimes wondered what Perry would say if she told him 'no' more often, but like a lot of things, that would create tension, an argument, un-ease she could really do without.

The solid front door closed with a thud and no goodbye from Perry. Still, at least another wretched corporate dinner wasn't planned; that much was a relief. And he'd be gone until the early evening at least, which meant she had a nice long, peaceful day to get things done. The plumber would come and hopefully sort the sink, and they were also having the lounge repainted and with the furniture moved out of there – she suspected that was why they'd had the dinners out and she hadn't had to entertain here – there was plenty of cleaning to do. Too much dirt lurked behind soft furnishings and only came to light when they were moved from their normal positions.

If her friends could see her now they would be appalled. Maybe it was a good thing that she had nobody close to her any more. Bethany's husband had moved to Wales for her when she needed him to. He stood by her side no matter what. Trinny had a partnership with her husband – Trinny ran her business, her husband was a police detective, and somehow they juggled everything: their son's activities, their daughter's dance schedule, their own plans. Her friends had spouses who supported them and in return they did the same. But for Margot it was all one-sided. It was all give on her part and take on Perry's.

She finally left the house and made her way to the supermarket to do the weekly shop. She had her list; she was organised. She wouldn't be more than an hour or so. But as she came out of the supermarket her trolley crashed into another. She apologised and was about to head for her car when she realised the other person was Juliet who lived a few doors down from her on the same side of the street.

'Margot, how are you?' Juliet's smile didn't seem forced. It seemed genuine, which was in a way much worse. She was another friend who had fallen away or rather, been driven away by Perry.

Margot gave her standard answer of, 'I'm very well thank you.'

'And how are your boys?'

'They're doing great.' She recapped where they both were and asked after Juliet's daughter, Sarah.

Sarah had been a good friend to Alistair, who had been at their house more than he probably should have, more than he would have had Perry not been so awful to live with. Margot had never heard Juliet or her husband talk to their daughter the way Perry talked to his sons, and it made her even more sad that their memories of growing up and family time were tainted with their dad's lack of interest or dis-approval.

'Well, I'd better go.' Juliet had a trolley full just like she did. 'I've got my in-laws coming for lunch. But it was good to see you.'

Margot's smile and spirits faded when Juliet waltzed off.

Despite only living a few doors away they hadn't

really known Juliet and her husband, Mike, until they bumped into them at the tennis club one day. Perry had wanted to learn how to play properly because one of his colleagues had suggested they have a match and by his own admission he wasn't very good. Margot had taken a chance and asked whether she could have lessons as well, and she must have caught him at a weak moment because he was all for it. So, while he had his lessons, she played other women at the club, and slowly Margot felt a connection to real life opening up to her.

Margot and Juliet soon became friends. They shopped together, they went for lunch or coffee at the weekends, and for a while it had been good. In fact Perry had applauded the friendship until he met Juliet's husband. Mike, a tactile person, had hugged Margot to thank her for the flowers she'd sent after his mother passed away and Perry hadn't said a word at the time. But his suspicions that the man was after his wife were confirmed when he cancelled their tennis club memberships without discussion, using the excuse that he had too much work. Perry didn't stop her going to see Juliet but Juliet worked during the day and Perry was home in the evening, so it was difficult. And if Juliet came to their house, Perry was so cold or abrupt that eventually she stopped coming.

Margot was only thankful that Alistair and Sarah kept the friendship they'd found as their mums got to know each other, a friendship that blossomed at Sarah's home well away from the tension at Alistair's.

Back at the house she hauled all the shopping inside, lingering for a moment in the doorway as she watched two women power walking past, engaged in conversation. Friendship, she missed it; she yearned for it.

But all she could do was close the door to the rest of the world she barely felt a part of any more.

* * *

Margot had filled her day with cleaning the lounge, now the furniture was out ready for the decorator to start in a few days, cooking and ironing, and although she had an evening meal prepared at the usual time, Perry waltzed in well after she'd finished and grunted that he'd eaten with a colleague. No apology, no thanks for her hard work. He just left the kitchen after dumping his laptop bag on the other end of the table.

Margot trudged up the stairs wearily once the

remains of the Bolognese sauce was packed away in the freezer and the dishes were done. She ran a bath and luxuriated in a long soak. Just what she needed. Although it didn't fix anything, did it?

When she came back downstairs she knew Perry was in the lounge – she could see him from the hallway, his long legs crossed in front of him. He was most likely kicking back with a nightcap. Heading for the kitchen she wished she'd thought to put the rubbish out before her bath – Perry rarely did it and so she'd have to make sure it was done. But it wasn't the bin she was focused on when she walked into the room. Her eyes were drawn to the pinboard. The near-to-empty pinboard.

All of Sebastian's postcards had gone. All that was left beneath a couple of discoloured drawing pins was a receipt for a new suit Perry had ordered and a takeaway menu.

She yanked off the lid to the recycling bin. But they weren't there.

She went to the bin praying they were inside and sure enough, they were. He hadn't even bothered to push them down to bury them amongst the rest of the rubbish.

She took out every single one of them, found a plastic bag from the drawer, put the cards inside and then went back upstairs where she stashed the bag beneath the bed.

How could he do that? How could he blatantly get rid of the postcards Sebastian had thoughtfully sent across the miles? Was it to get back at her? Or was it to get back at his son who he thought could do better?

She had no idea but this man wasn't someone she recognised. He wasn't a man she wanted to be around any more.

She put the rubbish outside in the bigger bins and once she'd washed her hands went down to the basement after checking Perry was still in the lounge. She wouldn't confront him. He'd said the pinboard needed clearing, end of story.

She opened up the cupboard where they kept their luggage ready for when it was needed for the next fancy trip. She looked at the suitcases longingly.

All she had to do was reach in, pull one out, put a few things inside and turn her back on her life.

She was the only person who could change things for the better.

Her hand touched the handle of the red suitcase but she withdrew it when she heard footsteps above, turned off the light and went up the stairs.

Could she really leave? Or was Perry right? Years

ago she'd told him she wanted a divorce but he'd shut her down, told her she would be nothing without him and would soon come running back. And ever since then she'd thought he was probably right. And if that was going to happen she'd rather not leave in the first place.

She went to bed earlier than usual and when she heard the creak on the landing near their bedroom that meant Perry was having an early night, she quickly put down her book, switched off her lamp and pretended to be asleep. It wasn't unknown for him to want sex if he wasn't falling into bed late. She'd avoided being intimate for months now and she had no intention of giving him any more of herself than she already had.

This had to stop.

When the snoring finally began, regardless of everything going on in her life, she crept out of the bedroom and down to the basement.

At last, it was time for the Midnight Book Club.

5

FAYE

Faye hadn't been as enthusiastic as usual when she'd logged on this morning. For the past three weeks her most hardy book club attendees, Howard and Margot, hadn't turned up. She hoped they hadn't left for good. But the way her luck was going these days anything was possible.

She'd chosen to do this book club session in a quiet café well away from her apartment and the town's main drag, away from the water-sports business, away from anyone who knew her and away from the salon, because even that had started to become uncomfortable. She'd thought she could manage, hold her head up high until the gossip died down, but she couldn't do it any more. She'd cancelled her clients for the next month, told the salon she'd be on long-term leave. It was all too much. Aside from the scandal and the fact that she was still furious with her sister for bringing this drama to their family, she also needed time to adjust to life now she wasn't getting married. She'd gone between being devastated about losing Brad, to angry at how he'd ended things, then she'd gone all the way back to being upset. She'd texted him; he hadn't replied. She'd called; he hadn't answered. She wanted to ask how he could throw away the last two years of them being together and the plans they'd made. But perhaps given he'd done it so easily and now wasn't contactable, she'd had a lucky escape.

She shivered as the temperature appeared to drop and a familiar scent hung in the air. It was going to rain – she was sure of it – and her hopes were fading that the book club was going to happen this week. The only consolation was that nobody here in the café was looking at her. People would think she was just another freelancer making the most of a day working from home, her laptop in front of her, sipping on a coffee as she got things done.

Within thirty seconds of her thinking it, a few drops pre-empted proper rainfall. It had been sunny when she'd arrived but now she watched each drop hit the ground and rebound off, creating a little dancing pattern all the way along the street. It wasn't even wet season yet, not in August, that would come between December and February when the humidity would hit too.

She pulled her table a little bit away from the edge so she was definitely fully under cover. The screeching sound of the legs on the ground announced to everyone what she was doing.

A waitress nearby rushed over to help her. 'You don't want your laptop to get wet.' She looked at the near-empty cup. 'More coffee?'

'Yes, please. Soy latte?'

If the waitress recognised her, she was kind enough not to say. That or the waitress had decided it was none of her business, which Faye wished everyone else could understand.

The rain upped its tempo in a way that suggested the Queensland weather gods liked to remind residents that they weren't in charge.

Faye listened to the downpour and took out her copy of Maeve Binchy's *Circle of Friends*, the book Winston had chosen last week when it was just Faye, Winston, and Joel at the session. Apparently Maeve Binchy was his mother's favourite author. He'd read *Light a Penny Candle* and loved it. She wasn't sure why his admission had been a little sheepish – men were after all allowed to enjoy whatever sort of fiction they liked, just as women were.

At least she had a good book to lose herself in while she waited to see whether anyone else turned up to this week's book club. Winston and Joel had already sent their apologies, and Sarah had said two weeks ago that this week she wouldn't be able to make it. So now it was just Howard and Margot who would possibly sign in but so far, neither of them were here.

She opened up the book as her second coffee arrived. Novels set in Ireland had a magic all of their own and the setting reminded her of her time in England. She remembered the flip of the seasons, clearly delineated from one another. Right now they'd be in summer with the long days they didn't get here in Queensland no matter the time of year, the bright colours of flowers and sunshine that the middle of the year brought with it, the coming alive of a country that had felt dormant over winter. She missed the seasons and she missed her dad and with the scandal going on and losing Brad as well as another clash with her sister, she felt so alone. She wanted to hide herself away until the vultures backed off.

She breathed in the smell of rain as she sipped her coffee, mesmerised by the weather. Petrichor, wasn't that the word for the smell that came with rain? It had been in a book they'd chosen for book club a couple of months back. She'd never realised rain officially had a smell. She'd thought it was her, imagining the earthy aroma, the scent she often detected even before the rain came, like she had some kind of superpower.

Did the rain smell different in England? In Dorset?

She was almost too preoccupied to notice she wasn't on her own in her Zoom session any more because here was Margot, wearing beautiful navy silk pyjamas with a thin white stripe around the collar.

'Margot! It's wonderful to see you!'

Margot beamed. 'You too! I've missed you. Where is everyone else?'

She explained about Joel, Winston, and Sarah. 'And Howard hasn't been here for three weeks,' she added lastly.

'Three weeks? That's not like him.'

Margot had sent her apologies each time she couldn't make it but Howard hadn't. 'He hasn't emailed me at all,' she shared with Margot.

'Have you sent him a message?'

'I sent him one last week and the week before. He didn't reply.'

Margot paused. 'You don't think...'

'Don't think what?'

'Well, he was being hassled by the developer. At first he sounded like he was taking their little drop-in visits in his stride, but the last time he mentioned it he sounded like it might be getting to him.'

'I thought so too.' And Faye hated thinking his life was being impacted by someone bothering him. She knew what that was like after all. 'But I'm sure he's fine.'

'Hopefully we'll hear from him soon,' said Margot.

'I'll send him another email later on. Perhaps he's just busy. The bookshop sounds popular.'

'It does, and do let me know if he replies, won't you?'

'Of course.'

Margot frowned. 'What on earth is that noise?'

'It's a different sort of ambience, isn't it?' Faye turned the laptop briefly to show the downpour, which looked all the more impressive as it hit the canopy and ran straight off.

'That sound is rain? It's so loud!'

'Tropical rain.' Faye turned the laptop back so

that she was on camera. 'And in the summer it's often way heavier than this.'

'I love the rain.'

She could remember a similar feeling when she was a little girl, dancing in and out of puddles with her sister, their wellington boots on, when rain was fun rather than a nuisance. When her twin was a little girl just like her and didn't come with all the drama she liked to surround herself with now.

'When I lived in England the rain always made me want to cosy up,' she told Margot. 'You can't do that here when it gets hot and sticky. You just have to shelter.'

'Well, it looks like you've picked a good spot to do that.' But then she frowned. 'It's odd with just the two of us. I don't think this has happened before, has it?'

'No, not that I can remember. I don't think it happened to Auntie Clare either. She built the book club for insomniacs like her and from memory she said there were usually a few of them attending each week.'

'Your auntie sounds like a real character.'

'She was, and I really wanted to continue the book club for her.'

'She'd be proud of you.'

'Not for how many members show up she wouldn't.'

Margot gasped. 'Please tell me you're not going to put a stop to the club?'

That was what she'd been thinking as members fell away and even her hardiest members hadn't shown for the last three weeks but seeing Margot's reaction, and remembering what the club had meant to Auntie Clare, how could she? 'Don't panic. I intend to keep it going and who knows, maybe next week there'll be a whole load of us.'

The rain upped its tempo and Faye had to speak a bit louder as they got to talking about their book choice *Circle of Friends*.

'I raced through the book,' said Margot. 'Beautiful Ireland, fantastic characters: it was brilliant.'

As they settled into chatting, Faye went to her happy place, a place that was far removed from her sad reality.

When it was time to say goodbye, Margot was first to notice that the sunshine was back for Faye.

Faye smiled. 'Queensland is a bit like that. Heavy rains one minute and the next? Well, you wouldn't even know it had happened.'

'Not like here. When the rain comes, it lingers.

But I love it though, it's always peaceful sitting inside and watching it pelt against the windows.'

Faye bet Margot had a beautiful home. Whatever room she was in was bigger than Faye's whole apartment, by the looks of things, and had a fully equipped gym in the background.

After she ended the Zoom session, Faye emailed Howard again to check in and ask whether everything was okay. She bet if he knew what was going on with her he would have something to say about the people harassing her and talking about her and her family. He'd tell them to butt out, or use words to that effect; she knew he would. They'd once read a book centred on a family scandal and Howard had been very strong in his opinion of the gossips. He, like a lot of readers, got so engrossed in the different worlds in their books; they were passionate about the issues they raised and the characters' behaviour. Howard had said that the people in that story should've focused more on their own lives than other people's and the world would be a happier place.

Faye couldn't help thinking he might be right.

* * *

She'd only been back at her apartment five minutes when the phone rang. It was Brad. And she couldn't help it, hope rose inside of her until he told her why he was calling.

'I'm sending Guy to pick up my things,' he announced.

Guy was a friend of his from work here in Queensland.

Her back against the wall she slid down until she was sat on the cold tiled floor. He didn't have much here, but she'd never once thought he'd send an errand boy for his belongings rather than coming to get them himself.

'It's easier this way,' he said before she had a chance to comment. 'Faye, are you there?'

She swallowed away the emotion. 'I'm here.'

His voice softened with the request she'd known was coming. 'The ring...' He was clearly grasping for the most appropriate way to ask for it back.

'I'll put it with your things.' And she hung up the call. What was the point in prolonging the conversation? They were over and the fact he wasn't even coming to pick up his things said it all. He was done; he was moving on.

* * *

After Guy left with Brad's belongings there was only one thing Faye wanted to do. She had to get out on the water where she could unplug from the entire world and take solace in nature.

She parked up as close as she could get to the access point where she would launch her kayak onto the Noosa River. She undid the straps securing the craft to the roof rack and carried it to the place she would launch from.

It was so serene and peaceful here now the rain had passed and in its place was a gentle glow of sunshine.

She launched the kayak, climbed in, and as her paddle blade dipped in on one side, then the other, the rhythmic motions did their best to bring her a sense of calm.

She paddled for a couple of hours on and off, stopping every now and then to savour the stillness, the quiet. She floated along the river, native birds sung their songs through the air, and she wondered what it would be like to do this in Dorset. Her dad hadn't been into water sports before he came to Australia, so as a family they'd never really embraced the love either, but yesterday he'd sent her a photograph of him in the English Channel on a paddleboard, and it looked pretty wonderful. He seemed to be

having a good time and she hated that he was worried about her and Steph facing the gossip over here,
being at loggerheads over what had happened.

He didn't yet know about Brad, that the engagement was off – he didn't need that added to his plate
– but she was glad he was where he was. When the
scandal first broke, he'd said that she and Steph were
welcome to join him in Dorset to get away. He'd said
they could stay in the static caravan their uncle
owned in West Lulworth. Faye had thanked him for
worrying, but she was fine. And she knew Steph
would never take him up on the offer – she hated the
climate in England and like her mother had no intention of returning, not even for a visit. How could
her twin sister be so different to her in every way but
her appearance?

She felt invigorated at the end of her kayak session, pleasantly worn out, and back at her car she
hoisted the kayak above her head and slid it onto the
roof rack.

'Need a hand?'

She jumped at the male voice behind her.

The man, middle-aged with a long greying ponytail and pockmarked skin that had likely had way too
much sun, had come out of nowhere and he put up
his hands. 'Sorry, didn't mean to startle you.'

She loved the solitude here, but she didn't much like it when she had company unexpectedly. She wished the kayak wasn't on the roof yet, as it would give her a degree of separation from this stranger.

'Are you lost?' she asked.

'No, just walking around, exploring.'

'Well, have a lovely rest of your day.' Keeping an awareness of where he was standing, she secured each of the straps around the kayak one by one.

She was unnerved when he seemed to follow her every step. She realised she hadn't put the paddle away and opened up the back door to stash it in the car.

'Aren't you her?' he asked as she closed the door. He reached out and gripped her upper arm. 'You are. You're her from the news.'

He thought she was Steph.

She shrugged off his grip. 'Are you a reporter?' She reached for the handle of the driver's door, but before she could open it he pinned her against the car.

'No. Not one of those. Do you wish I was?' The sleaze put a hand to the side of her face and rough, calloused fingers scratched at her skin. 'Or do you wish I was a politician?'

She lifted her knee at exactly the right angle to

have him yell out and double over. She pushed him roughly out of the way, jumped into the car and without even putting on her seatbelt thrust it into reverse and got out of there. So much for a month off work helping her find some sort of normality. This was getting worse.

Would this nightmare ever end?

By the time she reached her apartment, she suspected it wouldn't, and when she logged on to see there was still no reply from Howard she made a decision.

She was going to get far away. She was going to Dorset to escape, to see her dad, and while she was there she would try to find out why Howard, who had never missed a week of the Midnight Book Club since he joined, had all but disappeared.

6

MARGOT

Margot climbed into bed. She looked across at Perry who was already asleep. How could this man not realise what he had done to her? He was so self-absorbed, so selfish, and worse than how he acted towards her was the way he treated their sons.

When Perry started to snore she almost turned out the light, but she wasn't tired, because she couldn't stop thinking about those suitcases in the basement, how she could pick one up, pack it full of her things and change her life. The problem was, every time she thought seriously about going through with it and leaving him, she had Perry's voice in her head telling her she would never make it on her own; she would always come crawling back.

She had some money to her name but it wasn't a huge amount, and she had no job or skills to find employment. She was stuck with his voice telling her that if she tried to leave then it would be her fault that their family broke apart. He'd said that to her one day when they'd been arguing. She couldn't remember what the fight was about now, but she could remember him laying the responsibility of holding the family together firmly at her feet. Putting the boys through that hadn't been an option for her, but now they'd both left home, now they'd put distance between themselves and their father, was it finally time to think a bit about herself?

She picked up the book on her bedside table, romantic fiction and going by the blurb on the back it was about a man who was rough around the edges after being through a huge ordeal, and a woman who'd come to adore him anyway and change him into the loveable character that he was. She was happy to read this one. Romance would do what it said it would – there would be a happy ending. Whatever problems came along they would be solved between the pages.

If only real life were that easy.

She'd thought at one point that it really was.

That first night she met Perry, when he'd asked

her to leave the pub with him, they'd gone a bit further down the street and into the next pub, a much quieter place with no sign of any drinking challenges.

'I've never met a Margot before,' he told her.

She'd liked it when he said that. It was as if he was charming without knowing it. The demeanour seemed to come naturally, effortlessly and with no agenda.

They'd had another drink and then he'd walked her home, putting his coat around her shoulders as it grew colder. He'd kissed her goodnight – a gentle kiss with a lingering promise – and asked for her phone number. She was smitten. He'd said he'd call her.

And he did, less than forty-eight hours later.

Their first date was another seventy-two hours after that.

And thirteen weeks after the night they met, she was pregnant.

When she told Perry she was expecting a baby, he sat on the edge of the bed in her room at her shared flat in disbelief. She'd done the test the day before. She'd told one of her flatmates, unsure of what she was going to do. She'd had a plan, you see. She was in the first year of her four-year degree course. In the third year she would go over to America for twelve months. A baby wasn't even in the mix. Nineteen-year-olds and babies didn't go together, and a nineteen-year-old at university with a baby really didn't seem like it would work.

'You can't get rid of it,' Perry said when she told him she didn't know what to do. 'I mean you could, it's your body, but...' He turned to her and took both of her hands in his. 'But it's my baby too.'

She reached out a hand and put it against his cheek. Her kind, gentle Perry, who worked so hard at his graduate job and looked at her with eyes that pleaded for her to make the right decision. She'd decided then that she'd met her real-life hero. A man who was in this one hundred per cent.

'I'm going to go home this weekend,' she told him a couple of days later. 'I need to tell my parents. I can't do this alone.'

He rallied. 'But you're not alone. I'm here for you, Margot.' He cleared his throat, then he stood up before sinking down onto one knee.

'What are you doing?'

'Margot, would you marry me?' He huffed. 'I don't have a ring, but we'll choose one, a great big diamond if you like. Be my wife, Margot. You'll never want for anything.'

She'd thrown her arms around him. 'Yes, yes! I will marry you.'

They'd gone to tell her parents together. It had been hard. Her father cried, but with Perry at her side they had her parents' support. It didn't go quite as well telling Perry's parents three days after that.

'What the bloody hell were you thinking?' his father, Phil, roared. Margot could hear him shouting from the next room, yelling at his son as if he'd done this on purpose. She was sitting opposite his mother, Linda, in the lounge, watching Mrs York twist her wedding ring around her fourth finger. Margot's palms were clammy; the room felt too hot. All she wanted to do was leave. She wished that none of this was happening.

The shouting continued. Perry's mother shifted uncomfortably, offered Margot tea or a drink of water, talked about where she and Perry might live when they were married. She was behaving as if nothing out of the ordinary was playing out in this house, that there wasn't an almighty row going on in the next room, that this was a minor problem that would be dealt with when to Margot it was life-changing.

Over time, Margot saw Perry's father, Phil, for the

man he really was. Perry seemed to shrink in his presence. He was always telling him about his achievements, his successes, and for very little praise in return. She saw Phil snap at his wife many a time, he put her down in front of others, he was a bully. Linda waited on Phil hand and foot too, without so much as a thank you or gentle affectionate touch from him to show his appreciation. Margot didn't know how Perry's mum put up with it. And she'd never thought for one minute that she would ever become that woman.

Perry and Margot married when she was five months pregnant. She was slim and the bump, although there, wasn't enormous. They'd had a lovely wedding and her dad had been proud as anything, his daughter marrying into the York family who, unbeknownst to Margot when she met Perry, were prominent in the philanthropic sector as a result of a very successful business venture, which Perry's father launched two decades earlier and sold off for millions. The Yorks had paid for the entire wedding, and both sets of parents seemed excited about becoming grandparents despite Perry's father's initial bellowing.

When Sebastian was born things got harder. Perry couldn't take much time off work and Margot was bogged down with nappies, feeds, bathing, sleep schedules, and trying to stay sane. Neither set of grandparents could help out much as they lived some distance away and Margot wasn't keen on any of them coming to stay in their tiny flat. She'd rather deal with it all herself. But in those hazy days she'd leap on Perry the second he came through the door, desperate for some adult interaction and some help. Her uni mates visited for a while, which was company of sorts, but they had their own lives – they had the life that she should've had and she realised one day that she resented it. She stopped inviting them. Their lives had gone on different trajectories and she could barely stand to see them and witness what she was missing out on.

But oh how she loved Sebastian. With his big brown eyes, his shock of chestnut hair and the way he smiled with his entire face, his gurgles, his chatter. When Sebastian was a year old, they moved to a terraced house bigger than the flat but not by much. By then Perry had started to come out of his shell a bit and he was doing really well with his job. Margot hadn't really given it much thought; she'd been proud of how hard he'd worked and how he was growing up to take responsibility. She'd never once thought back then that he was slowly turning into a man very much like his father.

In the new rental property, Margot struggled with Perry being away for work so much. She had stairs to tackle with the pram, which was never easy. The neighbours on both sides were noisy – it didn't bother Perry when he was there because he slept like a log – but it bothered Margot. Her sleep was all over the place, she tried to sleep when Sebastian did, but their neighbours were loud in the day as well as the evenings and she was running on empty.

She almost had a breakdown when Sebastian was a toddler, brought on by the stress of it all, by lack of support and so little rest. Perry had stepped in that time. He'd taken leave from work, he'd sent her to a hotel for four whole nights and she was ordered to recuperate. She couldn't have been happier in that moment for despite his busy job in London, he really saw how things were for her. And by the time Sebastian turned three, they were in a much better position financially. Perry had had two promotions and started to receive an annual bonus, and they found a small house to buy to get them on the property ladder.

Family visits were always tense for Margot. She hated going over to the Yorks. Linda was lovely. She always fussed over Sebastian, always cooked them a delicious meal and never let anyone lift a finger, but

Margot began to resent how much Perry changed when he was in his dad's company. He'd drink more than he usually did, they'd have cigars like it was something Perry did regularly, and on those occasions, Perry seemed to Margot like a little boy craving the approval he'd always wanted. Perry would talk nonstop about his job, his achievements at work, and his dad would offer praise, but he'd talk about his own success too, then he'd ask what was next for his son as if he hadn't achieved enough yet. Margot saw the immense pressure Perry was under every time his father was in the room. The pressure seemed to drive Perry to be even better, to succeed, to get the next promotion and the one after that. But all the while Margot wished he was doing it for himself and for them and less for his dad. Slowly the young man she'd met that night in the pub was fading before her very eyes until he was almost unrecognisable.

Margot tried a few times to talk to Perry about getting back to studying or working part-time, but it wasn't practical when Perry's job took them to Europe, Canada, and finally back to London. And then when she really had a chance to do something for herself with Sebastian that bit older, she'd fallen pregnant with Alistair. And so it began again, the feeding, the sleepless nights, the weaning, and by that time Perry was in an even more demanding position and so it was all down to her. They bought this big house, and organising renovations, decorating, and holding get-togethers to impress Perry's business associates became her world, a world she'd never wanted to be in in the first place.

Somehow, she'd ended up much like Perry's mother, the woman she'd felt sorry for, a woman whose life she vowed she'd never let hers resemble. Any conversation with Perry about further study or her going out to work was flipped: she'd been made to feel like Perry was supporting her, telling her how good she was at being a wife and mother. She'd never once thought of it as a form of manipulation because he was so good at it. Instead, it had felt like a two-way conversation. It was only later she realised that was exactly how things had always gone for Phil and Linda.

And by that time, she was trapped.

Margot had learned over time that it was easier not to argue with Perry, but when he'd tried to enrol the boys in boarding school for their high school years, she'd had to dig deep and stand up to him. That day she hadn't been quite sure where her fury and her guts had come from, but she'd told him that hell would have to freeze over before he took her boys away from her. She'd expected him to retaliate, but he hadn't. She'd wondered whether her raw emotion had touched a nerve; perhaps he wished his own mother had been as vehement when he was sent away as a young boy for his own schooling.

Having a family was what had always stopped Margot from leaving Perry and so over the years she'd tried to make the best of things. She'd pretended she was content, told herself that things could be worse, and when Alistair was at school full-time she even started to look into study options. But Perry put a stop to any notion of her furthering her education or training in anything. He'd told her time and time again that the boys needed her no matter what age they were, and he knew that Sebastian and Alistair were her Achilles' heel in an argument. And so she hadn't sought out anything for herself. She'd been there whenever her sons needed or wanted her. And she'd been kept right where Perry wanted her too: at home without a life of her own to speak of.

A year or so after trying to find a study option Margot had floated the idea that she apply for a part-time job.

'The school is looking for a receptionist,' she'd said to Perry. 'I think I could do it.'

But she must've caught him on a really bad day

because rather than dismiss it and have her think she wasn't capable he turned around and roared, 'Do I not provide you with enough?'

'That isn't what I'm saying.' To him it was all about money but to Margot it was about carving out a little bit of life away from this house.

'Then what are you saying?' he spat. He'd followed that up with a tirade of remarks about how hard he worked, how his father had taught him to be the man he was, how she was ungrateful for this big house and this comfortable life he'd given her.

The name-calling and criticism didn't stop over the years and when Alistair announced his career choice Perry had turned to her and delivered a savage, 'You've spoiled those boys and made sure they are nothing like me.' And then he'd looked at his youngest son. A muscle in his jaw had twitched when he told Alistair, 'You could've been more.'

Alistair had left the room after the remark and Margot had followed soon after, up to his bedroom.

'Am I too much?' she'd asked her youngest son as she sat on the edge of his bed next to him. 'Have I mothered you and not let you make your own choices?'

He'd looked up from beneath his fringe. 'No, you're a good mum. The best.'

She put her arm round him and pulled him close. 'You're the best too.'

'Not in Dad's eyes.'

'Your dad is—'

'No, don't make excuses. It's not your job to do that.'

'I know, but I hate how he makes you feel.'

His voice caught when he told her, 'I don't know how to deal with him any more. I hate that he never seems to approve of what me and Sebastian are doing. I hate that he is horrible to you.' And then he wrapped his arms around her, him the protector rather than her. He sniffed, and she knew he was trying to hide his tears.

Her heart broke a little bit more on that day, because it was one of the first times she realised that, try as she might to hide what was going on in her marriage, her sons knew.

Sebastian had clashed with Perry plenty of times too. And they'd argued bigger and louder than Perry and Alistair had, and then her eldest son had taken a job that took him far away from the family home in an effort to avoid the man who should be there for him and his brother unconditionally.

Now, in her bedroom in the house that was far too big for two of them, Margot opened the book on her bedside table, ready to lose herself in a romance with a hero who considered his heroine and those around him rather than just thinking about himself.

Unfortunately, now she'd started replaying her history with Perry it was hard to stop. Those words to Alistair – *you could've been more* – weren't just applicable to his opinions about his sons, they meant something to her.

She could've been more. So much more than a wife who gave as much as she could and got nothing much in return from her husband.

She thought about the email she'd had from Faye a few days ago, saying she was going to Dorset to see her dad but also to check on Howard who she still hadn't heard from. Faye was concerned about him and as the days went on Margot was getting increasingly worried too. Howard was a man she liked, admired, a man she could talk to, and the sort of man she hoped her boys would turn out to be. One thing was for sure: she didn't want Sebastian or Alistair to take after their own father.

Her mind went back to seeing Sebastian's postcards in the bin, to the tears Alistair had shed over his dad's disapproval, the many times her boys had been made to feel not good enough. She thought of all the things Perry had taken from her, the friendships she'd lost, the marriage that was nothing like the partnership it should be, the way he spoke to her and treated her like she barely existed apart from to do his bidding.

Those suitcases were in the basement. They were waiting for her, and slowly she crept out of bed. Perry might think that their family was still intact but it wasn't, not when the boys didn't call much, rarely spoke to their father and no longer liked visiting. And definitely not with the fractured relationship they had with their dad. And only now did she really see that it was Perry who had broken their family apart. Not her, but him.

She could do this, couldn't she? The reason for her staying all this time was no longer there.

But she couldn't just walk out of here tonight; she needed a proper plan. And so at the kitchen table with a notepad and pen and her laptop, her heart beating wildly in her chest, she started to put one together. She didn't have much money, but over the years leaving Perry had always been at the back of her mind and so she'd been squirrelling away some cash, here and there so it wouldn't be noticed, and it was safely in an account Perry didn't even know existed. It wasn't much but it was enough to last her a couple of months if she was careful. She tried not to think of what would happen after that. She couldn't or it would stop her going. There would never be a perfect time – if she waited for that it would never come.

It was now or never, and at forty-nine years old, the thought of *never* absolutely terrified her.

7

FAYE

Faye had been travelling for thirty hours so far – thirty hours since she got into the hire car, drove to Brisbane International Airport, boarded her plane that went via Sydney and then Dubai, before landing here at London's Heathrow. She was exhausted but the excitement as the plane came in to land took over any other feeling. She was here, back in England, after all this time.

'I thought you'd be more tired,' said her dad after she finally let him go at the arrivals gate. Somehow she'd found the energy to race around past fellow travellers, and launch herself into an enormous hug.

'I'm too happy to see you to be tired.'

'It'll hit later on.' She gladly let him take her suit-case. 'Did you get any sleep at all?'

'I dozed; that was it.'

He put his free arm around her. 'It's lovely to have you here.'

They found their way to the short-term parking and were soon on their way, chattering about the weather of course – a top of twenty-four was ex-pected today – her uncle, Frank, the busy roads around the airport that proved plenty of people weren't still in bed, and after her dad had navigated his way from the terminal and they were on the mo-torway she knew it was time to be honest with him.

'I've taken a month off work,' she said.

'That sounds like a good idea. It'll give you time to enjoy being over here once the jet lag has passed.' He put a hand up to wave a thank you at a driver who let him into the lane he needed. 'Frank says you can use the caravan as long as you like.'

'It's good that you're here with him.'

'It is. He's had some bad days, unfortunately, but lots of good ones too, and it's nice to be in Dorset.' He grumbled as the traffic came to another halt. It really was like one big traffic jam on this motorway. 'You know I'd missed the green grass of home more than I realised.'

She sniggered. 'Can't see any green yet.' All she could see was the side of a long lorry and the rear windscreen of the vehicle in front.

'Just you wait until we get closer to Dorset.' The traffic had them moving at the rapid rate of fifteen miles per hour. 'So how are you *really* doing?'

The speedometer slowed to zero yet again.

She took a deep breath before she admitted, 'Dad... I'm not getting married any more.'

From her peripheral vision she knew he'd turned to face her but his action was short-lived when he got beeped by the driver of the vehicle behind as the traffic moved once more.

She told him all about how Brad hadn't only left Queensland with his family to hide out in Tasmania, he'd been applying for jobs there as well.

'And he didn't ask you to make the move with him?'

'No.' She looked out at the traffic, bumper to bumper in the lane next to them. 'I really thought we would spend the rest of our lives together, but this makes me feel like I never knew him at all. I thought marriage was about being there for each other even when it got hard, but he left, just like that.'

They moved from the middle lane to the outside one, passing other cars, and her dad maintained the quiet as he took the next exit, but once he was on the way and through a roundabout he spoke again. 'You've been all by yourself.'

'It's not been easy.' Although Steph leaving too had been kind of a blessing. Perhaps it was the one thing her twin sister might have done right. 'Actually, it's been really shit.' She explained about the reporters, the man the other morning after her kayaking session.

His grip tightened on the wheel. 'I'm sorry you've had to deal with all that. I wish I'd been there to—'

'No, Dad. It was good that you were away from it all.' She paused. 'I'm so angry with Steph. Her decisions have made my life difficult. They caused Brad to…' She couldn't even say the words again.

'I know you are really upset with your sister.' He waited a while before he said, 'She really fell for that man.'

That man. When the scandal broke and a reporter turned up at the water-sports business premises, her dad had had a lot more choice words than those, including pervert and predator. He'd apologised to Faye because the man was going to be her father-in-law but she'd agreed with everything he'd said.

'You've spoken to her?' she asked.

'I have. She's upset too. And it makes my blood boil thinking that man might have taken advantage of her.' He indicated to change lanes. 'But she gave me the impression that he didn't, that she honestly believed they were going to be together. And then he stood up on television and told the country and the world that it had all been a mistake. That hit her pretty hard.'

It almost burst out of her that Steph should've known or should've at least suspected the man would have wanted to come out smelling of roses. But Faye had long since given up being her sister's keeper, the responsible one, the one Steph could run to whenever things went wrong for her.

The girls were sixteen when their mother upped and left. The family had already emigrated to Australia as a foursome. They were living quite the life in Queensland; the girls had sunshine, freedom, and plenty of friends. Their dad's water-sports business was growing but a few months before their mother walked out for good Faye had noticed a change in Daria, who was spending more and more time away from the house with friends she'd met at yoga. Some of those friends lived in the hinterland in smaller country towns with rainforest walks, and soon Daria was spending nights there, then weeks, and drifting away both emotionally and physically from her family more and more.

Faye had seen her dad looking weary but trying to put on a brave face, and one night Faye had asked him whether they were getting a divorce. He'd sat her down and said that he honestly didn't know. This move to the southern hemisphere had been initiated by Daria all along, and Faye wondered then whether their dad had agreed to it in an attempt to save his marriage.

Their parents never really had a big row after that day or even a significant argument; they literally drifted a bit like a tide falling away from the shore but never returning again. Daria moved up to Far North Queensland, some eighteen hours away by car or a three-hour flight, leaving the girls with their dad. Steph took it really hard. It came as more of a shock for her because, unlike Faye, she hadn't really seen it coming. She'd been wayward as a teen, often in her own little world with little regard to what was going on for everyone else, so when their mother upped and left it came out of the blue.

Steph got progressively worse and the more trouble she got into the more Faye wondered whether her younger sister was just like their mother and only able to think about number one. She'd yelled at her once that she only thought about herself and Steph had broken down, sobbed, asked why their mum had had to leave, asked whether they were such terrible daughters. Faye had ended up crying that day too and had called her mother, telling her in no uncertain terms that her shitty parenting had consequences before she slammed the phone down.

Daria had turned up three days later, showering both girls with presents – little cloth bags with smelly soaps, decorative hair accessories Faye wasn't sure either of them would ever wear, some chocolates that had partially melted in her bag, a T-shirt each although Faye's had been far too small. The only good part about their mother showing up that day was that she'd apologised to Faye when Steph was in the bathroom, and later on Faye had heard Daria telling Steph the truth: that her leaving had nothing to do with her daughters and whether they were good enough, it was because she just couldn't be this person any more. She needed to be free, she didn't like the suburbs, she wanted the freedom and lushness she'd found up north. Faye hadn't really cared what she'd found, only that she put things right. But how could she?

In the years that followed, Steph liked visiting

their mother but Faye eventually chose not to. It never appealed to stay in a house with a bunch of strangers, her mother's so-called wider family who all seemed as lazy – or maybe stoned – as each other. None of them worked, they were happy to live in a mess, they all shunned technology and hated mobile phones. The only thing they'd allowed was a landline at the property so at least there was a way to know that Daria was okay. The lifestyle they chose was so cut off, but Daria insisted that was the brilliant thing about it. She was a strange woman to understand but slowly, over time, Faye had found it easier to deal with the fact.

Steph somehow managed to finish school with some qualifications despite her lack of interest and her partying, and she even got a job as a personal assistant locally while Faye trained as a hairdresser. For a while it seemed that Steph was settling down too, but her life outside her work had so many ups and downs that Faye felt like she was on the roller coaster with her at every single dip. Steph had been thrown out of a bar in her early twenties after she followed a friend into the toilets where they had sex – their dad had picked her up when the owner of the bar called the emergency contact on Steph's phone. Soon after that she made a pass at Faye's then-boyfriend, Charlie, and Faye had seen that one with her own eyes. It resulted in an almighty row, radio silence for over a month, and even though Faye had ended things with Charlie for reasons other than her sister, she'd never forgotten the betrayal. Of course Steph had been remorseful, said it was only a joke to see whether he could tell he was kissing the wrong twin, and she promised she'd do anything to make it up to her, but Faye wasn't interested. She was getting used to having a sister who acted first and thought about it later.

When Steph was twenty-one she got caught stealing a lipstick from a department store and because their dad was out on the ocean and uncontactable Faye had taken the call at home. It was she who called in to work to explain she was dealing with an emergency and she who had gone to see whether she could help. As she'd pulled up in the car park near the department store she'd wondered whether she should turn right around again. Perhaps if they came down hard on Steph it might teach her a proper lesson.

When Faye arrived at the office in the department store she'd gone in to see Steph with her red blotched tear-stained cheeks, a wobbly bottom lip and more regret than Faye had ever witnessed. The manager had given Steph a stern talking-to, Faye had explained that there was trouble at home and their mother had walked out – she didn't point out that that was almost five years ago. Steph was let off with a warning, Faye paid the money for the lipstick and apologised profusely, promising it wouldn't happen again, and they'd left the store in shock.

What shocked Faye more, however, was when Steph began laughing as soon as they were in the car. 'What a high!' she'd exclaimed. 'What a rush!'

Faye tried to distance herself from her sister after that. It pained her to do so but gradually, with less and less time spent together, Faye realised she had more individuality without Steph in the background. She wasn't heaving around her sister's personality as well as her own, making excuses for her, worrying so much, trying to fix everything. They saw one another, but Faye stayed away from Steph's dramas, and it was always a relief when Steph went away to stay with their mother for a while.

At least that was how it had worked until the scandal broke.

Faye smiled when her dad turned off the main road now. 'This is more like it.'

'England's roads, half the width of Aussie ones,' he said with amusement.

'And with two-way traffic.' A tractor was coming towards them and she almost breathed in as it passed. 'Did it take you a while to get used to these roads again?'

'You wait until we're closer to Moreton.' Moreton was the small village in Dorset where Uncle Frank lived. 'This road is like the freeway in comparison.'

'Steph wouldn't like it.' Her sister didn't like driving much at all. She was terrible at parking, and she would never cope with these dinky roads.

'She's been driving a ute around at her mother's. Can you imagine?'

'Not really.'

'I think she's staying on a while longer.'

'Hiding a while longer you mean.' Steph never had been one to face the consequences. 'And rather her than me.'

'You never were a fan of the outside dunny.'

His remark about the outside toilet at their mother's house had her lighten up a bit. There was an inside bathroom but if it was occupied, which it often was with between four and eight people living there on and off, then you had to go out in the elements. Bad enough that you had to go outside to the toilet anywhere, but in Far North Queensland with its wildlife it was no joke.

'Dad, would you mind if we took a bit of a detour before we go to Uncle Frank's?' Simultaneously they flipped their sun visors down at the change of light now they were trundling towards the Dorset village.

'Detour?'

She explained about Howard and Driftwick Bay. 'He never misses a book club, you see, and I'm getting worried about him.'

'You know where he lives?'

'Well, no, but he bought the bookshop, Driftwick Bay Books, so if we drive into the town I could pop in.'

Her dad was happy to take the detour and she reprogrammed the satnav as he drove. She couldn't wait to see Howard's face when she walked into the bookshop, took him by surprise. Meeting her friend in person was something she never thought would happen, but now she was actually going to do it and it would be wonderful.

As they came to a T-junction her dad carefully pulled out to turn right. 'Your sister is a lot like your mother,' he said. 'That may sound harsh, but—'

'I saw it when Steph was younger. I hoped she'd grow out of it.'

He didn't seem surprised that she'd realised it all along. 'You know when your mother and I first started dating, her waywardness was what I was drawn to. I was always calm and organised; I always did the right thing.' They'd met at Glastonbury one year and perhaps in the same way as he was drawn to her rebelliousness, she liked his assuredness and reliability.

'Talk about opposites attract,' said Faye.

'I think your mum liked the fact that I was a family man.' He smiled, perhaps remembering fondly the earlier years because they hadn't all been bad. When she was little Faye could remember plenty of family outings with all four of them, the journey over to Australia when she was in her early teens, the discovery of beautiful beaches and hidden places in the land down under. 'Your mum never had stability in her life until she met me. I think losing her parents when she was only six years old had a bigger effect on your mother than she ever admitted. She had nobody to show her what growing up meant and the responsibility that comes with having children. I'm not making excuses for her, but maybe that was part of what made her into the person she was and still is.'

'Steph has you, at least, to show her the right way.' She paused. 'Do you think she'll ever change?'

'I have no idea. But I'll love her anyway.'

'So will I.' It felt odd to think it, that you could love someone but not particularly *like* them.

Her dad was right; the quaint villages and roads that they passed by and through were quintessentially English and she was falling in love with the place already. It was amazing how much she'd forgotten – the odd brilliant red phone box still in situ, the corner shops with their coloured awnings, the cottage gardens, the thatched roofs on properties dating way back.

It wasn't long before he slowed to drive down the hill into the heart of Driftwick Bay. Faye could already see what must be Lulworth Cove in the distance and she knew she was smiling. Back in Dorset, all this beauty surrounding her, she already felt at home.

'This is the main street.' Her dad slowed up and pulled in on the left of the hill. 'I believe the bookshop is just in front of these few cars.'

She undid her seatbelt. 'You coming?'

'I'll wait here for you, love. I was up early; I'll rest my eyes.'

Out in the August sunshine that seemed to have already started to warm up since she got into the car at the airport, she walked down the hill past the other cars until she drew level with Driftwick Bay

Books. It was just as Howard had said, charming and with a character all of its very own. He'd shown them photographs of this place and now she got to see the shop for real, with its beautiful dark wooden Georgian windows, a display of books with novelty items beyond the glass, but... hang on...

She cupped her hands around her eyes and peered in through the window. Despite it being past 9 a.m. the bookshop was still closed, and Howard had told them all that he opened on the dot of 9 a.m. six days a week and if he wasn't there, his assistant would be.

But it wasn't the fact that the shop looked abandoned inside with no light and no sign of life that had her worrying all the more, it was the sign on the door.

Permanently Closed, it said.

Her heart sank. Had the developers got their way and hounded Howard so much that he'd walked away from his beloved shop?

And if that was the case, was he so distraught that he hadn't even been able to share it with his friends in the Midnight Book Club?

8
____

BONNIE

Bonnie's retirement had brought an enormous change to their lives, enabling them to travel and then move to the coast, but unfortunately she hadn't realised another change was on its way, one that would rock her world and make her question where she could possibly go from here.

Four weeks ago, she and Howard had been enjoying a beautiful July day together, one of many they both thought they had in their future. Happy with her painting of the elevated view of the town and the water from their back garden, she'd decided to gift it to Beverly and had taken the canvas to Dorchester to have it framed.

'You sure you're not keeping it?' Howard asked

her when she arrived back at the cottage with the finished picture in a beautiful graphite silver frame. He was pouring a tea and she'd declined his offer to make her one.

'No, I really want Beverly to have it. She used to holiday here in the town as a kid; I know she'll love it, and she was my closest colleague at work.' She set the wrapped picture down, leaning it against the far wall of the kitchen out of the way. The picture was protected inside the brown paper and all she needed to do was address it and take it to the post office.

Howard stirred milk into his mug of tea. 'I made you a sandwich. It's in the fridge.' As he returned the milk to the door of the fridge she watched him a little closer. He seemed more unsteady than usual, or perhaps she was imagining it. What she definitely hadn't imagined, however, was how tired he'd been in the last week or so. At the end of each day he was positively worn out and she'd wondered more than once whether he'd taken on too much – owning and running a bookshop when he was already in his seventies. But if she ever raised the point, he'd insist that working again and being surrounded by books kept his grey matter top notch.

He'd admitted yesterday, however, that the developers who were originally interested in the bookshop had been stopping by regularly in an attempt to persuade him to sell to them. They really weren't letting this go and had even upped their original offer.

'Do you think there are hidden jewels sewn into the upholstery of those nooks?' Howard had joked because of their persistence. They'd laughed about it but Bonnie wished they'd leave him alone and hopefully soon they would get the message that the bookshop was not for sale. It was special to the community. Plenty of residents remembered going to the bookshop as kids themselves, then taking their own children and even grandchildren there, and it was a popular hub for the local primary school who took groups there in support of literacy programs. When Howard first took on the shop, Wendy from the bakery had told them that she remembered sitting on the big rug as a child when story time came around every Saturday morning, and one of the men behind the post office counter had told Bonnie when she went in to buy stamps one day that he used to spend all his weekly pocket money at Driftwick Bay Books. The locals would be devastated if the bookshop ever disappeared and even now Howard still got thanks for coming to the rescue and saving it.

She leaned in and kissed Howard on the cheek as he picked up his mug of tea. 'Thanks for the sandwich, love. I suppose I'd better return the favour and make the syrup sponge I promised you.'

'I've told you I'm happy to give it a go.'

He'd take over all the cooking if she let him. They took turns most of the time but to be honest since she'd retired and they'd come home from their travels she needed to keep busy. 'Nonsense, you put your feet up. You know I love making it.'

And she did. She loved baking in this kitchen. It was cosy despite being a decent size with a window at the very end of the room, which looked out to the front of the cottage, and the little fence with its tiny low-down gate. They'd installed a new range cooker in here, which wasn't so modern it looked out of place but was modern enough that it worked and cooked things well. They'd redone the walk-in larder, which was tiny but now had floor-to-ceiling shelving on three walls and held more food than they could ever collect and need between them, and the wooden-doored cupboards suited a country-style kitchen. The oak table in front of the window had been the perfect way to complete the look and some-times Bonnie thought perhaps their kitchen looked as cosy as those you saw in a magazine.

She took ingredients from the larder and lined them all up on the benchtop before she pulled out equipment from the oak corner cupboard. She'd get started making the pudding first, then eat her sandwich while it was steaming.

But she turned suddenly at the sound of Howard cursing and saw the splash of tea on the floor and up the side of the cupboard. His hand wobbled as he successfully set the mug back down to safety.

'Don't get in a flap,' he warned. She'd already mentioned the other day that he seemed unusually tired and that hadn't gone down well at all. He'd never been one to fuss if he didn't feel the best, and at his age she didn't expect him to change now.

'I'll get a cloth,' she said without any more debate.

Because of her job, Bonnie had seen the rapid decline of patients Howard's age, and hers for that matter, and that had been a big driver behind them travelling. She'd wanted to do it while they both still could, before it was either impossible physically or travel insurance premiums made it too costly. They'd had eight weeks of travel that she would never ever forget, and for that she would always be grateful.

She wiped up the spillage with a damp cloth. 'I'll make you another.'

'It's fine. I had half.'

He hadn't. But she didn't want to upset him. So

she got on with measuring and cutting out the baking paper she needed to line the pudding basin as Howard sat at the table and picked up his Kindle. He looked exhausted again, but when he glanced her way she turned to put the baking paper into the basin.

'How's the book?' she asked as she worked, not wanting him to see how concerned she was.

'I only started it last night so the jury is out.'

'What's this one called?'

'*The Girl on the Train*. It's a psychological thriller.'

He was happy for now and Bonnie lost herself in her baking for a bit. She spooned golden syrup into the base of the pudding basin, beat more syrup with butter, sugar and lemon zest, added in the eggs and flour. And when she was done and the pudding was set over a pan of water to steam for slightly under two hours she set the timer and made them both a mug of tea.

Howard had moved to his comfier chair in the other room and she set down his mug on the table beside him. 'You read so fast. Does everyone in the book club keep up?' The prep and the baking had taken her long enough that it was quite acceptable to be having more tea by now.

'Everyone goes at a different pace, love. But we're all pretty fast readers most of the time.'

With Howard reading and the pudding steaming, Bonnie ate her lunch and then went through to join Howard again and make a start on her new painting, or at least the preparation for it.

'Would you like the back doors closed?' She didn't mind the fresh air, but she wanted Howard to be comfortable.

'No, leave them, it's lovely to bring the outside in.'

She opened up various drawers to find her supplies. She was going to start painting that view from the picture she'd taken on the hill near the bookshop. She'd already printed out her favourite shot from her phone and enlarged it, so with a length of masking tape she fixed it to one side of the easel.

She picked up a pencil and started to sketch some rough outlines of the road onto her canvas, then the pavements, the row of shops with Howard's beloved bookshop nestled in the middle as the main feature. She added the telephone box on the hill, the sea in the distance, and happy with her sketch for now she found tools including a detail brush, a palette knife and a spatula, a damp rag, a beaker of water, and her palette onto which she squeezed measures of different colours. She'd start with the sky, the palest part of the painting. Acrylics dried fast but she would layer it up with texture to eventually get the right shade, the right finish she wanted.

Her wooden easel had handy inset shelves at the top where she could put her brush momentarily if she wanted to use the knife to shift the paint around, or the rag to blend or smudge. The easel was ancient but special because every painting she'd done so far had been done on this very same piece of equipment Howard bought her when they first moved in together.

After an hour or so sat in front of her easel, the sketch complete and the sky beginning to gain some colour, she felt a bit of a chill come inside and so she closed the back doors. It was time to check on the steamed sponge anyway.

When she looked at Howard, he wasn't reading, he was dozing. Both of them got so absorbed with their different pastimes it was easy to forget the other one was there half the time. Friends of hers said they could never concentrate when their husband or partner was around, but for her it was as if Howard being there gave her extra energy. Neither of them disturbed the other; they were merely happy with each other's presence and carried on with what they loved doing.

Howard looked up when she rested her hand gently on his shoulder. His Kindle was still nestled on a cushion on his lap.

'I knew you were tired.' She leaned down to kiss him. 'How about a big slice of syrup sponge to wake you up after I sort these out?' She held the brushes and the container of water aloft. Acrylic paint dried quickly; you never wanted to leave brushes lying about, especially not these, which were the pricier kind and part of the set Howard gave her for their last anniversary.

Howard murmured an agreement of sorts and she went off to the small utility room at the far end of the kitchen, rinsed her brushes, and lined them up to air-dry. After washing her hands she took the opportunity to put on some washing, shoving the clothes into the machine along with a capsule of detergent.

In the kitchen she closed the door to the utility room to keep the machine noise away. She caught sight of the framed photograph of her in her district nurse's uniform. Howard had pinned this one to the pinboard that sat behind the end section of kitchen bench. It was taken with her friend and colleague, Beverly, their arms linked, resting against the bonnet of her car as they prepared to head out for the day.

Bonnie had been a district nurse for over twenty

years. When she'd started as a nurse, she'd worked in a couple of different hospitals and then she'd seen an advert for a district nurse and decided that perhaps it was the change she needed. She'd never regretted it either. In her new role she began to meet all sorts of people; no two days were the same. The struggles were often hard as she was visiting housebound patients, but she revelled in the support she was able to give each and every one of them. She could natter through a catheter change and make a patient feel at ease, and ignore any messes or smells as she dealt with continence care. She could tend to wounds that were not for the faint-hearted. Her job made her feel like she had a purpose and that she was delivering the very best of care. Even when she got the curmudgeonly patients, the ones who moaned or snapped at her, it slid right off her back. Half the time they couldn't help it; part of the time they were in such a bad way that she understood why they were so annoyed. And all she'd ever wanted to do was help.

Saying goodbye to some of her regular patients when she retired had been harder than she would've thought possible, especially when they got upset. Beryl, a ninety-year-old lady with limited mobility, had been the most distraught even when Bonnie handed over to Yvonne, a bubbly redhead who always had a smile and a kind word. She supposed that was what happened and what she'd loved so much about being a district nurse. You got involved; you developed a deeply personal connection to patients and their families outside a hospital setting.

Then there was Stephen, a fifty-two-year-old living at home with his parents after a motorcycle accident put him in a wheelchair. He had his name down to move to a specialist facility with people his own age but until then he'd been stuck at the house he'd grown up in and couldn't wait to leave. He'd always made her laugh with his moans about his parents, always very good-natured grumbles, and they were doing nothing but fussing over the son they loved, but he had a dry sense of humour and Bonnie had had a hard time remaining professional rather than giggling all the time.

She missed her work. She hadn't at the start. She hadn't when they'd been on their travels or busy moving into the cottage in Driftwick Bay, but now life had settled somewhat she missed a routine. Had she retired too early?

The timer buzzed, signalling the syrup sponge was ready.

She took the basin off the pan, set it down on the trivet and opened the top carefully to avoid any burns from the steam. The skewer she poked into the sponge's centre came out nice and clean, and she left it to stand for a few minutes while she washed up some of the utensils she'd left piled in the sink in favour of getting on with her painting. Howard always said she liked to use every pot. She hadn't but somehow, yet again, it did look like she'd done her best to.

The pudding was best served hot and so she wasted no time turning the sponge out onto a deep plate. She spooned some of the syrup from the bottom of the basin over the fluffy golden top and then cut two enormous wedges.

She'd take Howard his portion first, get him settled and happy and then come back for hers.

On her way to the back room she trilled, 'Now, don't eat this too fast; it's very hot.' But he'd fallen asleep again. 'Howard... pudding...'

But in seconds she knew.

He wasn't sleeping at all.

The bowl, the sponge, and the syrup fell from her hands, crashing onto the floor and sending splatters all over the rug and the side of her husband's favourite chair.

That day was four weeks ago and very quickly Bonnie had had Howard's assistant Iris put a sign up on the door to the bookshop saying *Permanently Closed*. Bonnie had no intention of ever setting foot in there again. It would be far too painful. Iris had brought over the post from the shop the day she put the sign up and sure enough there was another letter from the developer. She'd set it in the letter rack because she wasn't entirely sure she wouldn't get in touch with them. Driftwick Bay Books might not have been Howard's for all that long, but much like his bookshelves here, it was all Howard. She couldn't go inside the quaint shop with its warm dark wooden interior, its little antique-effect signs dotted around to point customers to the right section if they were lost, without expecting him to look up at her from the counter behind the till and beam a smile her way, a smile like he'd had that rainy day in Blackpool when they first met.

The town loved the bookshop; the community would hate to see it go. But without Howard, was she really going to hang on to it? Was she really a part of things around here anyway? Was living here still her dream without her husband by her side?

Howard had gone, and sometimes Bonnie wished she had too.

9

MARGOT

Margot couldn't believe it. She was here in Dorset. She'd left her home. She'd left Perry and come down to Bournemouth where she'd made some of her happiest memories with her parents and her boys. And she'd planned her departure so well that Perry wouldn't have realised it had happened until it was too late.

She'd really done it.

It felt unreal in so many ways.

She took her shoes off to feel the sand between her toes as she looked out to sea, the vastness of nothing but water, nothing but freedom. The boys had always loved their time here and she'd always felt at peace. It had been the natural destination to head for.

With their mum and their gran, the boys had experienced a freedom on the south coast that came without criticism, that gave them the ability to be young and to truly be themselves. The older they got the less easy that was to do with Perry around at home. When Alistair was tiny, Sebastian being so much older would make him laugh with the infectious giggle that had him and Margot doing the same. When Alistair reached the terrible twos, it was Sebastian who could calm him down and distract him. And when Alistair had felt the pressure of his exams as a teenager, Sebastian had taken him away from his books almost as if he intuitively knew he was feeling the same pressure he had felt from their dad, and they'd go kick a football around outside instead.

Over the last week, Margot had given nothing away about what was coming. It was as if flipping the calendar in the kitchen over to the month of September at the start of the week had marked a monumental change that she'd made cautiously but surely. Each day she'd got up and done her chores and anything else on her to-do list in record time to make sure that Perry suspected nothing by the time he came home from work. As part of her plan, she'd rented a storage unit less than ten miles away as it meant she could easily drive back and forth to get her most treasured things out of the house. She moved the items she wanted from home to storage over a few days so that it wouldn't raise suspicions. Luckily there was a rear access to the garage so she didn't have to come out through the front door as Perry would've got that on the Ring camera. She also couldn't take too long – everything would have to be explained and shorter outings were far easier: *we needed more coffee beans*; *I was out of eggs*; *I forgot to post a letter*. Unbelievably, as she was taking things she'd felt *lucky* that Perry hadn't installed CCTV cameras around the property. Lucky? Feeling that way had reminded her of how wrong her whole situation was.

She'd taken plenty to the storage unit: the coffee table that once belonged to her mother, and because Perry said it didn't go with their lounge furniture it had been relegated to the loft; a beautiful ornate Ming vase her mother gave her on her fortieth birthday; the boys' memories including magic sets and board games and all the sentimental things that were either in the bedrooms they'd once occupied or packed away in the attic. She'd taken all the photograph albums – if Perry argued about that at a later date she'd happily put what he wanted onto memory sticks and send them to him, but for now she wanted to safeguard them. She'd had to think carefully about packing her clothes. She hadn't wanted Perry to see empty rails in her wardrobe should he look inside, so she'd packed her favourite items and repositioned what was left so the wardrobes didn't look so empty.

She had a wonderful book collection, but it would be too obvious if she cleared those. She needed to get away from the house without having a conversation about leaving because she knew Perry would stop her. Whatever he said would get into her head and before she knew it he would've convinced her that this was a bad idea. He would've repeated all those things he'd said time and time again – she couldn't make it on her own, she had no money or job or skills, she was breaking the family apart. Sometimes she had those thoughts all by herself, which was why she'd never taken the leap before.

She put a few of her most treasured books into a box. Margery Williams' *The Velveteen Rabbit* was incredibly special, having once belonged to her mother. Margot had read it to the boys time and time again when they were little. Into the box went other childhood favourites she'd enjoyed and then shared with her sons including *The Tiger Who Came to Tea*, *Charlie and the Chocolate Factory*, and *The Lion, the Witch and the Wardrobe*. She slotted in ten to twelve other books – as many as she thought she might get away with – and then she positioned the antique humidor Perry's father had passed down to him from his own father further along and spaced out more of the ornaments so it wouldn't look like anything was missing. Sometimes she moved or rearranged a few pieces when she was cleaning so she doubted any of the things she'd done would rouse suspicion.

The day she closed up the storage unit with the possessions that mattered the most to her tucked inside, the adrenalin was flowing freely. Her escape route was in sight. She wasn't going to be this crushed woman she barely recognised any more.

Back at the house she'd put a couple of thick jumpers into a rucksack at the last minute when she decided she didn't want to leave them here, given some days could be chilly despite the summer season. As she'd taken the rucksack down to the basement to put with the rest of her things, she'd paused when she passed the photograph of their family of four on the wall of the stairwell. The picture was of her and Perry and the boys on a boat, all of them smiling as the boat skipper took them further out to sea. She stood there staring at the smiles, the happiness of the Yorks. She closed her eyes. They'd had some good times.

The next picture along was taken of the boys outside the tent they'd pitched in the back garden. It was when Sebastian was fifteen and preparing to do the Duke of Edinburgh award and he'd been desperate to camp out for the night. Margot had borrowed a family-sized tent from her parents, and just when she was laying out the poles thinking she would have to do it with Sebastian when she didn't have much of a clue, Perry had come home and taken over. He hadn't seemed himself. He didn't mention anything about his day; he simply got on with putting up the tent. He made a campfire and they sat around it telling stories until it was time to go to sleep. They'd all stayed in the tent that night and it had been like a snapshot in time that was never really repeated, as if she was nineteen all over again and cuddling up to that same Perry she'd met in the pub.

They never did put the tent up again after that day, even though Sebastian and Alistair had begged. Perry had never taken Sebastian orienteering like he'd promised, and over the years the distance between the boys and their father simply grew. Perry had made matters even worse when Sebastian got a job as a ski instructor. He'd called Sebastian's career choice ridiculous, a lark. He'd told his son that he was just a boy wanting to mess around rather than getting a real job.

Yesterday, before Perry came home from work, Margot had gone from room to room in the house. It had a warmth in some places. In the boys' rooms she remembered tucking them into bed, reading them bedtime stories; she remembered how she'd sit with them the night before a big exam. She'd take them hot soups in a mug when they were sick; she'd lie with them if they needed her to.

She'd asked herself yet again whether she was doing the right thing.

But deep down despite any hesitation she knew she was. She'd take her memories, the good ones of this house and her boys, and keep them treasured in her heart.

Inside a cupboard in the same room in the basement as Perry's bike was a filled suitcase and a holdall as well as the rucksack. It wasn't a lot to take, but it would do until she needed to come back to the area to access her storage unit. Her laptop was with the holdall, as well as the bag of Sebastian's postcards and when the clock struck twelve she would leave this house. She'd use the back door after turning off the alarm, she would go down the side path and out of the back gate where she'd meet an Uber that would whisk her to a hotel some thirty miles away. She didn't want Perry to see her go when he woke up and looked at the Ring camera to see where she was, and in the morning she'd get the early train down to the South Coast.

The evening she planned to leave dragged on almost painfully. Perry had come home from work with an instant complaint as she bumped into him in the hallway.

'What happened to the bush by the driveway?' He took off his shoes and set them on the rack in the cupboard behind the sleek handleless door to one side.

'The gardener trimmed it right back.' She headed for the kitchen and took the tuna casserole that had been keeping warm out of the oven.

'We can see the bloody neighbours now.' He tugged off his tie and sat at the table. 'Call the gardener. Find out what can be put in its place.'

She didn't reply. He didn't necessarily expect her to; he expected action. And he was going to get that. When she left.

Her heart fluttered with nerves despite the fact

he had no idea. Part of her was waiting for him to announce he knew and block her path.

'Remember the Petersons will be here in an hour for drinks,' he announced, barely looking at her. He'd obviously noticed her make-up-free face, the summer dress that was years old now and not the smartest.

She'd forgotten all about the Petersons and momentarily panicked that her plan would be compromised. But the good thing about the Petersons – a couple from eight doors down – was that they never stayed past 10 p.m. Perry and Malcolm usually talked business, then holidays, then investments before it came full circle back to business. Throughout, Priya, some twenty years her husband Malcolm's junior, usually kept a smile on her face and her ridiculously white porcelain veneers on display as well as one hand on Malcolm's knee, as if he needed to know where she was at all times.

Dinner with Perry went as predicted – quiet and without much chatter – so did the drinks with the Petersons, and Margot got through both with the excitement about her plan brewing inside her.

'You could've at least tried,' Perry moaned as he got ready for bed almost an hour after the Petersons left.

Margot was wearing an old nightie, one she'd leave downstairs after she'd changed into jeans and a sweatshirt and made her exit. She hadn't taken her watch off and set it onto the top of her bedside cabinet like she usually did. 'I did try, Perry. The house is clean as always; I was polite.'

'You didn't even try with the conversation.' He yanked on his pyjama bottoms. 'They're nice people.'

'I'm sure they are but we don't really know them.' She rubbed cream into her hands and left the pot on the bedside table. It felt odd that such a small thing reminded her that she would never pick it up again. She wouldn't feel this carpet beneath her feet after tonight; she wouldn't luxuriate in their spa bath with scented candles lined up in a row. Because she wouldn't be coming back.

He pulled back the bedcovers. 'We do know them. We see them every couple of weeks.'

To Perry that meant they were close. He seemed to forget that associating with someone meant nothing when the conversation between the men was always the same. Neither of them noticed the women were quite frankly bored, and Priya sat there inspecting her manicure or fiddling with her hair extensions and was just as spaced out if one of them asked her a question. Margot used to make an effort to remember people's names, recall things of interest to talk to them about, but tonight her heart wasn't in it and her mind was elsewhere.

When Perry was in the bathroom, she checked her phone. The confirmation for her bed and breakfast in Bournemouth had come through via email and she had three nights there before she would decide her next move.

Her heart thumped at the possibility of freedom after all this time.

Perry turned onto his side, almost but not quite looking at her over his shoulder as he said, enunciating every letter, 'F-Y-I, I hate tuna casserole.' And then he switched off his light.

She lay there in the darkness. This was the last time in this bed, in this room, in this house. Her last time sleeping next to Perry. Her Perry. Except he hadn't been that man for a long time. Maybe he hadn't ever been the man she thought he was.

When the time came, and she was sure he was asleep shortly before midnight, she crept downstairs and in the basement she took out everything she'd hidden away. She took it all up to the kitchen where she left it by the back door. She went into the hallway and disarmed the alarm, praying that despite his heavy slumber the little bleeps it emitted wouldn't alert Perry, and then she went back in the kitchen and exited through the rear door before walking all the way down the side path to the back gate.

The Uber driver was waiting for her. He got out and helped her stow everything in the boot, and when she climbed into the back seat and gave him the address of the hotel the adrenalin was really pumping. She disabled her location services on her phone – Perry probably assumed she didn't know how to do that but she did; she'd just never dared to do it before – and then debated whether blocking his number was a good idea in case something happened with the boys. She didn't debate it for long though. She blocked his office number, the home landline, and his mobile before they reached the hotel. She'd talk to Sebastian and Alistair soon and let them know what was going on, she had to, but for now she just wanted to be out of Perry's reach so he couldn't get into her head before she really got herself sorted out and knew in which direction she was heading.

No turning back now.

She was on her way. To a new life.

She wished she could tell her mum she was getting out, she wished she had her boys at her side, but most of all she wished she hadn't waited so long.

A tear briefly escaped until she swiped it away. Was this how every woman felt leaving behind a life of being trapped? You wanted to escape, and yet there was sadness for the good parts that you'd lost or maybe never ever gained in the first place.

She looked out of the window at houses as they passed them by, some with lights on, others in total darkness. Families, couples, lovers, behind closed doors. Some no doubt happy, others needing a way out.

Finally she'd found hers.

She bought herself an ice-cream after she'd brushed the sand from the beach off her feet and slipped her sandals back on. It felt wild to do whatever she liked, whenever she wanted.

Back at the bed and breakfast she logged on to her emails but Perry hadn't written. Of course he wouldn't be able to call, not unless he tried doing so from an unknown number, and she wasn't sure what was worse: an angry response demanding she come home or this, silence. This way she was waiting for him to make a move, and it wasn't a nice feeling. Or perhaps that was all part of the master plan he'd hatched the second he knew she'd gone.

Had she underestimated him? Had she made a mistake?

She felt a flutter of panic. What if he called the police? What if he reported her missing? What if she caused a whole lot of trouble and wasted valuable resources?

Oh my God, was what she was doing totally selfish?

Had she been so wrapped up in herself that she hadn't thought this through?

In a brief moment of guilt, she sent Perry an email to say that she'd left the marriage and that she would be in touch when she was ready. It was a short paragraph but the thought of the authorities trying to locate her was enough to drive her to send it. She gave him no hint as to her whereabouts.

She read more of her emails – Sebastian had sent through a whole lot of photographs and she clicked on those – he really did look professional, happy alongside the group he'd been teaching that day, their final day. Every single person in the photograph was smiling. Why had Perry never put happiness before career achievements for either of his sons? The Perry she'd met in the pub that first night might have done. The Perry with the young son and wife in the poky little flat, struggling to make ends meet, had seen the simplicity at the end of the day coming home to a little boy he could bounce on his knee and make laugh, to a wife who wanted his affections and who laughed with him. Somehow he'd got so successful that that had been all he could see. He was just like his father. How had Perry's mother lived that way for so many years? Had she felt trapped? Had *she* ever wanted to leave? Or was she happy with life the way it was? Maybe some women were.

She replied to Sebastian to thank him for the pictures. She wrote a sentence to say that things had changed somewhat at home, that they should talk soon. But then she deleted it. She wasn't ready to say anything and when she did, it would be on a face-to-face call. It was the right thing to do.

She thought about Faye. It was exciting to know that she was in England too, in the same county in fact. And she was a friend. She could reach out to her, have someone in her corner.

Except she wouldn't do it just yet. She wanted to eventually, but she needed to work things through in her own head before she talked to anyone else.

She began searching online at the wider parts of Dorset and the Jurassic Coast – Mupe Bay, Fossil Forest, Lulworth Cove, the Lulworth Estate, Driftwick Bay. She wondered whether Faye had been to the bay yet, whether she knew anything else about Howard.

She sent a brief email to find out if Faye might have any news.

She was surprised to get such a quick response and even more shocked at what Faye had to tell her.

Driftwick Bay Books was closed? Permanently?

She bashed out another email to ask whether Faye knew why, whether it was because Howard had given in to the pressure to sell up, but Faye quickly replied that she had no idea. And by the time their email exchange finished with Faye having to dash to accompany her uncle to the hospital for a checkup, Margot was even more concerned about Howard.

She suddenly felt compelled to help in some way. She was hiding in Bournemouth, but what if she went to Driftwick Bay herself? It was the least she could do to find out whether Howard was all right, whether she might be able to do something to help. She'd dealt with Perry her whole life, after all, and some of his less than pleasant business associates or clients. She might not have had the confidence to stand up to her husband, but this was different. Perry had manipulated her and got into her head before she knew what was even happening in her marriage, but maybe she could have a quiet word with this developer and ask them to please back off.

There were very few accommodation options in

or near Driftwick Bay given it was summer, but one place was available and caught her eye. It was a very cute one-bedroom cottage half a mile on from Driftwick Bay. She thought it a bit cheeky to claim it was still within Driftwick Bay because she wasn't sure that was strictly true according to the map, but it wasn't overly expensive – probably because it was one bedroom. The listing gave approximate walking distances to local amenities, which while being a distance some would moan about, she was quite happy with and already wanted to embrace the exercise.

She didn't hesitate for long. She could almost imagine some other online booker swooping in and booking it while she was dilly-dallying.

She booked a four-week period, which gave her a generous discount and quickly took out her credit card to secure the booking.

An uncomfortable feeling spread through her chest, however, right after she typed in the credit card number. Of course she couldn't use it. Perry was the primary account holder; if she used the card, he would check the statement and might somehow be able to work out where she was. She couldn't risk it.

From the back of her purse behind a photo of the boys she took out another card. This one was linked to the account Perry didn't know about. She hesitated for another moment, thinking of all she needed to do with the little money she had – she needed to live somewhere, she had to eat, pay bills and fund day-to-day living.

The enormity of it hit her all over again as she entered the alternative card number.

Margot stayed one more night at the bed and breakfast, getting a refund for the nights she hadn't used, which was kind of the owners, and the next day she packed her things and travelled by train to Wool, where she got in a taxi to go the rest of the way to Driftwick Bay.

She smiled to herself. She was going to meet Howard in real life. Howard, her kind friend with a heart of gold, Howard who might well be having his own tough time right now.

10

FAYE

Faye had stayed with her dad and Uncle Frank for a few days but today she let herself in to the static caravan at the site in West Lulworth. Her uncle had owned this caravan for a long time. It had been his and Clare's escape to the seaside or as close to it as they could get. He didn't come down here much now but had handed Faye the keys and told her it would be nice to know it was being used.

She opened a couple of windows in the lounge, which flowed into the kitchen area. Doors opened on to a balcony if the weather was nice and at the other end of the caravan were three bedrooms, one en suite, and a slightly bigger bathroom. It was compact but to have the space to herself was bliss.

She took out the groceries she'd picked up on the way here, then unpacked her things in the main bedroom, and by the time she came through to the lounge again the warm breeze of early September had done its job and freshened things up.

It was such a lovely day with no sign of rain, and it wasn't long before Faye headed out to explore on foot. It was a twenty-minute walk down to Lulworth Cove from her caravan and the sea seemed to draw her there faster. The air was so fresh, but that might have a lot to do with the fact that since she'd arrived – apart from that first day with the whistle-stop tour to Driftwick Bay, hoping to meet Howard – she'd stuck to walking around the village with her dad. This was her first time clapping eyes on the ocean properly.

The vastness of the ocean never ceased to amaze her, the sounds of the water and the gulls, the chopping of the waves you could see as you got closer. Back in Dorset after all these years, she felt something lift inside her. Rather than thinking of everything she'd lost, she focused on what she had to gain from her trip. She would have time with her dad, time in England after so many years, time to get used to no longer having a fiancé and the future she thought they would share together. And she had time to find out what had happened to Howard and why he'd closed his beloved bookshop.

Despite the summer heat, walkers were out in force, some taking photographs of the panoramic views afforded from this point. It really was quite spectacular. Towering white cliffs wrapped around the arc-shaped cove, contrasting against the calm clear waters below. A couple of little kids raced past with a woman hot on their heels requesting they be careful. They reminded Faye of the excitement she'd felt coming down here as a kid with a tiny coloured net – and if it was low tide her and Steph had been able to investigate the rock pools, to see what creatures they could find. She had good memories of spending time with her sister and nothing would ever take those away.

She watched the paddleboarders in the sea heading across the bay and wondered how far they would go – perhaps all the way around to Durdle Door, a place she would visit today on her nice long exploration of a county she'd forgotten so much about. There were three kayakers on the tail of the paddleboarders, and she wondered how easy it was on the water today, or rather, how difficult. Both sports were vastly different on the ocean to a river, although the weather always played a part. She'd brought her swimming togs with her, or perhaps while she was in England she should think in more British terms. What was it they used to say? Swimming costume? She'd been away so long she could barely remember.

She pushed open the wooden gate to access the South West Coast Path. She followed the steep hill, absorbing the most beautiful and very different views to those she had in Queensland. Everything felt so... well, British!

She passed a milestone and snapped a photograph of the face of it, which showed how many miles to Durdle Door, to Ringstead, to Weymouth and to Minehead. She wondered how long the stone had been there.

Walking on, it felt good to move her body, get air into her lungs. Lulworth Cove was now behind her and ahead she could see Portland Bill marked out by the red and white lighthouse she had seen in one of Frank's old photographs: him and Clare with the lighthouse in the background, their arms around one another, devoted to each other in a way perhaps she and Brad had never really been.

She had her first glimpse of Durdle Door but not much before she took the steep slope and then even steeper steps down to another Dorset gem, Man

O'War Bay. The crescent-shaped bay with aquamarine waters was utterly breathtaking and when she finally stepped onto the sand and shingle beach and the wind whipped through her hair she tilted her face up to the September sunshine and turned around on the spot, arms outstretched.

She almost lost her balance, but only because a large inquisitive golden retriever decided she was more interesting than anyone else on the beach.

She bent down. 'Hello you. Aren't you beautiful?'

'Careful, it'll go to his head,' came a voice from behind her.

When she turned, she couldn't see the man until she wrestled her windswept hair out of the way. 'What's his name?' she asked.

'This is Midas. Midas!' He groaned, because Midas had just put slobber on Faye's denim shorts.

She laughed and fussed the dog around his head and his neck. 'Well, Midas, if you weren't so gorgeous I'd be annoyed right now.' A tennis ball was clamped between his jaws, causing the slobber, and he looked at Faye, then at his master, before he dropped the ball.

The man picked it up and threw it far down the beach, further than Faye could've managed. He didn't have to yell fetch or anything because Midas took off.

'I'll bet this is his happy place.' Faye smiled. It was definitely hers. She had plenty of beaches to choose from in Queensland and was glad she'd come to Dorset where she could be near the water too. Anywhere else might have not felt like such an escape.

Midas was panting when he came back this time and dropped the ball.

When the man threw it again Faye asked, 'Are you trying to wear him out?'

He laughed. 'Something like that.' And then he fixed Faye with a look that had her a little bit uneasy beneath his stare, not because she felt threatened, but because the guy was insanely attractive and if she wasn't mistaken, looking at her like he had more to say.

She'd better go. 'Well, it was nice to meet you...'

'Theo,' he said, extending a hand.

'I'm Faye.'

'Yes, you are.'

She hooked her hair behind her ear with both hands and held it there as the wind coming off the sea picked up again. 'I'm sorry, have we met?' He seemed familiar but that wasn't possible – was it?

His eyebrows rose momentarily before he said, 'Let's just say I owe you some money for a haircut.'

Before she could reply, Midas charged over with the ball once again clamped in his jaw. He dropped it and Theo picked it up, lifted his arm ready to throw. But before he launched the ball into the air another ball from someone else sailed right past them and Midas charged after it alongside another dog who it was really meant for.

'Midas!' Theo growled, taking off after him.

Faye wandered along the beach, the water lapping gently against the shore, until Theo came back to her side with Midas who once again had his own ball.

'You do seem familiar,' she said to him. But he wasn't Australian and she would've remembered a British client at the salon if he'd ever been over there to visit, especially one as handsome as he was.

'I guess I've grown up a bit since we last saw each other.'

Still she couldn't place him.

The skin beside his eyes crinkled as he grinned. 'I was an innocent twelve-year-old boy and you cut my hair.'

That didn't make sense. Not at first, but then she gasped. 'Oh my goodness, you're Theo from school!'

He'd worn a backpack with his name written on the back in big white letters and he'd sat behind her in maths and once helped her when she had no idea of the answers. The haircut had been in return for helping her. 'I cut your hair in the playground.'

'You sure did. My mother was not best pleased when I got home.'

She grimaced. 'I doubt it was my finest work. I'm a bit better these days.'

He put both hands against his chest as if in shock. 'Don't tell me you're still cutting people's hair.'

'I'm a hairdresser.'

Now that made him really laugh.

'I'm not kidding,' she said when he couldn't stop. She'd forgotten that they also used to laugh a lot together at school. Not in maths, which she'd struggled with, not in English or history, but in assembly. She couldn't remember what they'd laughed at now, perhaps it was that they had to be silent, and that was enough to set them off.

How was it possible that funny, kind Theo from school was standing right in front of her now?

'Well then, the haircut makes more sense, given your career choice,' he said as they fell into step beside each other to head back up to the coastal path. 'I thought for years you did it that way to spite me.'

'No, I thought I was doing something nice, and I admit I wanted to practise.' She went first up the steps. 'You seemed like someone who wouldn't freak out if I messed it up. Funnily enough I hadn't had any takers before then. None of my family were willing to be victims.'

'Well I thought you did a great job. I was the talk of the school. You should've added colour to really get people talking.'

'I think your mother would've come and given me a piece of her mind if I'd done that.'

'No, Mum's gentle. She's got a sense of humour; she'd have seen the funny side. The only reason she didn't that day was because we were going to a family wedding at the weekend.'

'Oops.'

'Yeah.' He chuckled. 'Big oops.'

'So do you still live in West Lulworth?' she asked.

'Not any more. I left, studied in London, but always wanted to settle back this way and about ten years ago I bought a place in Driftwick Bay.'

'The bay is beautiful.'

'It is. And all of this is at my doorstep.'

She looked around at the ocean they were leaving behind, the beach, the beauty.

'You went to Australia. What brings you back to England?' he asked.

'My dad is here for a while staying with my uncle not too far away so I've come to see him. I'm staying in West Lulworth now.' They were part way up to the top already but she was getting out of breath. The steps were a lot steeper going up than they had been going down. She stopped. 'Can I ask you how you knew that it was me and not Steph?' They'd all been at school together, although Steph had been off with a different group of friends.

'I wasn't sure, not at first, but there are subtle differences between you both, and when I got closer I noticed the tiny freckle above your lip.'

Not many people noticed the differences unless they looked really closely to study the girls. The fact that he had pointed one out reminded her of how much time she'd spent with him at school.

'And your smile,' he said as they kept on walking. 'Your sister had a different smile.'

At the top she got her breath back and couldn't help but show him that smile now. 'It was really nice to bump into you today.'

'Likewise.' But he groaned when his phone went. 'I'm sorry, I have to take this.'

'No worries. I should get going anyway.' She lifted

her hand to wave. She still wanted to go and see Durdle Door and then had a decent distance to retrace back to Driftwick Bay.

She felt a little flutter in her tummy because seeing Theo brought back memories of the crush she'd had on him when they were at school, and feeling that way had her thinking of Brad. She felt uneasy, as if she was cheating by having any sort of feeling for another man. Of course she wasn't doing anything wrong at all, but it was an odd feeling being single, being allowed to feel that way, after being a part of a couple for a long time.

She followed the path in the direction of Durdle Door until at last the natural rock arch came into view. One of the Jurassic Coast's most impressive landmarks, it was a sight to behold. The water licked around the iconic arch, a kayaker passed through in one direction, a paddleboarder in another.

Brad had never wanted to come to England, let alone Dorset. She'd suggested it for their honeymoon – thought they might take in some of Europe too, but he'd wanted Bali, closer to Australia, and she'd seen the attraction. Now she wished she'd insisted a little more, although at the end of the day it wouldn't have mattered, because they weren't even together now.

Back at the caravan, she knew she couldn't put it off any longer. She needed to send out a link for the book club, which meant she had to end the moratorium on looking at her emails for a few days. After she'd emailed Margot to tell her about the closure of the bookshop and they'd had a couple of messages back and forth, Faye decided she needed an entire break from social media, email, everything that made her contactable. She hadn't found Howard at the bookshop. She had no idea what was going on there, but what she did know was that her time in England was a reset for her and she wanted to enjoy the outdoors, spend time with family, and get away from anything that caused her stress.

She logged on, expecting another message from Margot but there wasn't anything. She'd gone oddly quiet.

However, there was one from Howard. At last.

She was so happy to see his name. Now she'd be able to find out what was going on.

But her happiness faded when she clicked on the email.

The email wasn't from Howard at all. It was from his wife, Bonnie. And in the short message Faye knew now why the bookshop was closed.

Howard had passed away.

She was about to reply when she saw the P.S. at the bottom:

This email address won't be monitored as of today.

Her heart sank. She didn't know Howard's address in the bay. She wouldn't be able to go and tell Bonnie what a wonderful man her husband was, how much he'd given to the book club, how much joy he'd brought Faye and everyone else.

But something occurred to her – Howard had said that he and Bonnie lived up the hill leading past the shops and that their garden had a view of the ocean. Faye also knew he lived in a cottage with a white picket fence and an ocean blue front door because he'd told them that once during a book club meeting when they'd read a book that had a similar brightly coloured door on its cover.

Driftwick Bay couldn't be that big. She'd ask around, find out where the cottage was. She couldn't leave it like this. She had to at the very least go and pay her respects to Bonnie.

* * *

As she waited for the midnight hour and another book club to begin, she curled up on the sofa, the windows closed now the caravan had cooled with the absence of the sun. She hadn't held the book club in a few weeks and it felt odd to be doing this so late when she was used to doing it first thing in Australia. Maybe it was like Howard once said, the darkness and the late hour were all part of the adventure.

As far as she knew, everyone was coming to tonight's session; nobody had said they weren't. She'd contemplated telling Margot via email about Howard, but then decided that it wasn't the sort of news she ought to share in that way, so she would tell everyone together, tonight.

She read a couple more chapters of *Gone Girl* by Gillian Flynn, although it was hard to concentrate when her thoughts were still on Howard. He would say this book was a gripping read, and it was, and she tried to imagine him here, bossing her about, telling her to concentrate on it.

'Sorry, Howard, it's not happening.' She put the book on her lap and lay back, arms raised above her head, the backs of her hands resting lightly on her forehead.

She wondered how Bonnie was coping. Howard talked about her often, and one thing that had always stuck out was that his Bonnie didn't like to read. They'd all been shocked at the fact, given how much Howard adored books and had bought a bookshop. But, Faye supposed, everyone was different.

It felt like forever until midnight rolled around. She had a semi-decent internet connection at the caravan – apparently it could be touch and go – and with a milky hot chocolate to sip on and *Gone Girl* beside her, she was ready. Not that she suspected they'd talk about the book at all tonight because really this session was to tell everyone about Howard.

It was a full house apart from Howard, with Winston and Joel turning up as well as Sarah and Margot, and Faye got the news out as soon as everyone was logged on and microphones were working.

Sarah dried her eyes with a tissue. 'How can he really be gone?'

Winston shook his head. 'I'll miss his smiling face.'

Faye said, 'I'll miss seeing what pyjamas he has on each week.' They all laughed at that. He was a character – that was for sure.

'I'm really sad,' said Margot and she looked it. Her eyes had a telltale redness around them. Their dear friend had gone and all of them were left in disbelief.

Sadness and tears turned to laughter and fond memories of their favourite book club member, the man who was kind, funny, a true bookworm, a friend. Everyone was quieter than they'd been in previous sessions – as Faye had suspected no mention of this week's book was made – and as the time rolled on towards 1 a.m. the little rectangles on the Zoom session disappeared one by one. Eventually Faye had no choice but to attempt to get some sleep herself.

Faye had wondered whether Margot might stay on the call to talk a while longer but she didn't; her rectangle had disappeared quickly as well.

All of them felt the loss of a dear friend keenly and as Faye switched off her lamp she wondered whether the book club would ever feel the same again.

11

BONNIE

Howard had been gone for five weeks and waking up without him beside her was just as painful for Bonnie now as it had been the first time. Would it ever get any easier? These days she wanted to shut out the entire world; she wasn't sure she even wanted to be a part of it any more.

Bonnie had taken to sitting in Howard's chair to feel a connection to him. She'd even made it to midnight a couple of times, as if that kept her closer to her late husband. The one thing she wouldn't do, however, was set foot inside his beloved bookshop. She'd closed Driftwick Bay Books and really she would rather it just disappeared off the face of the earth. And yet, she still hadn't made the call to the developers. The letter was sitting in the letter rack and she'd deal with it eventually but not just yet. She didn't want to speak to anyone let alone them.

She swore her knees creaked as she climbed out of bed and shuffled into the kitchen. She was sixty-six. Shuffling wasn't for someone her age, was it? But that's all she could bear to do without Howard. It was as if the simple act of lifting up a foot to take a step and then doing it over and over so you could get where you were going was too hard.

She picked up the post from the mat. She hoped there wouldn't be something else to sort out – the paperwork and admin when someone died was never-ending. It was upsetting, stressful, and she'd dealt with enough of it to last a lifetime. She'd been on the phone to banks, insurance companies, the private pension company, the inland revenue. It made the loss of someone so much more powerful when over and over again you had to share the fact that they had died, the date of their death, their full name and date of birth, each word a tiny bit sharper than the one before as it shot pain through your heart at the knowledge this was permanent. Howard was never coming back.

The post brought nothing of interest, just some junk mail and a council tax reminder, so she put the kettle on and took two mugs out of the cupboard. She dropped a teabag into each.

And then she just stared at the mugs. Two mugs, not one, and she'd made the same mistake every day since her darling Howard died.

She could still remember the first cup of tea Howard had given her. It had been the summer of 1977, and on a rainy seafront in Blackpool he'd seen her waiting at the bus stop drenched from head to toe. She'd been staying at her uncle's and working on his ice-cream van. She was allowed free time when the weather was bad and tourists fell away, and the weather that day was dreadful. She'd gone in and out of the amusement arcades with her pennies, playing the slot machines, not winning much but enjoying herself and a summer of freedom in a new place, before she'd given up and gone to get the bus.

'Excuse me, miss,' came a voice next to her at the bus stop. It hadn't been raining quite so hard when she got here but the bus was ten minutes late and now the downpour was worse and she was soaked. She looked into kind blueish grey eyes when the man asked, 'Do you know when the next bus is due?'

'Should be any minute now.' She tried to smile, like it was perfectly normal to be standing here arms folded across her chest and shivering.

'Here.' He thrust his umbrella out and over her head, leaving himself to get wet.

'You'll get soaked.' She put her hand on the shaft of the umbrella and pushed it back his way.

He hesitated before he stepped to her side so that they were both under cover. 'Now neither of us will get wet.'

'Or wetter? It's a bit late for me.' And she was pretty sure the blouse she was wearing would be see-through now it was so soaked.

'I've got a thermos of tea. Would you like a cup?'

She barely hesitated because she was freezing. 'Yes please.' But she started to giggle.

'What's so funny?' He removed a thermos from his rucksack, took the plastic cup off the top, passed it to her to hold.

'Most guys your age would have alcohol in that, not tea.'

'If any of my mates walk past, it's beer, all right.' He filled the plastic piece with the hot liquid. 'We'll take turns to drink.'

'Thank you.' It was hot but not so hot she couldn't drink it gulp after gulp.

'Another?'

'No, your turn – you have one. You don't want to catch a chill.'

And so it continued until the tea was gone and the bus finally came into sight. But by then the rain had stopped, the sun came out and the man, who had introduced himself as Howard, pointed upwards. 'Look at that.'

'A rainbow.' She smiled. It was beautiful.

They got on the bus together and Howard insisted he get off at her stop to walk her to the front door. He told her which campsite he was staying at with friends and asked whether she would like to see him again. Bonnie had thought he'd make a move on her, try to kiss her or something, but he hadn't. And she'd told him that of course she would love to see him again. He was so polite, unexpected, she couldn't imagine not saying yes.

Bonnie visited the campsite the next day as they'd agreed – she was almost forty-five minutes earlier than the time they settled on though because she'd been worried about being late – and found Howard on a fold-out chair behind the toilet block after she'd walked around unable to locate him in the part of the field he'd told her his tent was pitched.

'Whatever are you doing here?' She pulled a face, looking up at the high windows at the back of the block.

'The boys think I'm still in the toilet.' He held up the book on his lap, a hefty tome by the looks of things. 'Only way I get some peace.' He stood up and offered her the chair.

'No thanks.' She shook her head. 'So, you have to pretend you've got alcohol not tea and you have to hide away to read?'

'Crazy, I know. I've had a brill holiday, they're good mates, just that I am a bit of a nerd really. Always was at school. Still am at twenty-four.'

'I'm nineteen.' She hoped that didn't make this a bad thing. She wasn't sure her uncle would approve or her parents, as it was quite the age gap.

'Good to know.' He smiled.

'I wasn't a nerd at school like you were,' she teased, 'but I'm working a bit harder now I'm training to be a nurse.'

'So the ice-cream van will lose you soon.'

She shrugged. 'I'm just helping out family with that. There isn't much to do here on a visit. What do you do? For work, I mean?'

'I'm in the civil service.'

'And what do you do in the civil service?'

'I'm in administration. Which sounds dull, but I don't mind it. I'm learning all the time. Who knows what I'll get into next.'

She liked his response. It sounded mysterious, like there was more to this man than she realised. She could imagine him in an administration role – he'd be organised, patient, do things right. She wasn't sure why she knew this; she just did.

She looked at his book. 'That looks heavy.' She took it when he passed it her way. She was right.

'Do you read, Bonnie?' he asked, relieving her of the weight of it.

'I had to for my studies, but not for pleasure, no.'

'You're missing out.'

'Am I?' She shrugged. 'I like real life, me.'

Except right now in her kitchen on her own in their cottage in Driftwick Bay she'd rather have anything but her real life.

She took her tea into the back room and set it on the desk. Howard's books hogged the shelves behind and his laptop was exactly where he'd left it. He'd had a habit of always leaving it open and she'd come along and close it so that dust didn't gather between the keys.

She picked up her mug of tea and turned to look at the painting of the ice-cream van she'd done in the summer of 1977.

On the day she'd gone to meet Howard at the campsite, she'd had a later shift at the ice-cream van.

She'd told Howard to stop by just after 4 p.m. as that was usually when her uncle took his break. She might only be nineteen, but had already been married once – something she knew she ought to explain to Howard sooner rather than later, because after the terrible time with her first husband, her family, immediate and extended, kept a watchful eye on her.

Howard had turned up promptly at 4 p.m. and standing behind three others in the queue he'd not taken his eyes off her. She knew he was watching her every move and she'd tried to act nonchalant, like she wasn't nervous at all. But her hand shook as she took the change from the elderly gentleman buying a cider lolly and a 99 before she looked up as if she'd only just realised Howard was there.

'Four p.m. already,' she said.

'Looks like it.'

She leaned onto the counter. She was way more nervous than she'd been seeing him that morning and she knew it was because she liked him so much. They hadn't spent much time together but already he made her feel safe, which was odd – she didn't know him that well, so how was that even possible?

She spotted the rucksack on his back again. 'You got a book in that bag?'

'Never leave home, or the tent, without one. And

besides, if the boys find my book back at the camp-site, it'll be destroyed and that would be a crime.'

'Where do they think you are now?'

'I told them I was going to walk all the way to the pier. That put them off.'

'You're on holiday with them. Don't you want to do things together, like go out and meet girls?' She expected that was what they were all here for like many of the big single-sex groups.

'I've already met my girl.'

Flustered, she served another lady three mini milks. A young boy wanted a tongue twister and a girl with dreadlocks rushed up with a request for a strawberry split.

When it was all quiet again, she asked Howard what he would like.

'What would you suggest?'

She smiled. She knew exactly what he'd like. She held a cone beneath a spout and pulled the lever to make the soft-serve ice-cream come out and as she moved the cone around the perfect ice-cream formed. She took a long chocolate flake, pushed it in the side and passed it to him. 'Try that.'

He fumbled in his pocket.

'No, it's fine.' She swished her hands, wanting to give him this ice-cream on the house.

She turned around at the sound of the van's door opening. Her uncle was back already. He pulled on the white coat he always wore when he was working.

The sound of coins being dropped onto the counter made her turn again.

'Keep the change,' said Howard in a sing-song voice as he headed away from trouble.

She could've kissed him right there and then, if she could reach down to his level the other side of the van that was, and if her uncle wasn't watching.

Once her shift was over, she skipped over to the bench where Howard had sat for the last couple of hours. She sat at the opposite end.

'Keep your book on your lap in case my uncle looks over,' she said.

'You're not allowed to date?'

The sea breeze caught her hair when she turned to ask, 'Is that what this is?'

'Maybe.' He looked suddenly shy.

Bonnie liked that Howard wasn't at all cocky, wasn't too big for his boots, not like her husband had been. She'd met Sean at a local pub near where she lived in Derby. He'd been wild from the start: he rode a motorbike, had tattoos all up both arms, and he was a couple of years older. He had jet-black hair, smoked, hung around with other lads equally up their own arses, but he'd had an air about him that she'd been drawn to. She'd been so young, so vulnerable when they met. Maybe everyone had to date a bad boy somewhere along the line. And he'd been hers.

She fixed her gaze on the sea stretching out before them from their vantage point. 'Before we decide what this is, I think I should tell you something.' She was worried he would walk away when he heard what she had to say so she blurted it out to get it over with. 'I was married.'

'Married?' He paused. 'But you're only nineteen.'

'It was a mistake. It shouldn't have happened. We were both young,' she rambled on.

'You were in love?'

She paused, trying to think of how to explain it when sometimes she didn't really understand it all herself. 'Looking back, I think we thought we were. We wanted to grow up too fast I suppose, move out of home and do the next exciting thing. It was soon clear that neither of us were ready and we went our separate ways, but not before my ex-husband burned through his savings and mine. Not that I had much, but I had some put by. My parents ended up getting me out of the dodgy bedsit we'd rented by paying the sum we owed to the landlord and they never let my ex near me again.'

'I'm sorry you went through that.' He closed his book as if he didn't care who was watching them both now. 'But I'm glad, in a way.'

'Glad?'

'You've had a relationship go bad; you've been with someone you can't trust. Maybe now it's time to take a chance on someone who's the complete opposite.' He cleared his throat. He'd sounded confident but only for a second before he was back to being unsure of himself. She loved that he wasn't at all arrogant when he said, 'I'm talking about me... you know, in case that isn't clear.'

'It's clear.' She shuffled a bit closer to him on the bench, eager to talk about something other than her failures. 'Tell me, what do you boys actually do when you're on holiday? When you're not running off with a book that is.'

'The usual – swimming in the sea—'

'It's cold!'

'Freezing,' he said. 'But we had to do it. You can't come to the beach and not get in the water. We've had fish and chips, been to the amusements many times. We've enjoyed a few beers, even me.'

'Beer instead of tea? So you are semi normal then.'

They stayed where they were, talking and laughing until it was time for her to head back to her uncle's for dinner.

Howard had come back to see her every day of his holiday after that. He'd spent the mornings with the boys, swimming in the sea, lazing on the beach, trawling the amusement arcades. Then after Bonnie's shift at the ice-cream van was over, he'd take her to the Pleasure Beach where they rode the Big Dipper, their hands tightly gripped together the whole time they were on it, a secret thrill zipping through her body at the closeness. They'd laughed their way through the fun house once they were past the slightly creepy grinning clowns outside and enjoyed the near-vertical slides, the wonky staircase, the moving floorboards and the rotating barrel that was next to impossible to stay on. They drank fizzy orange, then strolled hand in hand along the pier with the smell of fresh doughnuts, hot dogs and candy floss lacing the air. And as the sun went down the first evening they were together, they stopped on the pier, the lights illuminating the water and the boardwalk, and shared their first kiss.

On the last day of his holiday, Howard cut his

time with the boys short. He'd finally told them that he'd met someone and before they could ask who, or worse, follow him, he'd jumped on the bus near the campsite and come to meet her. That day Howard brought his camera with him and got a passer-by to take a photograph of them both in front of the ice-cream van, his arm hooked around her and across her chest from behind, holding her against him. By that time her uncle had been introduced to Howard, her auntie had come down to say hello to him, and she needn't have worried about her family thinking the worst of this man. From the very start they'd loved Howard, and her auntie had reported back to Bonnie's mother – she knew this because she'd over-heard the brief phone call – that this man was 'nothing like the last'.

When they both went back to their own lives, Bonnie wondered if she would ever see that photograph or the young man she'd met in the summer of 1977, the man who'd promised to write and come and see her. A week after Howard left Blackpool, she re-alised he'd meant every single thing he said and along with the photograph of them in front of the ice-cream van came a letter through the post. They wrote as much as they could – him from Coventry, Bonnie from Derby once she was back there to continue her nursing training, and they arranged to meet up as much as possible. And when she missed him more than she could bear in the winter, she painted the picture she was looking at now in the cottage in Driftwick Bay, the painting that hung in the back room, bringing the summer of love to the forefront of her mind all over again.

She let out a little laugh, putting her hand across her mouth as if she shouldn't have done it, when she heard the ice-cream van going down the hill in Driftwick Bay towards Lulworth Cove. It was as if Howard was saying hello.

And then she took her tea back to the bedroom, climbed beneath the duvet and hid from the rest of the world the same way she'd been doing ever since she lost him.

12

MARGOT

Margot's sleep had been all over the place since she arrived in the bay and found out about Howard. It had been as if the news had nudged the reality of her own situation to the forefront of her mind all over again. She had no financial stability, she had no job or experience that employers might recognise, and she still hadn't told her sons that she'd left their father. Her mind kept leaping from one thing to the next, like a monkey swinging from branch to branch.

She'd briefly thought about getting in touch with Faye as soon as she was here, but she wasn't ready to meet up with anyone yet. It was funny, here she was, free to do what she liked, and yet it still felt like she had to give herself permission. She wondered too whether when Faye saw her she would sense this was no holiday for one and somehow she'd end up having to admit the truth, and the misery of her marriage before she really felt ready to talk to anyone other than herself. Howard had been different, perhaps as he'd felt like a parent figure the night she told him the whole truth.

The cottage she was staying in was old but cosy. She was used to everything being modern, but loved the Victorian bathroom suite, the flagstone tiles, the small windows with iron fittings and framed with cute little curtains. She imagined it would be even cosier in the winter. There was a cast-iron flame-effect log fire in the little lounge, an old-fashioned trunk filled with thick woollen blankets at the side of the room, and a lovely slipper bathtub upstairs that she hadn't yet used.

She'd just had breakfast and once she'd done the dishes she sat down and lifted her laptop onto her knees. She logged on and although she should've expected the contact, her mind went into overdrive when she saw four emails waiting from Perry.

It looked like he'd given her what felt like a cooling-off period and now he wanted answers.

She abandoned the laptop and the blanket, got up, paced the room.

Should she delete them without reading them? Or was it better to know what they said?

She wished she could ask Howard and for one ridiculous moment thought about looking up to the sky to ask the question.

She'd look at the messages quickly she decided. She had to know what they said.

But they only said the sorts of things she'd heard already.

The oldest email asked when she was going to come to her senses, the next said to let him know when she was finished playing games, the one after accused her of breaking up a family and the final one demanded to know where she was and end this 'fucking ridiculous stunt' she'd pulled.

She deleted every single one of them.

And then her spirits lifted when she saw an email land from Faye. She must be online now so Margot replied straight away.

They chatted back and forth a couple of times, mainly about Howard, until Margot suggested they switch the conversation over to WhatsApp to make it easier. She'd blocked Perry from WhatsApp already and the only reason she hadn't done it on email too was in case she needed to correspond with him. If he got much more abusive she might have to stop him from being able to contact her at all.

She told Faye in her message:

> I've become an insomniac like your auntie.

Faye replied:

> I'm not sleeping too well either since I found out about Howard.

Margot continued typing without really thinking.

> I thought opening my window to hear the faint sounds of the ocean might help me to doze off.

It was only after she'd pressed send that she realised she'd let on that she wasn't in Berkshire right now.

And sure enough Faye replied with:

> My geography isn't great, but I'm sure Ascot is quite far away from the coast.

Margot moved to the other end of the sofa away from the glare of the sun streaming through the window, reminding her that across the entire country they were being treated to an extended burst of summer despite the month flipping to September. Perhaps the brightness of the days could pull her through if she felt she might go under with the enormity of what she'd done over the last week or so.

She typed back:

> I'm taking a break, in Dorset.

Faye asked:

> Whereabouts?

She hesitated. But she realised she owed it to herself to take the plunge some time, and she didn't want to miss the opportunity of meeting Faye in person like she'd missed meeting Howard. She replied:

> Driftwick Bay!

Faye's message flew back.

You're right near me!

She added a heart emoji.

You came to check on Howard just like I did.

Margot had escaped her marriage, run from it, and yes, she'd been so worried about Howard that she'd come to the bay to see what was going on, but she hadn't ventured out since the taxi dropped her at her accommodation apart from to get some food in the cupboards. She hadn't yet walked down to the bookshop or seen the beauty of the area again for herself, because she'd been in panic mode that she hadn't thought this through.

Faye's next message didn't surprise Margot and saved her having to be brave enough to write it herself:

We need to meet in person.

Margot's pulse raced until she realised she could do this. She could meet a friend without worrying that Perry would put a stop to it, follow her or turn up and ruin things. She could do whatever she liked.

She tapped out a reply.

> You know I think that would be a really lovely idea.

* * *

Margot and Faye agreed to meet outside Driftwick Bay Books an hour later. It felt fitting for Howard even though he was no longer around and they couldn't go inside. And Margot was glad to finally have a reason to go out and explore.

She recognised Faye instantly, of course. She had beautiful blue eyes and the fresh dewy complexion that came with being in your late twenties, and of course she was just as lovely in real life as she was online.

She hadn't been sure how to greet Faye, but Faye took the decision out of her hands when she flung her arms out wide. 'It's so good to meet you!'

Margot readily returned Faye's hug. 'It's lovely to meet you too.'

'I can't believe we're really here. I'd got used to being miles away from you and Howard.'

At the mention of his name, they both looked in through the window of Driftwick Bay Books and the darkness beyond. Howard had talked about the little nooks with comfy upholstery, the bustle of children in the story corner at the far end, the low lighting that showed off the books. Peering inside now, there was none of the warmth or the personality Howard would have brought with him when he took the shop on. It was all still, all quiet.

'Howard has really gone,' said Faye.

Margot knew both Faye's parents were alive. She was still so young, she might never have been through the pain of losing someone close to her, which would make this even harder to understand.

'He loved this place.' Margot looked once again at the sign on the door. 'He'd hate it being closed. I wonder if Bonnie will sell the business to the developers.'

'I hope not. Howard was always adamant that they wouldn't get their hands on it. He'd have hated that.'

'I guess it's Bonnie's decision to make,' said Margot.

'Do you really think she'd do it?'

'I've got no idea.'

Both of them were still looking at the shop like it might come alive in front of them.

They stood there for a bit and reminisced about

the way Howard had described taking on the bookshop, the first day he'd gone down the hill with the key and let himself in, how he'd felt like a kid in a sweet shop. They recalled how he'd always managed to keep up lively book club discussions every week despite the midnight hour.

Faye laughed. 'Do you remember he once told us you should read a book twice or even three times to really appreciate it?'

Margot remembered it well. 'We were discussing *Pride and Prejudice* from memory and I didn't get into it at all. I told him that reading it once was enough.' Howard had insisted that her dislike of the novel meant she might not have fully appreciated it, suggested maybe her mind hadn't been on the story.

'Did you ever read it again?'

'Not a chance,' said Margot, her smile fading as they both contemplated the loss of their favourite member of the group. 'Book club won't be the same without him.'

They peered in the window one more time. The shop was deserted but it didn't look like anything else had changed. The shelves were lined, the story corner he'd often talked about was still at the back from what they could see. Howard might be gone but this place was still waiting for something. Or someone.

'I think we need to go and see Bonnie.' Margot's comment took their attention away from the window of the bookshop.

'I think you're right. And this is a small town; it can't be that hard to find the cottage. I meant to ask around but I haven't done that yet.'

'Let's see how we go,' Margot replied. 'He talked about walking down this hill a lot.' She pointed up in the direction she'd come from earlier. 'Their cottage has to be up there.'

'I think you're right.'

They started to walk. They'd seen a picture Bonnie had painted once from the garden of their cottage and they both turned to look behind them a couple of times as they walked, sure that this was the same view they'd seen on canvas.

It took a while but after a couple of hundred metres they suspected they'd found the place that Howard had called home.

'This has to be it,' said Margot. 'Don't you remember he talked about the garden gate being so low he thought it might sometimes be easier to step over it than open it. As far as I can see, none of the other homes seem to have the low fence or gate he could've been talking about.' She looked to the right as they stopped. It was beautiful looking down and towards Lulworth Cove. She could just about hear the sea too.

A crazy paving path led to the ocean blue front door, to the cottage that was framed with planters on either side of an outside doormat, and had wisteria around the entrance that was already starting to lose its leaves. Faye knocked on the door.

'Perhaps she's out for the day,' said Faye after they tried a third time without success.

Reluctantly they walked away when they got no answer.

'We'll try her again another time,' said Margot.

They headed further up the hill talking about Faye's journey over to England, the long flight she'd endured, the village where her uncle lived.

And quite unexpectedly Faye confided, 'The story about me taking my engagement ring off because of chemicals at the hairdresser's was a lie.'

'It was?' Margot hadn't noticed before but she wasn't wearing the flashy diamond she'd showed off when she announced her engagement.

'I'm here to see Dad but I'm also running away.'

Her breath hitched. Because she was doing the same thing except unlike Faye Margot had kept her wedding rings on to stop unwelcome questions until she was ready.

As they walked Faye confided in her about her ex-fiancé, Brad, how he'd broken off their engagement, how devastated she was. She'd cried, apologised for being silly, cried some more with Margot as the sympathetic ear she said she'd needed. She'd told her dad, and her mum also knew, but she told Margot that she didn't really want to give them any more worry than they already had.

'I'm so sorry you've been through all of that,' said Margot when Faye's tears subsided and she brightened up as if relieving herself of the burden by confiding in someone else had a magic power.

Margot almost wanted to tell her about Perry, seeing as they were being so honest with each other, but she couldn't do it, not until she'd told her boys. And it must have taken a lot for Faye to share what she had tonight, so this moment was about her, not Margot.

'What are your plans right now?' Faye wanted to know. 'You could come back to mine, have lunch. I'm making a roast for my dad. I promise I won't cry all over you again.'

'Cry all you like. I don't mind at all.' It felt good to be invited and even better to have the choice to do exactly what she liked. But she had to turn the offer down this time. 'Lunch would've been lovely but I have a few things I really need to do and they can't wait.'

Luckily Faye didn't ask what. Margot was going to tell her sons what was going on because Faye's honesty had prompted her to stop putting it off. Perry might well have told them already to get one up on her, but somehow she doubted it. He wouldn't have initiated a call. He'd rarely made contact with them since they each left home, and he probably knew that they would take her side.

She was nervous the rest of the morning as she waited for the right time so that she could tell the boys together.

When the time came she clicked on Sebastian's contact number and then Alistair's to make a group call on her phone – there was a twelve-hour time difference between England and New Zealand and she was doing this at 11 p.m. Sebastian's time after he got home from a social event. It worked out well that it was a study day for Alistair so he was at home rather than in the classroom at the start of the new school year now they were into September.

Sebastian answered first and spoke softly. 'Housemates are all asleep, better not wake them.'

Alistair clicked in soon enough to hear his brother's remark. 'I thought it would be wild partying all night and après ski.'

'That's what Dad thinks.' Margot cringed at his comment. 'I was out, but one drink and that was it. We've all got to be on the slopes by 10 a.m. and we're expected to teach and communicate. Can't say a skinful would be a good idea.'

Margot hated the way he felt he always had to defend himself. He did it with all of them, even though neither she nor Alistair were the ones who doubted him.

Alistair cottoned on to something being different and asked her, 'What's that picture behind you?'

She turned and laughed at the painting of a scantily clad lady basking on a rock. She supposed that gave away that she wasn't at the house.

'I'm not at home,' she confessed, dread pooling in her stomach.

'Where are you?' Sebastian was peering at the screen as if the peculiar painting of the naked lady might give a clue.

'I'm in Dorset, in a lovely little town called Driftwick Bay.'

'Is Dad with you?' Alistair asked unnecessarily, because since when had their dad ever taken a holiday in England? Not for a long time; he usually arranged something abroad, the flashier the hotel the better. Margot had always preferred the simplicity of packing up the car and driving somewhere on the coast for a holiday – it gave her far more joy than a faceless five-star hotel somewhere too hot for her and the boys.

'It's just me.'

'Mum, what's going on?' Sebastian's concern was evident and she almost wished she was doing this without being on screen. 'There must be a reason for having to do this call tonight.' She'd messaged him earlier and usually she would've said they'd talk another day when he didn't have a social event, but it had to be now; she had to tell them.

She was still trying to grab hold of a decent sentence when Sebastian blurted out, 'Have you left him?'

She wasn't sure whether to be upset he knew or relieved. 'I haven't been happy for a very long time,' she said.

'Mum...' Alistair prompted and she looked at the screen again. She'd hung her head at her admission; part of her saw it as her fault that their family would never be the same again.

'I've left him,' she said, her voice as big as she could make it for now.

It was Alistair who spoke first. 'I'm glad.'

'You are?'

Sebastian didn't look triumphant but instead accepting, like he'd finally found the last piece of a puzzle to slot into place. 'You've been putting up with him for years.' His voice caught. 'It's been a lot. For us, but more for you.'

She almost wished she'd talked to them both like this before but she'd so wanted to give them a normal upbringing, a happy home. She'd failed at both of those things.

'What did Dad say when you left?' Alistair asked.

'I left in the middle of the night.' Neither seemed surprised. 'He's emailed me but I'm not contacting him. Not yet.'

'Have you left for good?' Sebastian asked.

She nodded.

Silence.

Until Sebastian said, 'You deserve so much more, Mum.' And then he broke. No matter that his brother was watching, his mother too, he cried, big fat tears that came from a boy who was now the man who had held it all in for far too long.

Alistair hated seeing his brother upset but for

once he was the one who consoled Sebastian with kindness and understanding. Perhaps he'd seen more of Perry's behaviour recently to know that this really was the right thing. Maybe Sebastian had tried to escape it by going so far away that it was all flooding back to him now she'd left the marriage.

They talked about the night she left, about Bournemouth and some of their happy memories there, then a bit about the bay until Alistair asked, 'Mum, do you have enough money?' They both knew where finances were concerned Perry held the purse strings.

She wiped the tears from her cheeks. 'Don't you worry about me; I have some put aside. I'll need to get a job but I'm going to be absolutely fine.'

'We're not kids any more, Mum.' Frowning, Sebastian asked her, 'How many months before you run out of money?'

'Mum...' Alistair prompted her when she failed to give a reply.

'Not that long, but it's not your job to worry.'

'You can have my money from Granny.' Sebastian delivered his offer firmly, adding, 'No question about it. I haven't spent a penny of it. I don't need it right now; you do.'

'Sebastian, I can't take your money.'

'I'll bet Granny left it to us so Dad couldn't get at it,' Alistair put in before he offered his share too.

'He's right, isn't he?' Sebastian asked.

She nodded. 'Your granny changed her will.'

'Do you have your own bank account?' Sebastian asked her. 'One that Dad doesn't have access to.'

'I do.'

And before she knew it she'd been talked into giving them both her bank details and agreed to receive the transfers. 'But it is a loan – I won't budge on that,' she said. 'Once I get a job I'll pay you both back every single penny.'

'Mum, as long as you are safe and happy, that's all we care about,' said Sebastian, his brother chiming in his agreement.

They stayed on the call. She recapped on how she'd left, that she'd emailed Perry, that her things were in storage. She assured them they weren't to worry about her, that for the first time in a long while, she actually felt a modicum of happiness about her life.

Her eyes sparkled with tears. Her two beautiful boys. 'I'll keep you up to date. With everything.' She took in both boys' expressions. They didn't seem shocked or even that surprised. Had she been blinkered for so long that she was the only one who hadn't seen how bad things were?

'Love you, Mum,' Sebastian said as they prepared to wrap up the call. She didn't really want to let them go. And then he asked, 'What did you do with all my postcards?'

His question brought a smile to her face. 'I brought them all with me.' He didn't need to hear that his dad had thrown them out, nor that that had been the final straw.

'Do you think you'll settle in Dorset?' Alistair asked her before they said their goodbyes.

'I don't know yet. For now, I'm here.'

And more to the point, she was no longer with Perry.

The world was opening up in front of her. Maybe at long last she would get to do something for herself.

13

BONNIE

Bonnie was still in her nightie standing in the back room of the cottage staring out of the window. The view was nothing like usual with a mist hanging so low the sea was no longer visible.

She turned round, put a hand gently against the urn on the bookshelf. The urn was filled with Howard's ashes. Howard's cremation had happened incredibly quickly compared to others she'd heard about. A friend of theirs who died last year had passed away a good six weeks before the crematorium had a slot available. Summer was obviously a better time to go – Howard would've laughed at that; he'd always had a good sense of humour. She'd invited all their closest friends to the cremation and the wake in Reading where they'd bought their first home together and where they'd stayed until they'd moved to the bay after their travels. It had made sense to do it there and her friend, Beverly, had helped her organise it and get through the toughest parts. Bonnie had gone through the motions, which was easy enough given Howard had already told her what he wanted when the time came – a humanist ceremony, cremation, and his ashes to be scattered in the sea. She supposed she was grateful he'd outlined his wishes – they both had.

She should get ready. She headed for the bathroom but as she passed the front door she heard a knock. She contemplated not answering it, she'd done that plenty of times over the last few weeks, but the person on the other side had probably seen her form pass by the window to one side.

She opened it to Iris who had been checking up on her frequently either in this way or with a quick phone call – quick because Bonnie always made it that way. She supposed she should be grateful that people weren't giving up on her when sometimes she felt like giving up on herself.

'Oh, I'm sorry, Bonnie,' she said apologetically. 'You're not dressed.'

'I had some letters to deal with this morning,' she lied. She didn't want to admit that this was an all-too-common occurrence these days.

'Do you need anything? Food, errands run? It's just that I'm at a bit of a loose end... without work, you know.'

'I'm sorry. I know how that feels.' Iris had been Howard's assistant in the bookshop on a part-time basis. She was three years younger than Bonnie and much like Howard, her love of books had drawn her to keep on working.

'Don't you apologise – I understand why you closed the shop.'

The September breeze was warm enough not to worry that she wasn't wearing much at all, although she kept slightly to the side of the door frame out of sight of passers-by. She didn't need strangers to see her in her nightie. 'I didn't know what else to do I'm afraid.' But in the long term, she had the developer making a very good offer. She had the letter waiting for her in the letter rack and all she needed to do was get in touch with them to get the ball rolling. Then she would never have to see or think about the book-shop again.

'You did what you thought was right,' said Iris. 'And that's okay.'

Bonnie knew what it was like to be without work, without an anchor. And Iris had never been anything other than a pleasure to be around. Howard had always found the same. She felt bad that whatever decision she had made so far and whatever change was about to come would alter things in a big way for Iris too.

'You could always team up with me?' Iris suggested with a cautious smile.

Bonnie wasn't about to admit that the thought of going inside the bookshop filled her with dread. It was bad enough with her own reminders here; she barely coped with those. Yesterday she'd been looking for some dental floss in the back of the lowest bathroom drawer and her hand had fallen on something soft. She'd pulled out Howard's shaving brush. He hadn't used it for years, instead favouring the speedy method of squirting foam into his hands, lathering it up and spreading it over his chin and upper lip. She'd sat hugging the brush, like she was some kind of lunatic, a brush that had been stuffed into the recesses of their bathroom drawer. She'd thought he'd thrown it away when they moved. What a crazy thing to keep. She wanted to ask why he had, but of course she couldn't.

'I'm not a book lover,' said Bonnie simply. 'Me teaming up with you would be silly.'

'You don't need to be a book lover.' She shrugged. 'Just good at keeping things tidy, chatting to customers.'

She was only trying to help but there was no way Bonnie was going inside the bookshop ever again. Did she have to spell it out to Iris? 'I'd better go and take a shower.' She moved to close the door.

'Bonnie…' Iris's voice stopped her before she could get away. 'I know you're not sure what you're doing with the shop. But how about I go in there and make sure everything is as it should be?'

'Well, I—'

'I know there were a few boxes in the stockroom that are still taped up and need unpacking, and we didn't leave the story corner particularly tidy after the last session. I definitely didn't sweep the floors as I always do. It means you won't have to worry about it.' She smiled. 'Howard was a stickler for leaving everything perfect so that if anyone was to peer in the window it would be as enchanting as ever. You know he always wanted the glass at the front cleaned to draw people to the shop – not that it needed to be any more enticing…'

And as Iris carried on talking about Howard, the bookshop, her memories of the pair of them in there together, it almost made Bonnie fall to her knees picking up on someone else's grief. Because that's what it was. Howard had touched other people's lives not just hers, but she hadn't really been able to see it, not even at the cremation.

She almost wanted to engage in conversation with Iris about Howard and yet at the same time she wanted to make her stop. She was depleted of energy, of enthusiasm and zest for anything at all.

Howard would be so disappointed to know she'd closed his bookshop without any warning, and so with Iris still talking, Bonnie made a snap decision. It was the only way to get rid of this woman.

She leaned around the door and lifted the book-shop keys from the hook where she'd put them ever since Iris dropped her spare set round once the sign was placed in the window.

'You want me to check on the shop?' Iris asked as Bonnie dropped the keys into her outstretched palm.

'That would be lovely.'

'And what will I tell people? Should I explain—'

'You know what, you can reopen.' Again, anything to make her go away and leave her in peace.

'Yes, reopen. It's the right thing to do. You know, until I decide on what to do with the place. Don't order more stock, not yet. Concentrate on selling what you have.' She cleared her throat. 'It'll all have to go.'

'What do you mean?' Her face fell. 'Are you going to sell?'

'I would imagine so.'

Iris didn't look too panicked but then the reality seemed to dawn. 'You're planning to sell to the developer.'

'I... I don't know what else to do.'

'I understand.'

Bonnie wasn't so sure she did, but how could she bear to keep something that had become so much a part of Howard?

And now she was desperate for Iris to go. 'Howard always said that if we wanted a week away he could trust you with running things at the bookshop. You'll be fine.' Please, just go.

'He did train me up on everything, I suppose.' But she didn't look confident and told Bonnie, 'The thing is, I can only work a certain amount of hours; it won't cover the times Howard used to put in.'

Bonnie, drowning in her own grief, had quite forgotten other people's circumstances it seemed. Iris couldn't do really long days because she had a daughter with special needs who was semi-independent but still needed a lot of help from her mum.

Howard and Bonnie had never had a family. It was just the two of them until recently. And now it was just her. After her first marriage ended, Bonnie was wary of getting too serious too quickly. She knew straight away that Howard was the one, but she didn't want to marry, not for a while and he respected that. She got her first job as a nurse and they moved in together and for a while they stayed that way. When they eventually married when Bonnie turned thirty they were both blissfully happy as a young couple with no responsibilities. The baby conversation came soon after their wedding but despite trying for a couple of years nothing happened.

When they were in their mid-thirties they contemplated adoption but settled on fostering and for ten years on and off they took in children of varying ages for short periods of time, doing their best to give whoever was in their charge a good home and stability before they found their forever home. Some of those children stayed such a short while that saying goodbye wasn't terrible, but others stayed longer and it was heartbreaking to have to say their farewells.

That was why they eventually stopped and decided it would be just the two of them from then on.

She looked at poor Iris, torn between racing down to the shop with the key and thinking of the family who still needed her. Howard had once said that Iris told him the bookshop had given her a little something just for herself since she'd retired from her job as an accountancy clerk. It seemed she loved being with her family but she needed that little bit of something extra in her life.

Bonnie felt horribly guilty that every decision she made about the shop was going to have a knock-on effect on Iris. And, she knew, the town.

But she needed to close the door now, to be alone again; she didn't want to think about the bookshop any more.

'Open it for shorter days,' said Bonnie.

Iris nodded decisively. 'I'll go and see what's what, shall I? I'll give you a call and let you know.'

Bonnie murmured her agreement as she closed the door.

How would Howard react if he knew she had kept a letter from the developers, that she was seriously considering selling his bookshop to them of all people?

He wouldn't have been happy, but would he really expect her to hold on to it without him here?

The thought had her looking around the kitchen and the cottage they'd made their home. Did she even belong here in Driftwick Bay without him?

Those thoughts overwhelmed her as she took a quick shower and then got dressed. Even doing those simple things was an effort these days. She hadn't left the house much at all in the weeks since Howard died. She'd made it to the bakery, her aim to get in and out as quickly as possible and avoid too much eye contact or sympathy. She'd gone at the busiest time on purpose to avoid Cathy trying to engage her in small talk, something she'd loved once upon a time as she and Howard tried to make the town their new home and get to know everyone. She'd driven to the supermarket furthest away from the town so she wouldn't bump into anyone she knew when she needed to do a proper shop, and on each occasion she'd got back home and locked the door behind her with a huge sigh of relief.

She went into the back room. Her easel was still standing by one wall, the sketch of the view from the hill and the bookshop still waiting for its proper start, but something was stopping her from doing the very thing she loved. She'd tried several times over the last few weeks to lose herself in her art but it was as if she was blocked. Her mind, her brain, her hands, none of them worked the way she wanted them to.

She ran her hand across Howard's laptop as though it connected her to him as much as when she touched his clothes, his side of the bed, his belongings that were still in their place in the bedroom. He'd loved books, his bookshop, his Midnight Book Club. The man had been book crazy. She'd told the book club that he'd passed; she'd almost missed notifying them completely until well after his cremation. When she realised she hadn't let anyone know she'd retrieved his little black book of passwords from the secret shelf beneath the desk that most people wouldn't realise was there, logged on and sent a short email to a woman called Faye.

Howard had gone quickly and without a fuss, in a way he would've approved of. It hadn't been from a long-term illness or a disease that changed his day-to-day life. Perhaps it was a blessing, although that was hard to remember when she cried herself to sleep and when she wished she could lay a hand on his arm, see his smile, have just one more conversation. Howard's heart had inexplicably failed, just like that, while he was sitting in the chair she was staring at now. She'd been in the kitchen turning out a syrup sponge, his favourite pudding, none the wiser of what was about to happen.

And now Howard's ashes waited in the pewter grey urn on the bookshelf. She'd slotted the urn into the only remaining space, like a bookend, and there it would stay until she scattered them. Initially she'd told him that whoever went first would have to wait for the other, but he'd told her he didn't want to sit on some shelf gathering dust, he wanted to be set free, and if she were to go first then he would set her free too.

She felt guilty that she still hadn't done it. She wondered, would she ever be able to let him go?

Bonnie might not be going outside much, but she was still keeping the cottage clean and orderly. She dusted, and then she vacuumed, although she hated it when she switched the vacuum off and the cottage fell into its silence once more.

She'd just put the vacuum away in the hall cupboard when a delivery arrived. She took in a big brown parcel from the postman and she knew exactly what it was before she even opened it. It was the books she'd ordered on grief. Yes, she'd ordered books. She wasn't a reader but the day she'd emailed Faye from the Midnight Book Club she'd sat at

Howard's desk for quite some time. And then she'd stood up. She'd gone to Howard's bookshelves behind and walked along perusing the titles, waiting for a book to jump out at her, demand to be read. She'd even said out loud, 'What will help me get through this, Howard?' But she hadn't been drawn to anything. So, she'd used her iPad to search for books on the topic and suddenly had a barrage of choices. She'd skimmed through some of the accompanying wording and plucked those that seemed the best. At least in her inexperienced eye.

She found the scissors from the kitchen drawer and soon had the cardboard package off the books. She pulled out three titles, all of which had seemed like a good idea at the time, and now seemed like the worst idea in the world.

When she'd first retired she'd loved how many hours she had in the day to get things done. Now it was as though the hours had doubled, tripled even. The days were too long when you were all on your own, and time stretched out in front of you, looming, like something to cope with rather than enjoy.

Another knock at the door made her jump. Who on earth was it this time? This was the third caller today.

Howard had never moaned about people coming

to the door, in fact he'd welcomed it. He'd loved an unexpected chat with someone he knew or a stranger who'd come upon the cottage for whatever reason.

Years ago when Howard found himself an in-person book club he'd urged Bonnie to join an art group, thinking perhaps she'd like the company. She'd tried it but as predicted it hadn't lasted. One woman sat there knitting and nattering the entire time, another two gentlemen were more concerned with what biscuits were available this week, and from what she'd seen there was very little art done.

'I won't go back,' she'd told Howard after trying it for three weeks in a row. She'd leaned down and kissed him on the cheek. 'It's not for me.' And when she'd explained the lack of focus of the other attendees he'd suggested they might be lonely and were looking for an outlet, anything, to get them out into the world.

Right now she understood it more than ever and yet she still couldn't find the impetus to let anyone in, physically or metaphorically.

She opened the door to Theo, Iris's son. In his late twenties, he was a lovely young man, always friendly and polite, handsome too, and a teacher at the local primary school.

'Theo, what can I do for you?' She tried to sound more like herself and at least she was dressed this time. She couldn't ignore his dog, Midas, who was looking up at her patiently, waiting to be included in this encounter, and she reached down to pet him.

Theo handed her a bag of something that smelt good enough to eat. And it was, because when Bonnie looked inside it was filled with wholemeal rolls, a loaf and some Belgian buns as well as a little note from Cathy at the bakery. She'd tried knocking but Bonnie must've been in the shower.

'Well, thank you, Theo. Someone might have stolen these had you not alerted me.' And actually, she really quite fancied a Belgian bun now she'd seen them lurking in the bottom of the bag, with their delectably sticky white-iced tops and currants poking out and a glacé cherry on top. Her appetite seemed to be returning at long last.

'I think Midas sniffed them out before I saw them,' said Theo.

She felt incredibly rude not inviting the young man in. But she hadn't invited *anyone* in since Howard died. Sometimes she even ignored the door. 'I saw your mum earlier,' she told him.

'She said. You know, she is made up that you've let her go into the bookshop.'

'I'm glad. I wasn't sure what to do. I'm not a book person you see, but I know it's popular.' They hadn't been here that long in comparison to other residents but long enough to feel a part of the community, which said a lot about the locals. 'I'll have to have a think about what to do long term I suppose.' Because long term, was she really *still* a part of things here without Howard? She hadn't been the person who saved the bookshop; she hadn't interacted with people the same way Howard had. Perhaps it would be best for her if she sold the shop, gave up the cottage and went back to Reading where everything was so much more familiar.

'It must be really hard for you,' said Theo. 'But remember people are around, whenever you need.' It was as if he'd read her mind.

She gulped back her emotions. It was harder to think about leaving when someone said kind things.

'Even Midas here,' Theo went on, patting his dog on the head. 'Although he hasn't enjoyed his sudden retirement, let me tell you.'

Bonnie laughed for what had to be one of the first times since she'd lost Howard and it took her by surprise at how good it felt to be sharing a joke with someone else. 'I know the feeling.'

Oh, the dog was gorgeous, he really was. She

hung the bag with the buns on one of the coat hooks inside so she had both hands free to make a fuss of him.

Midas was trained as a therapy dog and he often went into Driftwick Bay Books with Iris. From what Howard said he was a hit with anyone who needed his services and indeed anyone who came into the shop. Bonnie could see why. He was such a softie.

'I thought schools were back now it's September,' she said to Theo when she stood up straight again. The sudden observation had her realise she was starting to feel a part of the real world again. It sounded silly but for weeks she hadn't known what day it was, what month; she'd been in an abyss of grief, unable to crawl out.

'Inset day today,' he said with a smile. 'I'm on a quick break.'

She looked at Midas. 'Well, you can go into the shop with Iris whenever you like,' she said.

Theo looked embarrassed. 'I didn't come to ask for his job back; I really did pass by and see the bag of goodies on your doorstep.'

She laughed for the second time. 'Well, it's lovely to see you both. And people will enjoy Midas being back at Driftwick Bay Books.' But she wasn't sure how long that would be for.

When she closed the door she was happy she'd managed to keep her smile, keep up the pretence that she was coping.

Because she really didn't feel like she was.

The way she felt right now she wished the bookshop, the cottage and Driftwick Bay would disappear and she could somehow magic herself somewhere else away from all this pain.

14

FAYE

Faye loved Australia but when her dad decided he wanted to go to Dorset to be with his brother, she had started to feel more drawn to England, as if she might have unfinished business there. She'd told herself she was merely being nostalgic and in part she was because with England came fond memories of her and Steph growing up, the family that was once all together.

Faye hadn't been in Dorset for very long before she'd felt that same draw and it was more than nostalgia; it was a sense of belonging and peace. And quickly she decided she would stay here for a bit longer than she'd planned. It would give the gossips extra time to settle down before she went back to

Australia. Perhaps by then the shitstorm would be over. And now that Margot was around it was even nicer because she had some female company.

Faye put her change of plans down to the freedom she felt, the not having to look around every corner, duck her head, hide behind a cap and sunglasses. It was lovely to be close to her dad again too and with an open-return plane ticket she had options. However, those options meant longer off work and so a few days ago when she'd seen a cleaner disappear into the caravan next to hers, she'd gone into the site office and offered up her services if they needed an extra hand. They did; in fact they were short of help, and so once she showed them her British passport they were happy to put her on the casual roster. It would be on a day-to-day basis depending on what the caravan park's needs were, which suited her just fine.

The job didn't pay that well at all, and it would be hard graft, but Faye didn't mind any of that. In fact, when one of the cleaners got sick and she was given even more of the workload she relished the busyness as well as making some extra money.

As she started work that morning, she put her AirPods in and lost herself in a Lily Allen album. She squirted cleaner into the toilet in caravan number 28, which had thankfully been left pretty tidy – not all of them were, the one she'd cleaned before this she'd reported to the site office for the dirty dishes piled not only in the sink but on the coffee table, in the bedroom and even on the ledge in the bathroom. She gave the shower a clean until it sparkled – easy with this caravan; it was new – and moved on to do the kitchen.

She did a couple more vans and once her shift was complete she headed to her own caravan and stood beneath the shower for a while. Her body felt fried. Hairdressing was taxing, given she was on her feet so much, but cleaning was a lot harder. She'd scrubbed, wiped, vacuumed, cleaned windows, polished surfaces, but she'd somehow enjoyed all of it. It had taken her head to a totally different place, and she was earning money to fund her longer stay and keep her sanity. No gossips lurking, no reminders of a life she might have had with Brad, just a simple life she was making the most of.

She locked up the caravan behind her. Today Margot had her youngest son visiting and with Faye working part of the day she wouldn't see her until tomorrow at the earliest. It was odd that she had come on a holiday down here really – Faye knew she was worried about Howard too but Ascot was close enough that she could've just come for the day or overnight.

She went over to the lock-up unit behind the caravan's parking space and wheeled out one of the two bicycles that her uncle had told her about in a text message last night. He said he'd quite forgotten about them until now. She was going to knock on Bonnie's door again, see whether she would talk to her. It was worth a try, wasn't it? She and Margot had tried again already but either Bonnie wasn't coming to the door or she'd gone away.

The bike she wheeled out had to have been Auntie Clare's as it suited Faye's height and the saddle was too low for it to be Uncle Frank's.

She dusted off one of the helmets that were also in the unit and set off for Driftwick Bay. It wasn't that far distance wise, but it was a hilly route. She was glad of the September sunshine, the extension of summer and no sign of rain. According to Uncle Frank, they were already on the countdown to a long, cold winter, and her dad was getting excited, talking about making sure there were enough logs for the fire in the store to keep them both going through those cold months. Watching them together was nice but it also reminded Faye that she and Steph had once been like that, but not for a very long time.

She pumped her legs hard to get up the first hill, enjoyed coasting down the next and eventually pedalled past the sign announcing she'd arrived in Driftwick Bay. The wind had been against her, which meant it should be behind her on the way back at least. She went part way down the hill until she saw the cycle rack on the corner of a little street just as Uncle Frank had said there would be. Amazing how he could remember some of the most random tiny details.

She carefully cycled across to the rack on the opposite side of the road and dismounted. She locked up her bike and looked down the side street to a little bakery, which was emitting a smell that had already convinced her she'd treat herself before she did anything else. With cleaning and the cycling, her appetite seemed to be off the scale.

Inside the bakery she looked at all the tempting bakes in the glass-fronted cabinets.

The jolly lady, with a name badge that said *Cathy*, beamed a smile Faye's way. 'What's it to be, my love?'

'I'm not sure. Everything looks so amazing, it's hard to choose.'

'Well, you're not from around these parts,' the woman said in a Dorset accent much like her uncle's. 'Where are you from?'

'Australia.'

'You're a long way from home.'

'I am, but actually, I was born here.'

Cathy's eyes lit up. 'In the bay?'

'No, but I grew up in West Lulworth.'

'Is that right?' She smiled. 'And you're back now?'

'Just visiting.' She retraced her steps in front of the glass cabinet before she made her mind up. 'I'll take one of the glazed ring doughnuts please.'

Cathy popped one into a bag. 'You enjoy that and enjoy your visit to Dorset.' She had another three customers milling and with a smile moved on to serving them.

Faye didn't waste any time biting into the doughnut when she got outside, and it tasted every bit as good as she'd expected. She deposited the bag in the bin nearby and walked down the hill. Cleaning and spending time with her dad and her uncle had kept her busy so she hadn't had a chance yet to nose inside the telephone box library that Howard had mentioned. She'd told Howard about the similar initiative in Australia where they had street libraries: miniature sheds on top of a post pushed into the ground in front yards. They were there for people to take a book and leave a book. It was always such an adventure, finding new titles, wondering who had read the story before and what effect it had had on them compared to her. Faye believed that everyone read stories differently, that our minds processed facts in a myriad of ways. It was all part of the fun and it was why she loved hosting the book club, because the discussions gave you more than the book had already delivered. Sometimes she'd reread a book just to see whether she could experience it in a way another person had.

She opened the door to the telephone box which was, just as Howard said, filled with books. She rooted around in her bag. She had just finished reading a paperback, one of the few that had been left at the caravan park and she'd been allowed to take it from the site office. She put it in an available space and perused the choices. There was a biography about a cricketer, another one for a celebrity, a couple of colourful teenage books, a few Harry Potters, some historical novels, some romance books, and on the lowest shelf she found a book she'd wanted to read for a while, *Wild* by Cheryl Strayed, but for some reason had never got around to it. Perfect.

She popped it in her bag, closed the door to the telephone box library behind her, and then she crossed the road to make her way back up the hill towards Bonnie's cottage. But she didn't get far because as she passed the bookshop, expecting it to still be closed with the same sign on the door, she noticed it was open, and more than that, people were inside. She hadn't looked this way as she went down the hill; she'd been too focused on safely traversing the street to get to the bike rack and a bus had been blocking that side of the road ahead.

How had it suddenly reopened? Whatever the reason, this had to be a good thing, didn't it?

Howard had said that most of his allocated state pension probably went on books. When he'd said that, other members had chimed in with their encouragement to keep on doing what he was doing. He was such a lovely gentleman, not as old as her grandad who had passed away a couple of years ago, but he'd always reminded Faye of a grandparent, the way he treated others and talked to them, the way he listened, how he was never afraid to share his own opinions either.

She couldn't resist going inside the bookshop, and the smell instantly wrapped around her when she was through the door. It was intoxicating. This had been another topic of conversation in her book club, one that came up time and time again. They were all guilty of being book sniffers; there was something addictive about doing it and right now she was reminded of why she was such a bookworm. Between the pages she could escape, put herself in a different world far, far away from her usual one. Howard had joked when they talked about book sniffing that his Kindle didn't quite have the same effect and had even picked up his device and inhaled while he was on screen, making them all laugh.

She wished he was here now to talk to, to hug hello and watch in his element selling books or talking about books to anyone who was interested.

She walked past the shelves on one side of the shop, the scent of fresh paper fibres, the ink, the glue all used to bind these beautiful books together filling the air. Dark, wooden shelves lined the walls, all stocked and very neat, a dark wooden counter stood just left of the centre and cosy nooks here and there had cushioned seating. There was a big rug spread out at the far end in what looked like the children's corner with low-down shelves and plenty of colourful titles to fill them. She'd seen the bookshop through the window the first day she came here but actually being inside was something else.

She made her way around the shop. She stopped at the cookery section, then she moved to the romance books, then it was on to the travel section where she found books about Dorset landscapes and Australia's outback. She slotted the Dorset book back onto the shelf as the gentle tap-tapping of paws accompanied a golden retriever coming her way.

'Midas.' A harried woman with an armful of books came bustling over. 'Sorry, he's very friendly and likes to say hello to newcomers.'

Faye had already crouched down to make a fuss of the gorgeous dog. 'Actually, we've already met, haven't we, boy?' She noticed his collar, which identified him as a therapy dog. 'I didn't know you worked here,' she said to him.

The woman smiled. 'Midas here has been helping people for the last year or so. He's fully certified as a therapy dog.' She put the books she was carrying in a pile on top of the nearby table.

Faye had heard of therapy dogs – she had a client at the salon whose mother was in a care home and was delighted that a therapy dog had recently taken up residence there too.

'How old is he?' Faye fussed Midas round the ears as he looked right into her eyes, trusting, happy with the attention from a stranger.

'He's almost ten.'

'Well, he's beautiful.'

'Where did you two meet?' the woman asked her.

'On the beach,' said Faye.

'Ah, then you must have met Theo.'

'I did.' Was she blushing? She hoped not. At least Midas was a good distraction so she didn't have to look this woman in the eye. 'He's very calm and friendly.'

'Theo?'

Faye laughed. 'No, Midas.'

'Well, it's in his job description.' The woman neatened the books up into smaller piles on the table. 'Are you on holiday here?'

'Did my accent give me away? It just happened in the bakery too.'

'It's a bit of a giveaway.' She slotted a title onto the top shelf near Faye. 'So what brings you to Driftwick Bay?'

That was a long story. She'd go with an acceptable easy version. 'My dad is in England visiting his brother not too far from here. I grew up in West Lulworth and I'm staying at my uncle's caravan there. Free accommodation.'

'Ideal,' said the woman.

'Today I thought I'd come and see more of the bay.' A sadness washed over her that Howard was no longer here. 'I run an online book club and one of my members—'

'Oh my goodness, you're Faye!'

She hadn't expected that. 'Yes, I am.'

'You cut my son's hair!'

Now Faye knew she was blushing.

'I'm Iris, Theo's mum,' she said, hand against her chest. 'And don't worry, dear, you were young; it would've been funny had we not had a family function to attend.' But she was laughing now. 'And you run the Midnight Book Club! Oh well, this is quite splendid. Howard talked about you all the time.' She seemed to suddenly check herself, adding, 'Do you know about Howard?'

'I do. It's incredibly sad.'

'It was sudden. We're all so shocked. He hasn't lived in the town that long but he's one of those people who... well, he left his mark – put it that way.'

'I can understand exactly what you mean.' She paused. 'I came here to see the bay but also to pay my respects to Bonnie. Howard brought so much light into a lot of people's lives with his participation in the book club.'

'I'll bet he did. He raved about it, how it was international, under the cover of darkness, all this cloak-and-dagger stuff like he was writing his own book.' Her remark made them both laugh. 'Excuse me a second...' She dashed off to serve another customer.

Faye sat down in a nearby chair to flip through the first few pages of *The Fault in Our Stars* by John Green. There were just so many books and not enough time to read them all. She'd seen the movie of this one, but would love to lose herself in the book. She knew it would be a tear-jerker, but a powerful story with love at its core.

When Iris came back over, Faye told her how she'd seen the sign saying that the shop was permanently closed.

'I don't think Bonnie knew what else to do when Howard died. But the other day she handed over the key and told me to reopen. I think she might have felt guilty.' She added, 'I'm not opening for the full hours – I can't manage it all on my own – but I'm so pleased to be back here and I know the customers are happy to see Driftwick Bay Books open again.'

'Howard did love his books and this place.' Faye looked around. The shop had such character and a beauty that was impossible to see unless you came in here for yourself.

But she picked up on something else. 'Wait a minute, Bonnie is home? She hasn't gone away?'

Iris, in a bit of a flap, dashed over to help another

customer and when she came back to Faye explained that Bonnie was at the cottage; she just wasn't talking much or letting anyone in. 'I'm worried about her,' she said.

Faye could understand it and now rather than worrying about Howard, she was worried about his widow instead. She smiled at Midas who had settled at her feet.

'Is he bothering you?' Iris asked.

'Not at all.' She went over to the counter, Midas following as if they were lifelong friends. 'I never had a dog when I was little. I'm enjoying it.'

At the counter she chose a suitable bookmark and paid Iris for the book. There was no sign of Midas's owner at all and she found herself disappointed. He'd been thirteen when she left the bay, but Theo was a fully grown man now. And a good-looking one at that. Had her teenage crush returned?

She left Iris who had to be really missing Howard given she had a shop to keep tidy and customers to serve on her own, crossed the road, unlocked her bike and, helmet back on, she pedalled back up the hill towards Bonnie's cottage. It was a lot harder going up even though the wind was behind her, but she was soon opening the little gate in the middle of the white picket fence and walking towards the front door.

But she felt even worse when after knocking three times she got no answer. Since the scandal broke in Australia, Faye knew what it was like to be hounded, and so in the end she walked away.

Bonnie might not be there, or she might just want to be left alone. And to Bonnie she was nothing but a stranger after all.

15

BONNIE

Bonnie had been sitting in front of her easel for well over an hour. But she still hadn't managed to do anything with the canvas. She was waiting for inspiration to strike, but it seemed as though that was akin to waiting for a miracle.

Was this the way it was going to be from now on? No passion for the things she'd once loved, no desire for company, holed up in the cottage that should've been for two not one?

She'd cried a lot when Howard first died, then she'd got through the cremation, the return home, the many days that had passed since. And yet she still couldn't get herself back to functioning normally. Most days, with today being no exception, she felt as though she was going backwards rather than forwards. She felt stuck and unable to do anything about it.

She pulled out a big photograph book she'd had put together with all the pictures of her travel adventures with Howard. It was the sort where you sent your pictures online and a magic process turned those memories into a book. She'd thought she'd miss the traditional way with an album, but this really was quite beautiful.

She sat down in Howard's chair and flipped through the pages. The picture of the two of them at the front of their lodge in Africa beside a campfire gave her comfort, as did the rest of the photographs, which all helped her relive those precious moments. She'd never regret doing what they'd done. Everyone's retirement looked different – some wanted to potter in the garden, others revelled in looking after grandchildren, a few of their friends had downsized and got into renovations of their homes, but apart from retiring beside the sea, travel had been the main thing Bonnie and Howard had talked about doing together. He would've foregone the idea if she wasn't so adamant, being a bit of a homebody, but he'd had the time of his life in all those far-flung places, as had she.

When Bonnie heard a scratching at the front door, she put the book down and went to investigate. It sounded like some sort of animal trying to gain access but when she opened up it wasn't an animal; it wasn't anyone. It was the soon-to-be-completely-bare branches of the wisteria, which was dropping its leaves now summer had come to an end. Its woody framework structured around the front door of the cottage would need cutting back as winter came and it entered its dormant phase, and there wouldn't be a return of colour until spring.

No animal. No visitor. No Howard. No anybody. Just her. And as much as it irritated her when people came to check up on her, this time she felt the loneliness more than ever when she closed the door. She wondered who might have knocked the day before, because she hadn't answered it then.

She went back to looking at the photo book, moving on to the stunning photographs taken of the Norwegian Fjords. Howard and her, their arms around each other outside a store in one of the tiny towns they'd visited, which she couldn't quite remember the name of now. Perhaps it was Bergen as the next picture was of her standing outside one of the townhouses she remembered from there. She turned the page to see more shots of the narrow valleys in Norway, more of the jaw-dropping scenery and the ever-impressive Tvindefossen waterfall that had had her mesmerised. But most of all she remembered how lucky she'd felt to be with Howard and share those moments together.

Oh, this wouldn't do. She closed the book and went back to her easel, sure that something would unlock inside her and she'd put her paintbrush to work to produce something worthwhile. She knew part of the mental block was that it was the bookshop starring in the would-be painting, but it wasn't like setting foot inside there. Seeing it in a picture wasn't nearly as painful as doing that and in some ways she felt like she had to get it onto canvas if she was ever to move forwards.

She was overthinking everything these days. She shook her head, started to mix the colour on her palette to get the right shade of brown for the bookshop's frontage, which was all dark wood outside and matched the cosy interior's shelving. In the picture she'd taken, the shop was bathed with golden light coming from inside, and people milled on the street in front – a woman in a baby pink cardigan, a man wearing a flat cap, two children both wearing shorts were laughing at something or other.

But no matter how many times she dipped the

brush into the paint and it hovered in her hand in front of the stretched canvas, she couldn't quite get going.

When she heard the door again, she felt relieved at the interruption. Maybe that was a good sign?

She was already at the door when she noticed she still had a paintbrush in her hand. Too late now.

She flung open the door to find a young woman standing on the other side. She was pretty, blonde, and Bonnie suspected, an out-of-season tourist. She was probably looking for directions. Being at the top of the hill this sometimes happened as tourists arrived wanting to know where Lulworth Cove was – open your eyes! – or how to get to the coastal path or Durdle Door.

'Hello. Are you Bonnie?' The woman had sun-kissed skin and beamed a smile Bonnie imagined she'd never be able to replicate.

'Yes, I'm Bonnie.' She looked down when she realised she'd managed to get brown paint on the door-jamb. 'Damn it. Hang on.'

She brought a wet cloth back from the kitchen, and wiped off the paint, which hadn't been given a chance to make its mark.

'I'm sorry, dear, but I'm very busy. What can I do for you?' What was wrong with her? A moment ago she'd thought she might actually want some company, been excited about it even.

'I'm Faye.'

'Faye?' she asked with a depleted sigh. The woman definitely wasn't local or British by the sound of her accent.

'I've come a long way. I just wanted to… well, I wanted to say, I'm very sorry, about Howard.'

It took a moment before it dawned. 'Are you Faye from the Midnight Book Club?'

'I am, yes.'

'But you live thousands of miles away.' She was confused.

'I'm here visiting family. Well, kind of. I'm staying nearby.' She smiled. 'And now I'm waffling.' She turned, as if looking down the hill and her awkwardness made Bonnie glad she hadn't closed the door in her face. 'You know it's as beautiful here as Howard always said it was. I grew up nearby but had forgotten what it was really like. He always talked about Driftwick Bay with such passion.'

Bonnie knew Howard was well liked; that much was obvious at his cremation, which some of the locals from Driftwick Bay had gone to – although most of the day had been a blur to her. What she hadn't realised, however, was how much he'd touched other people's lives, people who didn't see him day to day. She should've known really. He had that special quality.

'I have to go,' she fibbed, clutching the door frame because all of a sudden she was desperate to close the door. Hearing about Howard from a stranger had left her discombobulated. 'I've something on the stove.' Couldn't she think of a more original excuse?

And she closed the door just like that before rushing to the side where she was out of sight if Faye peered in through the glass.

Oh, she'd been so rude. And Faye seemed as lovely as Howard had always said she was. Faye, along with Margot, another lady in the group, had been the pair Howard mentioned most often. He must've thought a lot of them and he would be devastated if he was here to see how she'd treated someone he'd come to like, someone who had brightened his life.

She should go back, open the door again, and yet she couldn't. Her legs, no longer like jelly, now felt as if they were refusing to work and she stayed in her crouched position leaning against the wall, trying to focus on breathing in and out.

Would Faye come to the cottage again? Or had she frightened her off for good?

A tear strayed down her cheek. What had happened to her? Was this the way she was now? A miserable, cantankerous woman who didn't want to be disturbed?

She went through to the back room again and looked out at the view she and Howard had never stopped appreciating. As the days of September rolled on, each one held a little less warmth but the weak sunshine and clear sky highlighted the pots dotted about the garden. They all needed attention, none of them held anything other than dead plants or weeds inside.

When her tummy rumbled she remembered she had to eat. Even that wasn't something that came easily right now.

In the kitchen, she took the bread from the larder, and dropped two slices into the toaster. She found the remaining portion of soup she'd made yesterday in the fridge and went through the motions of making herself a meal.

While the soup was warming and the bread toasting, she picked up one of the grief books that kept getting shunted around the cottage, as if leaving them in a different place might urge her to pick one up. They were at the end of the kitchen table now.

She opened up the book on top, but was only halfway through one of the initial pages when a phrase jumped out at her, claiming that grief would visit again and again.

This was never going to stop.

It was already flooring her. She didn't need to be reminded that that would never change.

She turned off the gas beneath the soup pan when it seemed hot enough, flipped up the bread from the toaster, and after buttering it she sat at the table and eyed those books with distaste.

She went into the back room, sat in Howard's soft leather chair and closed her eyes, going right back to the happy days after she met the love of her life.

Howard once told her that he found it fascinating watching her get lost in her painting or drawing and likewise she loved to watch him read. He was always so engrossed it would take a lot for him to look up.

Two months after they met, Howard had been for a browse in the library while Bonnie stayed outside to finish her can of cola. When Howard emerged from the brick building, he'd handed her a book.

She looked at the cover. *The Thorn Birds* by

Colleen McCullough, but shook her head until the way he was looking at her had her take it from him.

'It's popular,' he said. 'I was very lucky to get a copy.'

'Then I'm afraid it might be wasted on me. I won't appreciate it nearly enough.'

As they began to walk he took her hand. 'It's been described as an Australian version of *Gone With the Wind*. A love story. A powerful one at that. Not as good as our love story, but you might enjoy it if you try. Give it a go, for me?'

She couldn't resist his request but had to point out, 'You know this is like me making you draw a picture.'

'I don't have your talent for drawing, but I know you can read.'

'All right, I'll try.' She'd do anything for Howard.

When they were together the weekend before that she'd had the desperate urge to sketch out a picture of the fields next to the bed and breakfast where they were staying. They'd gone for a walk and while she sat on the fence taking in everything she could see in a way she always did before she committed anything to paper Howard had run back to the accommodation for her little bag filled with her art supplies and his bag with his book. You see, while

Howard never went anywhere without a book, she rarely went anywhere without a sketch pad and tin of pencils. She was going to be a nurse, a job she loved, but this was a different part of her that she couldn't ever give up.

As Howard sat on one side of the stile leading into the field and read, she sat on the other with her sketch pad on her knees and tin of pencils balanced on the fence. The scenery here was incredible. In the distance was an old shed. Sheep dotted the hills. There was a beautiful gate a little off centre, and a stone wall to the left, which ran higgledy-piggledy all the way to the top of the hill.

When her neck ached from leaning down over the pad of paper she'd put a hand to it but almost as soon as she did she felt Howard's larger hands taking away some of the strain with a gentle massage. 'It's coming on,' he'd said, looking down at her sketch so far. 'I don't know how you manage it.'

She flipped the paper over. 'Give it a go.'

'Me, no.' He climbed over the stile so they were together again. 'I can't draw at all.'

'Have you tried?'

'Every kid tries,' he said.

'You're not a kid.' She handed him the pad with the fresh sheet showing and passed him a pencil.

'Draw what you see.' She looked out at the view; it really was beautiful. And the sheep gave a wonderful detail to the landscape.

When she looked down to see what he'd done so far she started to laugh and he put a hand around her waist, pulling her body closer.

'Howard...' He'd drawn a big heart and written their names inside. But she'd dipped her head and kissed him until he eventually let her get back to her drawing.

They found a café and she took *The Thorn Birds* from Howard when he handed it to her. For almost half an hour – a very long half an hour for Bonnie – they sipped on hot chocolates and as Howard read *The Shining* by Stephen King, Bonnie did her best.

'Well?' he asked.

'It's well written,' she said brightly. 'I'll persevere.' His questioning glance had her admitting, 'It will feel like a chore, like reading for my nursing studies except not as useful.' She covered her face. 'I'm sorry, it's not what you want to hear.'

'It's fine.' He slipped his book and hers into his bag. 'Come on, the library isn't closed yet. We'll pop your book back. It's heavily in demand.'

Outside she hooked her arm into his. 'Are you very upset with me?'

'Of course not. But that doesn't mean I won't keep trying with you.'

He didn't push it much at all over the years, just a gentle nudge every now and then, and sometimes she tried, sometimes she made it through a few chapters of whatever he suggested for her. It was only when they were married that she told him what had put her off reading. They'd been ripping off old wallpaper from the master bedroom of the Victorian terraced house they'd managed to buy in Reading and Howard was already talking about an old bookshelf he'd seen for sale in the second-hand furniture shop down the end of the road.

'It'll look good if I re-stain the wood,' he'd told her. 'I'd say it could fit fifty to sixty books.'

'You're going to fill this whole house with books, aren't you?' She'd turned, wallpaper scraper in hand, her hair beneath a paisley headscarf to protect it from the debris involved with decorating. 'Admit it.'

'Only if it's all right with you. We could allocate you a shelf perhaps. Just in case you get into reading some day.'

'Maybe I'll have an art shelf instead. You know I'm not bothered about books.' She carried on scraping but turned at a thud.

He'd fallen to his knees, hands clasped against

his chest. 'Not bothered about books?' he breathed rapidly as if her comment had wounded him.

'Get up, you daft man.' She laughed. 'I didn't say I wasn't bothered about you.' She hesitated. She didn't meet his eye. She carried on with scraping the paper from the wall. 'At school, I struggled... to read. I was later to learn than most, and I was always really embarrassed because my friends all got it and I didn't.' She could feel him watching her. 'I wasn't dyslexic, I was just slower to pick it up. I had difficulty working out the sounds of the letters and the longer it went on the worse it got because I felt stupid.'

She felt his hand on hers and he gently tugged so that she stepped down off the stool and stood facing him. He took the scraper, set it on the windowsill and reached for her other hand. 'You were never stupid. Please don't ever say that.'

'I know, but I felt it. My friends didn't laugh, nobody in class did, and I know I was lucky for that. But I never felt the enjoyment that my peers would when they opened a book, because I'd be faced with another battle.'

'But you learned in the end.'

'I did, but by then, I suppose, I associated books with struggle. And I never really wanted to try for pleasure. My favourite room at school was the art room. In there, I felt I was myself. I could be free; I could do anything. I was a different person. But art was a small portion of school, the rest seemed to involve countless books to read to learn everything.'

'So reading became necessity not a pleasure.'

'Exactly, I did it for my nursing studies but there was a purpose for that.'

'But pleasure is a purpose.'

She leaned in and kissed him firmly on the lips. 'I'm happy, Howard. For me, painting is my joy; even painting this ceiling tomorrow will be fun.'

Howard raised his eyebrows in doubt. 'Remember you complained of neck ache after painting the lounge ceiling.'

Her nose scrunched in realisation. 'I'd forgotten that. But do you understand?' Suddenly coy she looked down at the bare floorboards. 'About the books.'

His fingers lifted her chin up so she was looking him in the eye. 'Of course I do. Painting is your joy; books are mine.' Then he smiled. 'You know what else is my joy?'

She began to giggle as he trailed kisses all down her neck. He opened the buttons of her shirt, they peeled each other's clothes off, and they made love there and then on top of the sheets piled in the corner ready to lay over the floor before they painted.

As she laid her head against his chest and ran her fingers through the hairs, she reminded him of the bookcase he'd talked about buying. 'Where will you put it?' she asked.

'I think it'll look really good in the dining room.'

'Then you should go and get it, before someone else does.'

She'd never seen him pull his clothes on quite so fast. After he gave her one more kiss of course.

Now she realised that she was smiling at the memory as she sat in his chair in this beautiful cottage in Driftwick Bay. He would hate the way she was now. He'd want her to pull herself together and re-join the world. He'd remind her that this cottage and this town were her home. And she knew he'd be devastated that she was even considering selling the bookshop to the developer.

But a piece of her was missing. Things had changed. The world was different now without Howard.

And it would be different for the rest of her days.

16

MARGOT

Margot took a seat in the Georgian-style tearooms to wait for Faye. It had a charming wooden interior and was hidden away on a side street just along from the bakery. Despite the onslaught of rain overnight, the sun had come out again.

Alistair had come to visit her. At first she'd not wanted him to disrupt his routine and his hard work, but when she saw him she realised how much she'd needed to see his face. They'd got Sebastian on FaceTime too and even though nothing had really changed since they last spoke, it made Margot feel as if things were going to be okay. She'd thanked them both again for the money and despite her anxiety at how she was quite going to do it, she assured them that she would be paying every single penny of it back. She felt a camaraderie between them that they'd likely always had but one that was coming to the fore now she'd left Perry.

Margot popped a napkin under one of the legs of the table, on top of a questionably levelled floor with flagstone tiles, and when she looked up again Faye had arrived.

They hugged each other hello and with the waitress so attentive immediately ordered scones with jam and cream plus tea.

'How's work going?' Margot asked Faye. No matter that she'd done enough cleaning in the house near Ascot to last her a lifetime, she still envied Faye. The world of work felt alien to Margot, but she longed to do something useful, earn her own money, be able to support herself. She had to believe that she would, eventually.

'I've had some extra vans to clean and I'm a bit knackered, but it's all good.'

'I don't suppose they need any more help there, do they?' She might as well ask. She had experience after all.

'I'm not sure. I'm only filling in and the regular people are back today. I'll ask though.' Faye poured them both a glass of water from the carafe on the table. 'Do you work back near your home?'

'No, I've been a housewife for a very long time.'

'So you do work, just not outside the home.'

Margot liked that distinction.

Thankfully Faye didn't focus on Margot and her life because she leapt onto another topic. 'So... the bookshop, open again. How about that?'

Faye had sent her a WhatsApp message to say that Driftwick Bay Books had reopened. 'It's a good thing,' said Margot. 'I'll have to go inside and see it for myself.'

'I think Howard would be glad it's open again, even if the hours are limited.' She sighed. 'It's such a shame that the three of us never got to meet.'

'I know. It would've been incredible.'

'I went to knock at the cottage again earlier,' said Faye. 'And this time I saw Bonnie.'

'You did? How is she?'

'She's okay. But she didn't talk much, and it felt like she couldn't wait to get rid of me.'

'That's a shame. But I suppose Howard always said she loved her own company.'

'He also said how bubbly she was.'

Faye had a point. 'He'd hate that she's struggling,' said Margot. 'But it's early days.'

'Maybe. But then there's your own company some of the time – which is great, don't get me wrong – but if it goes on for too long, it can be a bad thing. It really can affect you. You know, mentally.'

The waitress brought over their scones and mini pots of jam and cream. 'Jam first?' Margot asked.

Faye laughed. 'Is there any other way?'

Margot smeared a generous helping of jam on top of one warm half of scone. 'Howard would never have wanted Bonnie to close herself off from the world. Remember when Sarah lost her sister earlier this year and she came to the Midnight Book Club and admitted that she hadn't left the house in three weeks?' Sarah hadn't told them for three weeks either; she'd just shown up at book club as if nothing out of the ordinary had happened.

'It all burst out of her that day, didn't it,' said Faye.

'I'll never forget it.' One minute they'd been talking about Arthur Miller's *Death of a Salesman* and the next thing they knew the rectangle on the screen with Sarah's face showed a woman in turmoil. Her sister had been a retail salesperson in her younger years and the title had been what set her off. Sarah told them all that she'd been holding it together be-cause she wanted to feel normal again, but she'd asked how that was ever possible with such a devastating loss.

'It will be hard for a while,' Howard had said. 'You *will* go on,' he'd told her. 'You *will* find a new sense of normality.' He'd admitted then that he would be lost without his Bonnie and made them all laugh when he said she'd probably be fine without him as she was the organised one, paying the bills, sorting out what meals they ate, dealing with all the admin that came with a house.

Margot dolloped cream on top of the jam on her second half of scone with big juicy sultanas bursting out of its surface. 'Do you ever hear from any of the members who dropped out of your book club so suddenly?'

'No, never.'

'It was like we'd had a hex put on us or something.' Margot was laughing but Faye wasn't.

Faye didn't remark on the people she'd brought to the group, people she knew personally. 'We're a smaller group now than we were, but you and Howard were the two who were the most reliable.'

'I feel I should get a gold star or something.'

Faye grinned. 'I'll think about it.' And then she changed the topic. 'Now, about Bonnie. Iris at the bookshop said it's hard to get her to talk when she goes up there to the cottage to check on her. So it isn't just me.'

'That's kind of reassuring to know.'

Faye picked up the last morsel of her scone smothered in jam and cream and, after she popped it into her mouth, got back to the pressing issue. 'It's one thing not being very welcoming to me, or to us – we are strangers after all – but Iris knows her.'

'When you put it like that it does sound very odd.'

'Maybe she's not managing at all. I don't want to poke my nose in, but...'

Margot paused thoughtfully. 'Howard wouldn't want her to hide away from the rest of the world.'

'I don't think he would either.'

'What about you?' Margot asked, because ever since Faye told her about the broken engagement, their focus had been on Bonnie, and she hadn't asked how Faye was doing. 'How are things?'

'After being dumped, you mean?'

'Sorry, should I have avoided bringing it up?'

'No, don't apologise. I'm actually doing all right. It helps being here, away from Queensland, away from my apartment and work, and the places we used to go together.'

'I think you were right to come.'

'Yeah.'

When you were with someone you were in a routine, even if it wasn't an official routine. Your life revolved around them and if you were lucky theirs might revolve around you just a bit too. 'It's not very nice for you at the moment, but it's far better to split up now than further down the line.'

Margot wanted to ask whether there was more to the story of the broken engagement than Faye had previously let on, but she didn't feel it was her place. They didn't know each other that well; they were linked by books and by the brief conversations they'd had, and she didn't want to pry.

Rather than dwelling on relationship talk, which Margot had no desire to ignite either, Margot got Faye talking about Australia. Other countries fascinated her; they always had.

'I've never been to Australia,' said Margot. 'I always wanted to travel. I almost did a degree that would've taken me to America for a year.'

'That would've been an awesome experience.'

Margot smiled at the sound of Faye's Australian accent when she was enthusiastic about something. 'Awesome. Yes, I think it would have been.'

'So how come you never did it?'

'I got pregnant instead.'

Faye tilted her head to one side. 'Do you regret it? Not the babies, but not doing the degree?'

'Yes and no. No, not at the time. But yes, perhaps lately I've been thinking about it more.'

'Would you go back and study? Or study from home?'

She hesitated. 'I thought about it.' But Perry had dismissed it of course. She'd let herself be bullied for far too long and she hated herself a little bit for it.

'You should do, if that's what you want.'

'Maybe...' Although really she needed something a lot more immediate; she needed to earn money. She had the funds from the boys but hated the fact she'd taken them in the first place. The sooner she was bringing some money in the better.

Faye leaned to the side as the waitress took away their empty plates and then she poured them both another cup of tea from the teapot. 'Your husband would support the idea, wouldn't he?'

'My husband wasn't keen at all when I mentioned it.'

'The husband who isn't holidaying with you.' She set the teapot down.

Margot, in the presence of a friend for the first time in far too long, found it all tumbling out. 'I'm not just on a holiday,' she admitted. 'I've left my husband. My marriage of almost thirty years is over.' It felt surprisingly good to unburden herself to a friend at last.

'Margot, I...'

'It's okay. Well, it's not, but you know, it kind of is.'

She explained some of the moments that had led her here – Perry's obsession with work and being the best, the way he was with their boys, seeing them as not achieving their full potential and the light that dimmed in their eyes every time they faced their father's scrutiny and disapproval. She told Faye about her life since she'd given up her degree – the home-maker she was, the mother, the entertainer when it came to Perry's business associates, how she felt no warmth in the house when the boys weren't there, how Perry didn't show love or affection any more, how he criticised her and made her feel like she'd never make it on her own. And she told Faye that slowly her friends had fallen away one by one.

'I can't imagine what it must have been like for you, Margot.'

'It's why I joined the Midnight Book Club. It was at a time I knew Perry would be asleep and I could sneak off. It was something just for me.'

'I'm glad you got that.'

'Honestly, things have been the same way for

such a long time that it became my normal. And it was always about family for me. It was always about my boys. I couldn't bear them getting hurt in all of this, and so I put up with the way things were. My sons were my saviour in the toughest of times. Even if they weren't with me, they were in the background. Without them...'

'Are they the reason you never left?'

She nodded. 'I never wanted to break up the family, and I didn't think I could manage on my own. Perry took my confidence along with everything else.' Perhaps it was better that she didn't know Faye all that well. It was more like telling a neutral party. Maybe this was what therapy was like, confessing all your secrets, having them pouring out just like the tea from the teapot on the table.

'What changed?' Faye asked.

'You know, despite so many years falling into the place where Perry wanted me, I think *I* changed.'

'Have you spoken to your husband?'

She shook her head. 'I blocked his number. He's emailed but I haven't written back. It's almost worse that he's gone quiet. I don't know what his next move will be.'

As the tearooms were getting busy, they went Dutch to pay their bill and left. Margot put on her chunky knit cardigan and as they stepped outside they went back to the main street and the hill that passed through Driftwick Bay.

Faye zipped up her hoodie. 'Is this why you were asking about a cleaning job?'

'It is. I've got some money set by, but I need a plan for the longer term.'

'How long will the money last you for?'

'Not long enough.' They stopped on the street corner, Lulworth Cove to the right in the distance, the hill leading up and out of the bay on their left. 'And I'm worried to tell you the truth. Faye, I'm trained for nothing. I haven't had a job since I worked in a shop when I was nineteen. I'm trawling through online listings every day and I've applied for a couple of things – waitress jobs – but so far no joy. And I'm looking for a rental property too.' Now she had the money from the boys she'd be able to pay for six months to a year up front to give her some stability.

'Have you filed for divorce?' Faye asked.

'No, not yet.'

'I don't know much about it, given I didn't even make it to the altar, but going by things I've heard in the hairdressing salon from other couples in the same boat, I'd get in touch with a solicitor as soon as possible. You need to make sure you get a fair split of the assets. Just because you didn't work outside the home, it doesn't mean he can take everything. You looked after the house; you raised your kids.'

'You're very wise for someone in her twenties.' She grinned. 'I keep thinking you're really young, but you're not; I'm just getting older.'

Faye laughed. 'You've got years ahead of you yet.'

Margot was worried about the cost and voiced her concern. 'I'll bet solicitors are hideously expensive.'

'Cheaper than your husband taking everything and leaving you with nothing,' said Faye.

'You know what, you're right.' She looked down the hill. 'I'm desperate to go and see the bookshop but first, should we try Bonnie again?'

'Good idea.'

They walked up the hill and were soon outside the gorgeous little cottage but it took a few knocks before Bonnie opened the door, and even then it was only a crack.

Faye, a brilliant smile on her face, launched in with, 'Hey, Bonnie. It's me... Faye again. Howard's friend from the Midnight Book Club.'

'And I'm Margot,' Margot quickly added in a jolly voice that even to her sounded like a teacher trying to cajole her class into showing enthusiasm in a subject they all hated.

'Well, I'm afraid I'm just about to pop out.' Bonnie opened the door a little more. She lifted her handbag up from the floor as if to prove her claim. 'I can't stop.'

Had Faye noticed the slippers too? If Bonnie really was going out, she wouldn't still be wearing those surely.

'Shall we come back another time?' Margot suggested.

Bonnie looked surprised at the question. 'Yes, yes, do that. Now I'd better get going.'

Margot and Faye left her to it and Margot closed the little gate behind them. Bonnie was still lingering at the door and Margot gave her a nod.

They turned to head down the hill in the direction of the bookshop.

'I really don't think she's going anywhere,' said Margot to Faye. 'Do you?'

'No, I really don't.'

17

———

FAYE

'Good afternoon!' Iris trilled the second they went inside the bookshop. She swiftly passed them, a cloth and a bottle of spray cleaner in her hand. She went outside, sprayed the glass, gave it a good old wipe and came back inside very quickly. For some reason she'd only cleaned the lowest panels.

Faye assumed she'd been staring because Iris confided, 'I like to be discreet. Kids press their noses against the glass so I nip out and give it a good clean at least twice a day. Howard was a stickler for keeping this place shipshape.'

Margot looked around. 'The window and the lighting make it magical in here. I get why kids are drawn to it. And all the big picture books over there in the story corner look wonderful.'

'Well, thank you for saying something so kind,' said Iris. 'I only hope I'm doing it justice, you know, since Howard…'

'Of course you are,' said Faye.

'Well don't either of you go pressing your noses against the glass.' Iris wagged her finger in warning but added a big laugh for good measure. She had a friendly warmth and patted the super high bun on top of her head to ensure it was still in place.

Faye introduced Margot to Iris. 'She's a member of the Midnight Book Club. She knew Howard too.'

'Oh, then it's even lovelier to meet you,' said Iris. 'And welcome to Driftwick Bay.' She excused herself to go over and help a man who was in the section dedicated to thrillers. Faye had noticed him when she came in because he kept looking over as if he wasn't sure what he was doing.

When the door to the bookshop opened a couple of minutes after their arrival Faye wasn't sorry to see Theo coming inside. And when he smiled her way she felt the same flutter she'd had when they bumped into each other on the beach.

She focused on Midas instead, who must have been in his basket behind the counter but emerged at the sight of his owner. It was easier to focus on the dog than look at Theo although he was busy anyway ushering a group of children inside.

There had to be at least ten kids here and they obviously all knew Midas because after Theo greeted his loyal pet, little hands reached out to the dog, who let them stroke his coat, around his ears, give him cuddles.

'You're a teacher,' she said to Theo after Iris had said hello to her son and he'd instructed the kids that they must be quiet and well behaved and they were to go over to the story corner.

'I sure am. I work at the local primary school.'

'How old are this lot?'

'Mostly six-year-olds; some of them have turned seven.'

Faye could imagine him in front of a class, especially a class in this age group. He had a way about him, a patience and a kindness. It felt, even though she didn't know him, that he might want to make a difference for people who needed it. It wasn't something Faye had known before, certainly not with Brad.

A cute little girl with red hair in plaits came to Theo's side and tugged on his arm, but when Midas trotted back to the story corner with her it was clear it was the dog she really wanted.

Theo explained, 'That was Amelia. She won't read out loud to anyone but Midas.' He gently reprimanded two overexcited little boys running circles around a book stand.

'She reads to a dog?' Faye asked quietly.

'Give them a minute to settle, but you'll see.' And then he was back to his job.

Faye looked around for Margot and spotted her standing in the self-help section. Faye wouldn't mind betting she was looking forward to reinventing herself after being trapped in a marriage for so long, playing the role of wife and mother with little else in the way of friends or closeness.

She turned back to watch Theo with the kids and indeed, there was Midas lying next to Amelia who had opened up a book on her lap and was reading.

Iris leaned in and confided, 'Amelia is one of many children who don't like to read out loud to a class or to their peers. It sounds strange but dogs don't judge, they sit and listen, they won't make fun.'

'How long has Midas been a therapy dog?'

'For a few years now. My daughter has special needs and her therapy dog, Roxie, was a godsend for her. Theo already had Midas and when he saw how Beth was helped with Roxie by her side, he decided that Midas might be a good candidate to go through the training. He passed with flying colours of course, then started working at the school some days and here on others.'

'He seems really content,' said Faye, her focus at the back of the shop.

'Midas or Theo?' Iris asked.

Faye turned to see the light layer of amusement on Theo's mum's face. She only hoped she wasn't blushing. 'Midas, of course.'

'Well, I wasn't sure.'

Iris went off to sweep the floor by the entrance and Faye watched Amelia close her book and join the group of children on the rug. She realised she might be staring a little bit too much, so gave Theo a nod and went over to Margot who was engrossed in a book about changing your career.

'Find anything you like?' Faye asked her.

'I can't seem to narrow down a choice.' She put the title she had hold of back and looked over at the group of children. 'Aren't they cute?'

'Very.' Faye picked up a book near the window and noticed the same man who had been in the thriller section earlier peering in through the window. He didn't seem to be looking at the books, but at her.

She turned away, uneasy.

'Watching these children reminds me of when the boys were really little,' Margot shared. 'When Sebastian was at school, I'd go in to hear him and other kids read. I did the same with Alistair too. I really enjoyed it.'

'Why don't you try teaching?' Faye suggested.

'I don't really think it's me.'

'You never know.'

Margot's lips twisted in thought. 'I suppose I should keep an open mind.'

Faye looked across at the window again but the man who had been staring must have moved on elsewhere.

Iris interrupted them briefly. 'Have you two been to see Bonnie again?'

'We have,' said Faye. 'But no luck getting her to talk, I'm afraid. She came to the door, but she quickly made her excuses to get rid of us.'

Iris frowned. 'She was always so jolly and friendly. I know she's not going to just spring back to normal, but I worry she's closing herself off.' She paused, lowered her voice. 'And I think she's going to sell the shop.'

Margot shook her head. 'Not to the developer.'

'You know about that?'

Faye explained how close they were in the Midnight Book Club and that chat often centred around a lot more than books. 'He kept batting them away,' she said, 'but they just wouldn't give up.'

'They're not hassling Bonnie at home, are they?' Margot wondered.

'I wouldn't think so. I expect she has the correspondence they've previously left for Howard. As far as I know they never turned up at the cottage.'

'Let's hope they don't do that,' said Margot. 'I mean, that's the last thing she needs.'

Iris confided, 'I really think she'll sell. She's not thinking clearly at the moment. She knows what the bookshop means to this town.'

'She's in survival mode,' said Margot.

Iris sighed. 'I know, and it makes me feel really bad for thinking about myself.'

Faye sympathised. 'Howard always said you loved working here and he enjoyed your company. Try not to panic, perhaps Bonnie will change her mind.' Although books had never been Bonnie's thing so maybe this town really was about to lose their beloved bookshop after all.

'She might feel differently when she comes in here,' Margot suggested.

'Oh no,' said Iris. 'Bonnie told me when she closed the bookshop after Howard died that she didn't ever want to set foot in here again or even think about it. I don't think there's any chance of getting her to come down here before she makes the decision to sell.' She shook her head. 'I sound like I only care about the bookshop but I'm concerned about her too. She needs people around her but nobody has bumped into her in the street, a few people have seen her but she scurries away from the bakery or wherever she's nipped out to. She seems to go right back and hide at the cottage without seeing or speaking to a soul.'

'Why don't we try visiting Bonnie again tomorrow,' Margot suggested to Iris. 'I'm not sure there's anything we can do if she's made her mind up to sell the bookshop, but at least we might be able to check whether she's all right.'

'Oh, would you? I don't want to be too much of a nuisance.' Iris explained, 'I've called her enough times already to ask her questions about this place.'

Margot and Faye left the bookshop but not before Faye turned again to wave over at Theo who seemed very aware that she was leaving and gave her a nod and a smile.

'Bit of interest there,' said Margot as the door closed behind them.

'Sorry?'

'Theo. He was undressing you with his eyes.'

The comment sounded so out of character for her new friend that it made Faye laugh. 'He's with a bunch of kids, teaching them. I'm sure that me and my state of dress were the last things on his mind.'

'I don't know,' said Margot, enjoying this. But then her teasing faded. 'Do you really think Bonnie will sell to the developer?'

'It sounds like she wants nothing to do with the bookshop,' said Faye. 'We have to respect that, but Howard would hate it, wouldn't he?'

'He never wanted them to get their hands on it.'

'Perhaps she could wait, find a buyer who'll take it on and keep it the way it is,' said Faye.

'Sometimes you just want things to end. And it seems like there's an easy way out for her with the developer. It'll be a done deal, over with quickly, and she can move on.'

'But she belongs here. Howard said they both did, that since they came to Driftwick Bay it felt hard to imagine either of them ever being anywhere else.'

Both a little despondent with the thought of Howard's beloved bookshop nearing the end of its days, they said goodbye. Margot headed further up the hill and on to her accommodation, ready to get back to the online job search, house hunting and now, looking for a solicitor, and Faye went back down in the direction of Lulworth Cove to get her bike from where she'd locked it up.

She'd only just popped the lock into her bag when her phone rang, and she answered it automatically before she registered the WhatsApp call was from her sister.

'Faye… please don't hang up,' came Steph's voice.

Faye had woken up in the night, ruminating about her life as it was now. She'd put thousands of miles between herself and her home to get a sense of normality and she'd realised that lately she felt more herself than she had in a very long time. Even before the scandal, she'd had her sister in the background and perhaps she'd always expected something to happen. And now here was Steph again, making contact and eclipsing the piece of happiness she'd managed to find with her dad close by, a few hours work each day, and now a new friendship with Margot.

'How are you?' Steph asked when Faye didn't say anything.

Standing next to her bike, Faye gave up trying to wrestle the helmet on one-handed as she held her phone. She set it back on the saddle. 'I'm fine.'

'How's Dad?'

'Have you called him?'

'Of course I have,' Steph snapped. But then her tone lightened again. She knew Faye could hang up at any time. 'It's just that you've seen him in person; it's different.'

'Dad is good, Uncle Frank is okay and glad that Dad's here.' She paused after her summary. 'How's Mum?'

'The same.'

Faye let a smile escape. She knew what that meant. Wearing the floaty clothes, living her life freely the way she needed to, which meant in a chaotic house-share with people equally devoted to 'taking it easy'.

'I'm sorry, you know,' said Steph.

'Yeah, well.'

'I'm trying, Faye. That's why I called.'

'What are you sorry for?' She tried to zip up her hoodie and managed it by hugging the phone between her shoulder and her ear. 'Sorry for having an affair with a married man? Sorry that what you did caused trouble for me and Brad? Sorry that I've been hounded in the street and gossiped about and had Dad been in Queensland it would've been the same for him?'

'I'm sorry for all of it! Okay!' Steph's voice rose in her determination to get her point across.

'Well, I hope that man was worth it.'

Steph didn't say anything at first. Then: 'I thought it was real. I thought he *was* worth it. He told me he was going to leave his wife.'

'That's what they all say. And how did it even happen anyway?' But then she quickly added, 'Actually, I don't want to know.'

The silence lasted so long, Faye had to look at the phone display to see whether her sister was still there.

'Have you talked to Brad lately?' Steph asked.

'No. I haven't.'

'Dad told me the engagement was off. He thought I should know. As if I could feel any worse.'

Faye had told her dad that she wouldn't be telling Steph about Brad but that when he spoke to her he could fill her in. At least it was done now and her calling showed perhaps she did have a conscience after all.

'Faye, I'm so sorry about Brad.'

'Yeah, well, he ran off to Tasmania at the first sign of trouble, so perhaps you did me a favour.'

'Dad says he's applying for jobs in Tassie.'

'That's right. And he did that before he told me things were over.'

A gasp. 'The absolute bastard!' Now this Steph she could get on board with – the Steph who was in her corner and supporting her rather than the other way round, the twin sister who had once gone to detention after school for a whole week in her place so that she could still make swim club and prepare for an upcoming competition.

Somewhat more willing to talk since she answered the call, Faye asked, 'Did you really think that man would leave his wife, Steph?'

Her voice sounded so small across the miles when she said that's exactly what she'd thought. 'He told me they were talking divorce; he said he loved me. And now he's bloody well come out on the news to say that he and his wife are working through this and requested that the public please allow them to do so for the sake of their family.'

That had to have hurt. No matter whether Steph did the wrong thing, thinking someone loved you, planning a future with them, and to have it all thrown back in your face was hurtful. She should know.

'So… am I forgiven, Faye?' And there it was, the lighter tone, the slight smile in her voice and the presumption that a little apology would fix everything and make it all go away. 'Come on, I've said sorry.'

She was never going to change.

'We'll talk,' said Faye.

Steph whined, 'I miss you, sis.'

'Yeah, you too.'

She ended the call before dropping the phone into her backpack and shrugging it on again. There was no point trying to argue about anything, trying to point out how what Steph missed the most was having someone to turn to when she made a mess of things. They were twin sisters, always would be, but Steph was just like their mother and fighting it was only going to bring pain and heartbreak to Faye when trying to change her didn't work.

She put a foot over the crossbar of her bike and picked up the helmet but jumped as a figure stepped out of nowhere. The man who'd been staring at her earlier at the bookshop was suddenly right beside her.

'You're her, aren't you?' he said with no preamble.

'Excuse me?'

'Her. The one who shagged a politician and destroyed a family.'

'I...' The helmet fell from her hands. 'No, I'm not.'

'Liar!'

'Please, just leave me alone.' Claiming to be an identical twin seemed futile at this point; she just wanted to get out of there.

He sneered. 'I'd recognise you anywhere.' It was then she noticed his Australian accent. 'I keep up with the news back home.'

'Leave me alone, please!' She didn't want to get off the bike and reach for the helmet; she didn't want to bend down in case she lost her balance or he pushed her.

'Like you left that man alone? I don't know him, but my own family was ruined by a slag like you shagging my dad. So, I know what it's like.' He jabbed a finger in her face.

She pushed her foot onto the pedal. But starting off uphill was hard let alone when someone was walking beside you determined to badger you. She tried to get some purchase on the pedals and get away from him.

Luckily for Faye, she had fitness on her side and was soon going faster than the man, although she could hear him running after her. Her heart was pounding. She was going as hard as she could.

She got some way up the hill and turned to look over her shoulder to see where he was and that was when she swerved. She lost her balance and fell onto the hard tarmac.

She heard more footsteps. She felt a warm trickle and put a hand to her head. There was blood.

And then she heard a woman's voice yell, 'Bugger off! Go on, get away! I've called the police!'

And when she looked up it was into the eyes of someone much nicer than the horrible stranger.

18

BONNIE

Bonnie tried to coax Faye up from the ground. 'It's all right; he's gone.' Faye wouldn't stop trying to look around her, moving her head even more. 'Come on, up you get. A car could come over the hill at any moment.'

Faye got to her feet but Bonnie took her over to the kerb rather than letting her get her bike.

Once Faye was safely sitting, she went back and quickly got the bicycle out of harm's way. She wheeled it inside the back gate where she left it before going back to Faye's side.

'Come into the house. I need to make sure you're all right.' Blood was coming from one side of her forehead. Bonnie suspected it was only a surface wound but with head trauma you could never be too careful. 'Faye, do you know who I am?'

'Of course. You're Bonnie.'

At first glance she didn't appear to be concussed but of course concussion symptoms didn't always occur immediately.

Bonnie pulled a tissue from her pocket. Luckily she had one. 'Hold this against your head to stem the bleeding.' She held Faye's arm as she led her through the back gate.

Inside, Faye went to sit on the stool but Bonnie ushered her over to Howard's chair – there was less danger of her falling out of that if she suddenly felt dizzy.

Bonnie looked beneath the tissue to check that the bleeding was indeed subsiding as she'd suspected it would, and then went to get her first-aid kit from the kitchen cupboard.

She'd been in the back garden getting in the washing when she'd moved closer to the stone wall at the side of the garden because she recognised Faye. She watched her cycle uphill but something was off because there was a man chasing after her on foot. Bonnie had dropped the basket of washing and dashed out of the gate, yelling whatever she could think of to get rid of the man, but unfortunately by the time Faye came into view she was on the ground.

She held a small bowl beneath the tap at the sink and filled it with water, which she took to the back room. She soaked a piece of cotton wool in the water then gently dabbed it against the wound on Faye's forehead. 'Can you tell me your name?'

'I remembered yours so I definitely remember my own.' She winced as Bonnie finished cleaning up the cut on her forehead for her. 'I'm Faye.'

'And where are you?'

'Driftwick Bay.'

'Who was Howard?'

Faye smiled. 'He was one of the kindest men I've ever met... well, online-met.'

Bonnie's emotions stirred but for once it didn't make her want to run and hide. 'You're going to be fine. The bleeding has stopped; it's only a surface wound.' She noticed the tear in Faye's hoodie. 'How's your elbow?'

Faye looked at her clothing and tutted. 'I really like this hoodie.'

Bonnie helped her ease her hoodie off so that she could check her elbow.

'Only a slight graze.' Bonnie gave it a gentle clean. 'You're lucky you didn't hit your head harder, you know. Where's your helmet?' She surprised even herself with her question. She'd been hiding from the world, only going out to get the essentials, and now she'd been outside, yelled at a man, and here she was delivering a lecture on cycling safety. 'I apologise,' she said. 'I was a nurse once. I saw my fair share of injuries.'

'It's fine. And I do have a helmet. I dropped it when that guy was harassing me. I just wanted to get away.'

'Dropped it where?'

'By the bike rack near the road to the bakery.'

She couldn't very well send Faye out to get the helmet but equally she didn't want to walk down to get it. 'Where's your friend?'

'Margot?'

'Yes, Margot, that was it. Has she gone already?'

'Back to her accommodation about half an hour ago,' said Faye.

Bonnie had hoped she was still around so she could step in and take over. But she wasn't. And this young woman needed her help.

She gestured for Faye to pass her the hoodie. 'I can mend that quickly.'

'Oh no, I couldn't ask—'

'You're not asking, I'm offering.'

'I'll go and get my helmet. Although...'

'He might be hanging around,' Bonnie finished for her as she found her little sewing box. 'We should call the police.'

'No, I don't want that. It's... well, it's complicated.'

Bonnie sighed. 'Why don't I make you a cup of tea. That'll make you feel better.'

After she took the tea to Faye, Bonnie found the appropriate colour of cotton from her sewing box, took a seat at Howard's desk and got started on the repair to the hoodie.

Faye sipped her tea, surveying the room with a smile. 'So this is where Howard sat when he came to the Midnight Book Club. It feels kind of special to be here.'

Bonnie murmured an agreement.

Faye's smile disappeared. 'I hope I don't sound like a stalker.' She looked so panicked Bonnie almost laughed.

'You don't, dear.'

Faye set her cup down. 'Think about it, this man joins a book club hosted by a woman who lives thousands of miles away, and then she turns up on his doorstep?' She held out her hands as if to ask what did that tell you?

'You know that sounds an awful lot like a plot in one of Howard's books.'

'A book Howard would've enjoyed,' Faye added conspiratorially. 'I could imagine it as the plot of a psychological thriller. Not my favourite genre – a bit too scary for me, you know.'

'The world can be a bad place,' Bonnie agreed, 'why be reminded?'

'Exactly,' said Faye.

As Bonnie darned the hoodie she asked Faye, 'Where are you staying? Are you local?'

'I'm in a caravan in West Lulworth.'

Which meant she would need someone to take her home just in case a concussion was lurking. She didn't think it was, but Bonnie would never be able to forgive herself if she sent Faye on her way and something happened to her. She clocked her wine glass on the desk and knew she couldn't get behind the wheel. She wondered whether Faye had seen the glass too. She probably thought Bonnie was drowning her sorrows, but she wasn't. She'd opened it on a whim that afternoon. It was the first time she'd had a drink since she lost Howard, and she'd drawn comfort remembering their first night here in the cottage when they'd opened a lovely Cabernet Sauvignon, which Howard had been given on retirement and was saving for a special occasion.

'Can someone come to meet you?' Bonnie asked. 'It's wise not to be alone after a possible concussion. Just in case.'

'I could get my dad,' said Faye, 'but then…'

'Then you'd have to explain what happened.'

'I'll tell him about it. But I would rather he didn't have to worry just yet.'

'What about your friend? Would she come back to escort you?'

'Margot?' Faye shrugged. 'Maybe. She doesn't have a car, but we aren't far from each other really.'

Bonnie handed the hoodie back to Faye. 'It's a fix, but I'm not sure you'll approve.'

'Are you kidding?' She turned the garment to all angles. 'You can barely make out the tear. The coloured cotton is a perfect match.'

Bonnie was happy she'd done a good job, but she felt uneasy with the company all of a sudden. 'So, your friend?' she prompted.

'I can call a taxi, then I'll be safe.'

'No, you need someone with you.'

'But I feel fine. Honestly.'

'I know you do. But if you won't call your dad then it'll have to be someone else.' Bonnie was firm on that and it reminded her of when she'd had to set the ground rules at work. She quite missed the responsibility.

'I suppose I could call Margot. She might come here and get a taxi with me to make sure I get back all right.'

'That sounds like a plan.'

Faye pulled the bag from behind her, the bag which she'd had on over her hoodie. It was one of those small backpacks that almost sat flush against the body so she couldn't have much inside. She took out a bottle of water, some tissues, a book. 'Why does whatever you need fall to the bottom?' But she soon added a gleeful smile when she retrieved her phone from the bag's depths.

She tapped away on the phone screen for a few seconds. 'I've messaged her.'

A bleep came almost as soon as Faye put her phone on the arm of the chair. She picked it up again. 'Margot is on her way. I told her that I've fallen off my bike and need a hand getting home, and that my helmet is somewhere near the bike rack down the hill.' She smiled. 'We've not known each other that long, at least not in person, so it's really nice that she's coming.'

'Howard told me you were a closeknit bunch in the book club.'

'We are. And we miss him so much already.'

But Bonnie wasn't listening because she'd noticed the paperback on Faye's lap, the book that had been pulled from her bag in search of her phone. *Wild* by Cheryl Strayed. And it had the same little tear in the bottom right-hand corner of the cover that she recognised.

'Bonnie?' Faye's voice came into her psyche softly. 'Are you okay?'

'I should be asking you that,' Bonnie replied.

'You look like you've seen a ghost.'

'It's just... that book...'

'This?' Faye held it up. 'I grabbed it from the telephone box library and left one in its place.'

Bonnie put a hand against her chest. 'Does it have an inscription inside?'

Confused, Faye opened it up. 'It does.' She read it out: '"From Miriam, safe travels". Wait, how did you...'

'It was Howard's.'

Faye looked at the book, placed her palm on the front cover. 'Then I feel honoured to have it. But... if you want it back, I will totally understand.'

'Oh no. Howard loved leaving books in the telephone box library – you keep it.'

'I will treasure it.' Faye looked once again at the cover. 'What was the story behind the inscription?'

'Miriam worked with Howard in the civil service. When he retired she knew that he and I planned to travel one day when I stopped working, so she bought him that for inspiration.' Bonnie rolled her eyes. 'I'm not quite sure what she thought we would be doing – I haven't read it but by the sounds of it, I'm lucky he wasn't so inspired that I ended up long-distance hiking and sleeping under canvas.'

Faye's laughter filled the walls of the cottage and it was so delightful Bonnie found herself feeling happier than she had in a long while.

Faye told her, 'I'll take care of the book and put it back in the telephone box when I've finished. Someone else can enjoy it then.'

'Howard would've liked that. He was of the view that libraries of any kind lead you to find some of the most interesting titles around, books you'd never think to read.'

'I'm inclined to agree with him,' said Faye.

A warmth settled inside her. 'Howard told me that reading what you and some of the other members recommended made him feel younger.'

'He said that?'

'I believe he even used the word "hip".' She chuckled.

'He was very *hip* in his pyjamas each week.'

That had Bonnie laughing even more until a knock at the door interrupted them. 'You finish your tea; I'll get that.'

She stood back to let Margot, who was holding what had to be Faye's bike helmet, in, out of the cold. 'I'll let Faye explain,' she said as Margot wiped her feet on the mat. And feeling lost as to what else to do she offered Margot a cup of tea after she pointed her in the direction of the back room.

She'd trapped herself now. They'd at least be here until Margot finished her drink. But was she a tiny bit glad about that?

When she took the tea through Faye was assuring Margot that she was all right, that the man had called her names but nothing else.

'You need to call the police.' Margot looked at Bonnie as if to suggest she should've thought of that.

Bonnie held up her hands in defence. 'She didn't want to. I did say that she should.'

Margot pulled over the stool to sit next to the chair where Faye was resting comfortably and

Bonnie sat on the desk chair. 'Why wouldn't you want to, Faye? That man could've hurt you.'

'He just wanted to say his piece,' said Faye.

'Which was what exactly?' said Margot. 'It makes no sense.'

'Something happened in Australia.' She looked down into her lap.

'Something other than the break-up?' Margot prompted.

'Break-up?' Bonnie enquired, suddenly wanting to know more.

Margot briefly recapped on the fiancé, Brad, and the broken engagement.

Faye found her voice. 'What happened was the main driver to me coming here. My sister, Steph, was involved in a scandal involving a married politician. It was all over the news, on social media. People talked about it in the street. I've been shouted at and called names ever since, asked questions, expected to answer to everyone, it seems.'

'But why?' said Margot. 'Why are people hounding you?'

'Because they want a story. And because I'm her twin sister. And that complicates things.'

'You have a twin?' Bonnie asked.

'An identical twin,' said Faye. She harrumphed. 'I

left Australia and came here to get away. I thought I had. That man took me totally by surprise.'

'He thought you were her,' said Margot.

'Yes.'

'It sounds like a nightmare for you.' Bonnie wondered whether Faye realised she was shaking, and she pulled a blanket from the sideboard to put over her lap.

'It's been really horrible.' And then Faye's shaking turned to sobs, uncontrollable crying that close to broke Bonnie's heart. It must be the shock as well as everything else.

Bonnie found the box of tissues; Margot wrapped Faye in a hug.

'I didn't do anything and yet I'm being punished.' Faye dabbed at the tears beneath her eyes. 'It's the reason the Australians left the book club.'

Margot put her hand over Faye's. 'Is that really why?'

'Most of them I knew personally. Two emailed me and said they didn't want their names to appear anywhere online alongside mine. I mean, that wouldn't even happen. I had another email with an excuse not to attend for the first couple of sessions, then she just fell away. Even those I thought were friends.'

'I'm confused,' said Bonnie. 'What does any of this have to do with your broken engagement?'

Faye explained that Brad, her ex-fiancé, was the son of the politician involved.

'Well, that makes more sense,' said Bonnie. 'But he must have faced the same flak as you did.'

Faye looked up at her wide-eyed. 'He buggered off to Tassie – Tasmania – as soon as the scandal broke. He said it was to be with family.'

'He left you to deal with it alone?' Bonnie exchanged a look with Margot. 'Well, it sounds like it was better to break the engagement before you got married.'

Faye still looked shaken. 'That man who chased after me… I can't bear the thought that he's hanging around the bay and might confront me again.'

'Hopefully my threat of the police has scared him off,' said Bonnie. 'We can still call them. It might be wise.'

'Not yet.' But she added, 'If he ever shows his face again then I promise I will.'

'Fair enough.' In Bonnie's days as a district nurse she had seen her fair share of women like Faye who were innocent victims but didn't want to cause trouble by reporting anything to the authorities. It was wrong to be afraid to do so but she understood why it was so hard.

Margot took out her phone. 'I'll call a taxi. Let's get you back to the caravan.'

'Actually, I'll need to go to my dad's,' said Faye. 'I'll stay with him tonight. Bonnie says it's wise in case I have a concussion. I'll pay for the taxi fares. The driver can drop me and then take you back to your accommodation. I just didn't want to be in a taxi alone or have my dad panic and worry. This way I get to tell Dad about what happened face to face and he'll see that I'm okay.'

'Sounds like a good plan,' said Margot before making the call.

Bonnie thought she might have asked why Bonnie herself couldn't have gone in the taxi with Faye, but thankfully she didn't.

With the taxi ten minutes away Margot got up and finished her tea while she perused the book-shelves at Bonnie's suggestion. These women knew her husband; they shared his love of books.

'I wish we could've met Howard in person,' said Margot. 'I'm so sorry for your loss, Bonnie.'

'Thank you.'

'He was so kind and always had time for every-one.' Margot's fondness was evident. 'And his bookshop is beautiful. We've both spent time in there; it's lovely.'

Bonnie stiffened at the mention of Driftwick Bay Books. 'Howard loved that place.'

'He did,' said Faye. 'I still remember when he was toying with the idea of buying it.' She beamed a smile Bonnie's way. 'He was like a big kid discovering treasure when he picked up the keys.'

'I remember,' said Bonnie, basking in this particular memory rather than trying to push it away. 'We thought he was done with work, and then he just got this new lease of life when he took on the shop.'

'He never looked back, did he?' said Margot.

'No,' said Bonnie almost to herself. 'He never did.' And now here she was with the developer's contact details still in the letter rack. She'd picked up the phone that morning to call them, to get the ball rolling, but before she dialled the entire number she put the phone down again. Something stopped her; she just didn't know what.

'My Howard loved the Midnight Book Club. You both brought him a lot of happiness with that,' she told the women who up until now she hadn't had time for. She felt ashamed for ignoring the door, being so rude. She could see why Howard had gelled with them both. They seemed genuine, they weren't over the top, there was a friendliness without being too intrusive.

'He brought us plenty of happiness too,' said Margot. 'You know at one book club session Howard got into a real heated discussion about banned books.'

Faye's eyes widened. 'I remember that.'

'My Howard had some very clear views on banned books.' Bonnie could well imagine him participating in a fiery conversation on the topic. 'He said that as soon as he heard a book was banned from libraries it sparked his curiosity and he had to get his hands on it.'

Faye recalled the argument with another member. 'This other lady thought that books *should* be policed. She was adamant that parents should accompany their children to a library and heavily monitor what they chose.'

'Well, where's the fun in that?' Bonnie asked, getting into the conversation. This was the most alive she'd felt in weeks.

'Exactly!' Faye laughed. 'Howard said she had a funny idea about reading. The whole point, he said, was for your imagination to run wild, for you to experience a book your way, and part of that was choosing a book in the first place.'

It sounded so much like Howard that Bonnie felt a tug at her emotions all over again. Sitting here with these women as they talked about her husband was hard in some ways and in others she needed it.

And there was more. Margot asked, 'Do you remember when someone chose *Fifty Shades of Grey* as the read of the week?'

Faye looked at Bonnie. 'Your Howard read it.'

'I remember!' Bonnie said. Howard had been shocked at a lot of it, but read it just the same. He'd told her he wouldn't be trying to persuade her to read it either because it might give her very weird ideas. 'He told me that Christian Grey should be locked up. He did!' Bonnie could still remember his vehemence.

'Oh, he was so entertaining, Bonnie.' Faye's cheeks were red from the laughter.

Margot noticed the time and picked up the two empty mugs. 'The taxi will be here any minute. I'll pop these in the kitchen.'

Faye put her hoodie back on and picked up her backpack and bicycle helmet as they made their way to the door.

Before they could even step over the threshold, Bonnie found herself asking, 'Will you two come back?'

'I'll need to come back and get my bike,' said Faye.

She would, and rather than be annoyed by the intrusion, Bonnie was rather looking forward to it. 'Would you come too, Margot?'

Margot gave her a winning smile. 'I would really like that.'

'Does tomorrow afternoon suit you both?' Bonnie said it so quickly she hoped it sounded less desperate to their ears than her own.

'That sounds perfect,' said Margot with Faye readily agreeing.

The taxi came, the girls left, and when Bonnie closed the front door and locked up, she felt as though she might just have taken a very big leap back into the world.

And she went into her bedroom, picked up the framed photograph of her and Howard taken in the sunshine on their travels, and told him, 'If I believed it was possible, I'd say you sent me these women for a reason, Howard.'

Maybe in a way that was exactly what he'd managed to do.

19

MARGOT

Margot had barely slept. She'd been too preoccupied wondering why Perry hadn't been in touch. And now she was on her way to an appointment with a solicitor. She'd found details of a few but hadn't done anything with them since and the longer the silence from Perry went on the more uneasy she felt. It had been three weeks since she left and she had no idea what her husband was thinking now or what he might be planning.

At the solicitor's office she just had enough time for a quick WhatsApp exchange with Faye to check up on her – she was fine and resting at her dad's – before she was called in. She had a free thirty-minute consultation and she needed to get as much advice as possible in that time because once it went to an hourly rate it was going to eat into her money.

Margot left the solicitor's with her head swimming. They'd covered the basic process of what filing for divorce would look like, discussing everything from pre-marital assets, current assets, pensions, property, and all the nuances around each of those things. She had a headache when she ventured outside to the street and into gloomy rain that made her feel worse. The only bright thing was that the boys were grown up now, which did make part of the divorce process a little easier.

Margot arrived at Bonnie's before Faye. Bonnie answered the door quicker than she had done previously but she still seemed a little cautious.

'It's not a very nice day out there,' said Margot, peeling off her coat and allowing Bonnie to take it and hang it on the coat stand.

'I can tell.' She looked at the drips on the garment. 'I pulled this coat stand out especially for this purpose. It sits in my spare room a lot of the time but come the winter months it'll be by the door for wet things.'

'I quite enjoy the rain,' Margot admitted and her casual claim had Bonnie looking at her differently.

'Howard always did too. Oh, he was a pain making me go out in it.'

'Would he at least let you have an umbrella and wellies?'

Bonnie chortled. 'I wouldn't have gone out without the proper attire. You know the day we met it was raining.'

'I bet he held an umbrella over you.'

Bonnie's cheeks flushed with warmth. 'As a matter of fact, he did.'

They sat and talked over a mug of tea about the day Bonnie and Howard had met in Blackpool and Bonnie told Margot about the painting of the ice-cream van and the story behind it. Unsurprisingly, Bonnie asked how Margot had met Perry and Margot recapped the happy early days, how head over heels she'd been with him.

Bonnie didn't know that Margot had walked out on her marriage and right now Margot didn't want to share the other side of Perry, the side she'd wanted to get away from, the side that was the only one she'd been seeing for a long time.

She changed the subject. 'Howard told us all at book club that you didn't like to read.'

'Well, I don't suppose he thought we'd ever meet,

let alone have a cup of tea together.' They both smiled at that. 'I never got into it, no.'

'And those?' Margot spotted the books on grief piled on top of the coffee table. 'Are they as bad as they look?'

She laughed. 'Worse. I bought them and haven't bothered reading any at all.'

'I could be a pain and say that it isn't that you don't like books, it's that you haven't found the right one.'

'Howard told me that often enough.'

'I'm sorry. I'm overstepping.'

But Bonnie shook her head. 'Not at all. It's nice to have you here.'

'Shame Faye had to fall off her bike to get you to let us in,' Margot said with a grin as a knock at the door announced their third companion had arrived and Bonnie went off to answer it.

When Bonnie came back into the room Margot was standing beside the easel. The same photograph of the view from the hill taking in the bookshop and Lulworth Cove beyond was there but the canvas hadn't changed since Margot had seen it yesterday.

'This will be beautiful once it's finished,' said Margot. 'Howard's bookshop,' she added, hoping she wasn't overstepping the mark by continuously mentioning the bookshop. They needed to be subtle but having spoken with Faye and Iris again they had all agreed that if Bonnie wanted to sell then it was her right, but what none of them wanted was for her to make a rash decision in the midst of her grief.

'I've barely started it let alone finished it.' Bonnie had made a good start on the sky and the sketch of the rest of the detail was there ready and waiting.

'Artist's block?' Faye ruffled her damp hair to smooth it out.

Faye looked stunning, whatever her hair was doing, unlike Margot who felt like a drowned rat if she ever let her mousy strands come into contact with drizzle.

'You could say that,' Bonnie answered.

'Have you painted at all since Howard...?' Margot's voice trailed off. She didn't need to finish.

'I keep trying.' Bonnie sat down and looked into her lap as if it was something to be ashamed of.

'No judgement here,' said Faye.

'When my mum died, I didn't read a book for months.' Margot's admission had Bonnie looking up. 'I didn't. I couldn't. Either the text reminded me of death, or of Mum, or of families that were still intact. I saw her in between the pages of everything.'

'How did you move forwards?' Bonnie wanted to know.

'One day at a time. I kept busy at home, which was easy; there was always a lot to do, and I ignored books for a bit.'

'I keep sitting in front of my easel,' said Bonnie. 'I've even mixed paints, but then I lift the brush and I can't quite carry on.'

'You will, eventually,' Faye encouraged. 'Creativity isn't something you can force. It will come.'

'In the early days when Mum died,' said Margot, 'not only did I stop reading, I lost my ability to follow a basic recipe. I messed up quite a few meals. Put the wrong ingredients in, mixed up a gravy instead of a cheese sauce. I suppose cooking is creative, and I couldn't do it when my head was elsewhere.' She looked to Bonnie. 'Keep sitting in front of your easel when the mood takes you, mix the paint if you feel like it, give yourself permission to do a bloody awful piece of art.'

They all laughed at that.

'The rain has stopped,' said Faye. 'Why don't we put our coats on and go down the hill to look at the view ourselves.' She addressed Bonnie. 'You might find being outside and looking at the real-life scene, taking in your Howard's beautiful bookshop rather than looking at a photograph, is enough to make you want to paint.'

But Bonnie shook her head. 'Oh no, I think actually I might be getting a cold. Best I stay inside today and keep warm.'

Margot fought the urge to tell her perhaps the outside air and exercise might ward off the cold if there really was one coming. They'd got this far – getting Bonnie to invite them over was a major milestone and she didn't want to ruin anything.

'Would you girls like to see some photographs of our travels?' Bonnie asked them in what was, Margot suspected, a tactic to stop them talking about leaving the cottage.

For the next hour they went through page after page of pictures, Bonnie talking through at length what the picture was of, what she and Howard had done that day. She added animated anecdotes, tales about Howard that fitted the way they knew him already.

Margot closed the last of the photo books Bonnie had had made rather than printing out pictures and using a traditional photo album. Margot longed to have her own versions of these, and maybe some day she would. 'I really wanted to travel, you know.'

'So why didn't you?' Bonnie asked.

'Babies and marriage. And not in the right order. I got pregnant and had to give up my university place. I was doing English and American studies and would've had a year in America.'

'That would've been quite the experience.' Bonnie didn't leave it there. 'Do you have regrets?'

'I'll never regret the boys, but the study and the travel? Yes, I have regrets.'

'And your husband, would he travel with you?'

Margot toyed with her wedding band and engagement ring. When she met Faye's gaze and looked at Bonnie she knew she was among friends.

She could tell Bonnie too. 'We're separated.'

'Oh, I'm sorry,' said Bonnie.

'No, don't be. I left. In the middle of the night without a word. Less than a month ago.' She looked down at the cover of the photo book and only looked up when she sensed Bonnie sitting forwards, closing the gap between them.

Bonnie reached across and put her hand on Margot's. 'Then you had a good reason to leave. And you are very brave.'

Margot, eyes glistening with tears she pushed away, nodded.

Then Bonnie said, 'Well, you girls have such interesting lives it quite takes my mind off my own troubles.'

Her remark took away a lot of the tension and embarrassment that Margot felt. And in the comfort of Bonnie's home she told them both more about Perry, how he had changed from the man she'd first met. 'I put up with it for so long,' she said. 'And I hate that I did. I hate that I let him talk to my boys the way he did, or does.'

'I'll bet they don't resent you one single bit,' said Bonnie.

'Actually, they don't. They weren't very surprised about what's happened either.'

'Is he in touch with them?' Faye asked.

'He hasn't been so far. I don't want them to cut him out of their lives, but that's what will happen if he doesn't accept them for who they are.' She looked at Bonnie. 'I envy you and Howard. For your marriage.'

'We did all right. Oh, we had our ups and our downs, everyone does, but it sounds as though your relationship was very different. If I'm allowed to say it, given I don't know you all that well, I think you've done the right thing.'

'You have, Margot,' said Faye.

'I feel like Perry took away a part of me,' Margot

shared and both women looked at her with a sympathy she wasn't always sure she would get. It sounded so dramatic. But perhaps for too long she'd thought of it that way, when really it was just the truth. 'I was a wife and mother and those roles were incredibly important to me, but the way Perry treated me, it overshadowed everything else. I stopped joining in with things unless Perry was there; I never went away on my own unless it was to see my mother with the boys; Perry put an end to the tennis club; he made friends feel so uneasy when they visited that they stopped altogether. I didn't go back to work or carry on with study. There was always a reason not to – his job, his business clients, the boys – and now I'm trained for nothing. I am going to need to work to support myself but who would take me on? And... I really hate admitting this, but I've borrowed money from my boys to help me do this.'

'And that is okay,' said Bonnie, without hesitation. 'You sound as if you're very close to them both.'

'I am. I'm lucky.' She put her head in her hands. 'I need to find work soon. But there's nothing suitable and I've had a few rejections already.' Her eyes filled with tears she wouldn't shed, but the emotion behind them caught her by surprise. 'What if my money runs out before I find something? What if I have to go back to Berkshire? Oh, I'm so silly. I didn't think this through.'

'Go back and let that man convince you you're not good enough?' Bonnie said firmly. 'I think Faye would agree that we can't possibly let you do that.'

Margot wondered whether she would have much choice in the end, but she appreciated Bonnie's encouragement. 'Howard knew, you know.'

'About Perry?'

Margot nodded. 'It was his voice in my head that finally gave me the ability to see that this is my life, nobody else's, and somehow I managed to walk away. I just wish I'd made a better plan, perhaps found work first.'

'And what do you think Perry would've done if you had tried?' Faye asked.

'Probably sabotaged my efforts.'

'It must be terrifying,' said Bonnie. 'But you can do this. All of it. Finding a job, going through a divorce, moving forwards.'

'She's right,' said Faye. 'It's all out there for the taking, although putting it that way makes it sound far too simple.'

'I appreciate the vote of confidence from you both. I honestly do. It means a lot to me.' Margot felt her face flush, her emotions heightened at the kindness of women she barely knew really.

Faye brightened the conversation. 'So, job wise, do you have any idea of what you'd like to do? You didn't like my suggestion of teaching?'

'I don't think that's really me.' And Faye had asked about any more cleaning work at the caravan park but unfortunately they didn't need any more help.

'Then what is your thing?' Bonnie asked.

She'd given it a bit of thought on and off and last night she'd begun to investigate online. 'Promise me you won't laugh...'

'Spit it out,' Bonnie urged.

'Come on,' said Faye.

'I'm considering looking for jobs as a flight attendant.'

'Cabin crew?' Faye asked. 'That's great.'

She looked at both women. 'Do you really think so?'

Bonnie was grinning. 'If you want to do it, then I say go for it. What appeals to you about the job?'

And it all came out, her enthusiasm lacing the words: 'I would be a part of a team – I would be doing something totally different. I was trawling through article after article about older women entering or returning to the workforce, losing hope, until I read an article about a lady in her late fifties who'd got her first job as part of the cabin crew. It jumped out at me; it got me excited. I'd be meeting new people from different countries; I'd visit far-off places. I'm not silly. I know I might not get to see a lot of the places we stop at, but just being there and having a better sense of the world really appeals to me. And let's face it, I'd be good at serving on board. I'm used to doing that, and I'll probably get a lot more thanks from passengers than I ever did from Perry.'

'Then what are you waiting for?' Bonnie encouraged.

Margot had more confidence than she'd thought possible. 'Okay, I'll go for it. Maybe start applying.'

'Do it,' said Faye.

Margot thought Bonnie had so much more colour in her cheeks these days. It was hard to marry her with the woman who'd answered the door that first time Margot had come to the cottage when Bonnie wanted to get rid of them as soon as possible. Was there something more out there for her too? 'What about you, Bonnie?'

'What about me?'

'Howard said he thought you might miss working?'

'He said that?'

'He did,' said Faye. 'He told us that you loved the travel, the time you got to spend together, but that you were a bit lost. Do you really miss being a district nurse?'

'He said you were brilliant at it by the way,' Margot put in. She loved that they could bring new snippets to Bonnie about the man she'd adored.

'I do miss it, yes. But I retired.'

'And...?' Faye prompted.

Bonnie harrumphed. 'People don't un-retire.'

'If they miss what they once did, then of course they do,' said Margot. 'And Howard un-retired by taking on the bookshop.'

'That's a point.'

'You've got nothing to lose by looking into it,' said Faye.

'Oh, I'm too old now.'

'You travelled very recently,' Margot reminded her. 'We've seen the evidence. All your photos show us how active you are. You're in your sixties, you have a lot of years left, and if you miss working, go back to it. Take it from me, missed opportunities aren't all they're cracked up to be.'

'I'll think about it.' Bonnie smiled slightly. 'You two are very persuasive. Sometimes I would swear Howard asked you to watch out for me.'

It did feel a bit that way and when they left the thought had Margot saying, 'We'll pop in tomorrow, if that's all right?'

And Bonnie replied, 'Any time. I would love to see you both.'

20

FAYE

Faye had had four vans to clean this morning. She'd been late to bed – just one more chapter she'd kept on telling herself, thoroughly enjoying *Wild*, the memoir about a young woman's solo hike after her life fell apart – but four vans wasn't too bad. That, she could manage. And it worked out well. Rather than going to Bonnie's together Margot had said she would pop in to see Bonnie before lunchtime and before she finalised her job application, which she'd been working on ever since she talked to them about it yesterday, which meant Faye could go this afternoon.

As they'd walked up the hill after they left Bonnie's yesterday, Margot had gone into more detail about the early years of her marriage and the years between then and now. Perry didn't sound like a bad man, and Margot acknowledged that he wasn't in a lot of respects. He'd done a lot of things well and she said she'd never felt unsafe. But she had felt unseen, ignored, and taken advantage of, and Faye had to wonder whether that's what would have happened with her and Brad. If at the first sign of trouble he thought about himself and ran for the hills, what did that say about his ability to commit to a long-term relationship? Not a lot in Faye's eyes.

As she finished up at the fourth van, mopping the floor and reversing out so that she didn't step onto it while it dried, she thought about the change she'd made in her own life. She'd felt forced into it when she boarded the plane from Australia but now, rather than feeling like she was getting away from something, it felt like she was discovering a whole new world. Her dad had been contemplating whether this might be a longer-term move than he had originally planned and Faye was almost beginning to have some of the same thoughts. Steph and their mother would hate the weather here, they'd moan about it all the time, but Faye didn't mind it. As long as she had the right gear then she was sorted, rain, hail or shine.

She put all the cleaning paraphernalia away and went to her own caravan to get ready. After a shower she made a sandwich and with that plus a drink in her backpack she got onto her bicycle and headed for Driftwick Bay. She was a bit nervous about that man confronting her again and had her eyes peeled but so far, thankfully, no sign of him.

Before she went to Bonnie's she wanted to go all the way down to Lulworth Cove and take in some of the scenery, sit and read her book for a while and appreciate being in Dorset with her dad and now, friends. She didn't much care that it was cold either; she was bundled up with a fleece-lined coat and a waterproof jacket just in case.

She had a good ride down to Driftwick Bay and after she'd locked up her bike the walk on to Lulworth Cove filled her lungs with much-needed fresh air and ignited a smile at the prettiness of this slice of Dorset. She sat on a bench, read her book until the wind flapped the pages one too many times before she headed back towards the hill.

Before she headed up to Bonnie's cottage she stopped off at Driftwick Bay Books. Cleaning didn't

involve the same chit-chat that came with hairdressing, and so this morning as she'd worked, Faye had
let her mind wander, and she'd come up with an idea
she wanted to share with Iris. Faye had seen Bonnie
go from someone who would barely open the door
let alone talk, to someone who had laughed with
them and chatted like a friend. What if the same happened with the bookshop? What if avoiding it was
the worst possible thing Bonnie could do? Perhaps if
they could get her to come inside again it might just
help her to heal a little after losing Howard.

In the bookshop Iris was crouched down beside a
young boy who looked like he wasn't at all sure about
Midas, who was obediently sitting next to him. Faye
smiled. Midas was a softie; the dog would soon make
this little boy fall in love.

As she waited for Iris to be free, Faye browsed the
shelves and plucked *My Favourite Mistake* by Marian
Keyes as a treat for herself even though she hadn't
got onto reading the last book she'd bought from
here yet. She hadn't finished *Wild* either, and swore it
was taking her longer to read because she was trea-
suring the knowledge that it had been Howard to put
it in the telephone box library. She waved away Iris's
concern that she might want to pay and called over
that she would browse until Iris was free, and five

minutes later Iris was at the counter and Faye had found another couple of books to buy.

'Midas has another fan.' Faye watched as the same young boy, next to a man likely to be his dad given how much they looked like one another, giggled at Midas's wagging tail when he petted him.

'You'll have too much in your suitcase when you fly back with all these books.' Iris laughed as she began to ring up the purchases. 'They'll charge you more.'

'I was worried about that when I first got here, but I think I'll be fine. As long as I don't go too crazy.' Mind you, she was pretty sure she was going to have to buy a new jumper or two because this morning when she'd stepped outside the caravan it had been the first time she'd seen a dense fog that gave the county a chilly feel. The summer had been beautiful, and autumn was off to a pretty good start, but the chillier months would be here soon enough. She wasn't sure yet whether she would be too.

As Iris finished ringing up the purchases Faye told her that she and Margot had been managing to get Bonnie to talk a bit.

'She told us about the day Howard came here with the keys and showed it off to her.'

'She spoke about the shop?' Iris asked.

'Yes, and for a while too.'

'Usually she shuts the conversation down,' said Iris. 'That's a good sign.'

'Very.' Because Bonnie had been remembering some of the nice days she'd had with Howard, helping him unpack some of the stock, watching him talk with customers.

'Did she mention the sale again?'

Faye shook her head. 'No, but the letter from the developer is beside her phone.' She quickly added, 'I wasn't snooping. I went to use the bathroom and it must've fallen to the floor as I passed by.'

'Did you mention it to her?'

'No, it didn't feel right. But I do have another idea to help Bonnie out and maybe at some point get her back to the bookshop.'

'You do? Come on then, let's hear it.'

Once Faye had explained, Iris was all for it.

And the plan could start right now. The young boy who had Midas's attention was about to leave the bookshop and after Iris passed Faye the dog's lead, Faye got Midas ready and they left the shop to walk the rest of the way up the hill to Bonnie's cottage.

She let them both through the little front gate and closed it behind them. Already the cottage on the hill had taken on a much more homely feel compared to the first time she turned up here. It was as though the warmth in Bonnie's eyes the last few days made the whole place feel that much brighter even without Howard around.

Bonnie's smile didn't falter when she opened the door. 'Hello, what's all this?' She indicated Midas before stepping back. 'Bring him inside. Are you thirsty, boy?' She immediately went to fill a big bowl with water that she set down inside the front door.

Faye had had a suspicion that Bonnie wouldn't be able to resist Midas, who was a big part of the master plan.

Midas lapped vigorously at the water, sending droplets all over the tiles, but it made Bonnie laugh. *Midas, you have the magic touch,* Faye wanted to tell the dog. As she'd cleaned that morning she'd thought about Theo, which led to thinking about Midas and his therapy dog status. That had led her to thinking: what if Midas could help someone like Bonnie? As soon as she'd got back to her caravan she'd done some reading online. She found case studies using therapy dogs who could indeed help people who were anxious, and that was Bonnie, wasn't it? She was nervous talking to people now; she didn't seem to want to go out. Maybe Midas could help her. And perhaps some day he'd be able to entice her back inside the bookshop. She just wasn't sure how that part of the plan would work yet.

Bonnie crouched down and made a fuss over Midas. 'Now, what are you doing with our Faye, here?'

'I offered to take him for a long walk. He's working at the shop today and Iris won't get a chance to take him out much.'

'I told her not to open for so long. She could've closed for a long lunch, taken him for a stroll.'

'I don't think she felt right doing that. Everyone is pleased to see the shop open again, you know. She's got a steady flow of customers.'

Bonnie smiled tightly. 'She said. She's rung me twice already today fretting...'

'About what?' Faye asked when Bonnie stopped talking.

'Doesn't matter.' She distracted herself with Midas. 'So where did you take him?'

Faye wondered whether she'd been about to mention selling the bookshop to the developer, and that was what Iris had been fretting about, but she didn't know Bonnie all that well so it was a balance between being there for her without interfering.

'I haven't taken him anywhere apart from here yet,' she told Bonnie, 'but I thought I'd take him down to the cove, along the coastal path a bit, then loop back up the hill.'

'Well, that sounds lovely.' Her eyes were for the dog and the dog only. 'You'll enjoy that won't you, Midas.'

'We thought you might like to come?'

'I think I'll give it a miss this time, but you two enjoy yourselves.'

'That's a shame,' said Faye. But she'd planned for this. 'Would you mind if I nip in and use your toilet quickly.'

'Of course I don't mind.' And when Faye headed for the bathroom she heard Bonnie tell Midas, 'You can stay right here with me for a bit, can't you.'

In the bathroom Faye texted Iris who was in on the plan and sure enough after she flushed the toilet and used the sink her phone rang about a minute after she got back to talking to Bonnie in the hallway.

'I'm coming straight away,' Faye said urgently, her acting skills not too great but hopefully enough. She told Bonnie, 'Iris has caught someone trying to take my bike.'

'Oh, dear Lord. You don't think it's that man again, do you?'

'What? Er... no... it's a young lad apparently.' She hadn't banked on Bonnie asking her any questions, especially not about her previous unpleasant encounter.

Thankfully, she didn't ask any more. She ushered her out of the front door saying, 'You go! Scare them off. But be careful!'

Faye ran from the cottage. She had to make it look real and when she was out of sight further down the hill, just in case Bonnie was looking out of her window, she slowed to a walk. She'd hang around down in the high street for a bit, give Bonnie and Midas some time together. Iris had approved of the idea when Faye shared it and they hadn't been able to ask Theo whether it was okay because he was at work. 'As long as Midas is safe and happy, he won't mind,' Iris had told Faye.

Faye wanted to give Bonnie and Midas some decent time alone. Her reading on therapy dogs had suggested that a dog might have a calming presence, increase feel-good hormones with companionship and at the same time reduce stress and anxiety. Bonnie was grieving too and Faye had everything crossed that Midas's unconditional love might be just what she needed to help her with that as well. She got the feeling that Howard would've approved of this part of the plan.

She headed for the bakery to pick up some afternoon tea for her and Bonnie. She opted for Eccles cakes and if Bonnie still wouldn't go for a walk they'd have some time together, with Midas too, and then Faye would leave her to it. But she would try again and again until this worked. Howard would hate to think of his wife hiding away from the world.

Outside the bakery she gave Bonnie a quick call – Iris had given her her phone number. She told her that everything was fine, the kid trying to take her bike had run off, but she was just going to see if Iris needed a hand in the shop. Bonnie replied telling her to take her time, that her and Midas were fine.

Faye smiled. She'd known they would be.

She was just turning from the side street to go back up the hill when she saw Theo come out of the bookshop. She crossed over.

'You kidnapped my dog?' he asked.

She grinned. 'Kind of. It's a long story.'

He spotted the bump on her head. 'And that? Is that a long story too?'

'I'm afraid so.' She grimaced. She really didn't want to explain that one.

'Mum filled me in on your plan with Midas.'

'You're fine with Midas being a part of it?'

'Of course. He enjoys being with people and when he's not needed at the bookshop it's better he has company. That's why I showed up. It's my lunch hour and for once I can escape – not always the case as a teacher.'

'Oh, I'm sorry – you planned to walk him?'

'It's really not a problem.' He zipped up his coat. 'Autumn is here.'

'It sure is.' She looked down the hill towards Lulworth Cove. 'It's so beautiful even when the weather is the opposite.'

'Do you miss the English winters? Or is that a silly question? I bet you don't give them a moment's thought with all that Australian sunshine.'

'Actually, it's not such a silly question. I do miss it sometimes, the cosy winters, a huge fireplace like the one I remember having as a kid, the dark and snuggling up.'

'All sounds very romantic. Then of course there are the howling winds, the heavy showers, the fact you can't feel your face because it's gone numb with the cold.'

She began to laugh. 'All right, those are things I don't particularly miss.'

'Is your dad enjoying being back?'

They stood for a good fifteen minutes talking about her dad, her uncle, her parents' marriage, or rather divorce, her life in Queensland, and they even talked a bit about the book club.

'Howard was a lovely chap.' Theo stepped off the kerb to let a lady with a pram walk past on the pavement.

When he checked his watch she asked, 'Do you need to go?'

'Not just yet, so we could walk if you like.'

'Sure.'

They began to head down the hill towards the coastal path and when they reached it Theo said, 'So, the bump on your head?' He was still looking in the same direction as her, out across the water.

'I fell off my bike.' And with the soothing sounds of the waves crashing in the distance she found herself telling him all about her sister, the scandal, what led her to coming here, all the way to being chased by that man.

'You should've called the police.' She could feel him watching her now.

'I will if I see him again, or rather if he hassles me again. So far I've not set eyes on him.'

They didn't stay watching the sea for long and when they set off back up the hill they'd moved on to talking about his job, how much he loved being a primary school teacher, and how settled he was here.

'I always thought that I'd want to stay in London,' he admitted. 'It was great being there for a while, having the city right on my doorstep. It was a lot of fun but when a job came up here I took it as a sign.'

'Any regrets?'

'None.' They'd almost reached the bookshop when Theo told her, 'Be careful. You know, in case that man is hanging around again.'

She liked that he cared. 'I think Bonnie scared him off.'

'Good for her.'

'I'd better get going, take Midas on the nice long walk I promised him,' she said. 'Don't worry, I'll return him to the shop in plenty of time for his afternoon shift.'

'I bet he's loving all the added attention he's getting.'

'I hope in some way he can help Bonnie.' She shrugged.

'Hey, don't doubt yourself. It was a good idea.' He put a hand briefly to her shoulder for reassurance and the touch, although light, sent her a little bit giddy. She hadn't expected to have feelings for anyone so soon after Brad, but she did. It had felt weird at the start but now it felt normal. Now it felt right. But she was leaving, and that thought did the opposite of making her feel giddy; it made her feel sad.

'Carers often bring adults with learning difficulties into the shop,' Theo went on, oblivious to the storm of feelings brewing inside her. 'Midas seems to be good with everyone so I've no doubt he'll be good for Bonnie.'

When they reached the point where he had to cross over to head back to the school and she carried on up the hill, she wedged the bag from the bakery under her arm so she could check her emails. She usually paid a fixed monthly fee to the salon for renting a chair there and had been allowed to put it on hold, but they had written yesterday to ask whether she would recommence payments for the following month. She'd said that, at the moment, she had no idea how long she would stay in England. She wanted to see whether they were going to give the chair to someone else or whether they would wait a while longer. The email was there and she replied to negotiate a date that would give her another four weeks before she would have to either start renting the chair again or give it up.

Her life was in Australia, wasn't it? She was on holiday here, which wasn't the same thing, but it wasn't as clear cut as it had been when she first came here to get away. Already she was beginning to feel ties form. And she had to admit Theo might be a part of that.

She was about to close her email when another one jumped out at her. It was from one of the customers at her dad's water-sports business in Queensland and so she clicked on it assuming this would be about booking more lessons, or asking whether her dad had a certain piece of equipment for sale. But it wasn't. This was from Daryl, a lovely man in his seventies who had learned to kayak with her five years ago at the age of sixty-eight and had fallen in love with the sport.

She smiled. Daryl was lovely, great company.

But the smile fell away when she read on.

He had written because he was aware that Keith and Faye weren't around at the moment. He thought they should know that the reporters had been asking questions to everyone who came to the business and that morning he'd been hounded himself for comment when he was only a customer. Faye knew what being targeted was like and felt for him. But hadn't the gossip died down now? Weren't people tired of the story?

It was only when she stood at the side of the pavement moving out of the way of the same lady from earlier pushing her pram uphill that she did a bit of reconnaissance on her phone. And she didn't have to do much to find out why this was happening.

The headline:

Politician Leaves Wife for Lover Half His Age

said it all. She didn't need to read the body of text beneath it to know that her sister, Steph, and Brad's father were back together.

21

BONNIE

It was the fifth day in a row that Bonnie had seen the girls – Margot usually came in the mornings, Faye in the afternoons, and sometimes their visits overlapped. Other times, like today, they showed up together. During the visits the girls liked to talk about Howard, the book club, and the bookshop, and rather than inducing more pain, the memories were slowly becoming more of a comfort.

Faye had brought Midas with her again today and they spent a bit of time outside wandering around in the sunshine, inspecting the state of the flowerbeds.

'They're terrible, I know.' Back inside in the

warm, the doors to the garden closed, Bonnie made them all a cup of tea.

'The pots won't take much sorting,' Margot assured her. 'I could do them if you like. You could have something winter-flowering or you could pop in some bulbs – how about daffodils or tulips, and they'll bloom come spring? You'll have more colour than you can imagine.'

It did sound rather good. 'I'll have a think, decide on something.'

'Good,' said Margot. 'That's settled then.'

Midas happily curled up next to the radiator in the kitchen while the girls sat at the table. 'He likes it here,' said Bonnie, almost to herself. 'He reminds me of Patsy, our German shepherd when I was a young girl. German shepherds aren't known for being docile, but Patsy was.' She stirred a spoonful of sugar into her tea from the little bowl she'd set in the middle of the table. 'I think it's the amount of time Dad spent training her that did it. And the exercise.'

'The exercise?' Margot shook her head at the offer of sugar.

'Those sorts of dogs need mental and physical stimulation,' said Bonnie. 'You don't want them getting bored; that's when they misbehave. At least that's what my dad told me.'

'Did you ever think about getting a dog?' Faye blew across the top of her tea.

'Me and Howard?' She shook her head. 'Not really, not when we both had work. Howard did talk about it when he retired but it was always one of those "maybe one day" things. Then I retired, and we travelled.' Life went by far too fast.

'What is that on the stove?' Faye was curious about the large deep saucepan that was making a low rumbling sound.

Bonnie smiled. 'I thought it might be nice to make you both Howard's favourite pudding.' She'd made the syrup sponge before the girls turned up and it was happily steaming away inside the saucepan in the pudding basin she'd placed on top of a trivet.

Margot's eyes widened. 'The famous steamed syrup sponge?'

'He told you about it?'

'Oh yes,' said Faye, 'he was forever talking about how delicious it was.'

Bonnie had wondered whether she would ever make it again after the day he died, given she'd taken him a piece and promptly thrown it everywhere when she realised what had happened, but something about these women had made her want to try.

And the thought of her Howard sharing this part of their world with his friends touched her more than she expected. It brought him closer again, the same way that had been happening since these two women walked into her life.

While the pudding cooked, talk turned to Faye's family and specifically her dad when Bonnie asked after him.

'He's taking it all in his stride. I think it's the only way he knows how when it comes to my sister.'

'So are the stories definitely true about Steph and that politician?' Bonnie asked. Faye had told her all about it and she had to say having a sister like Steph sounded hard-going. 'It's not salacious gossip?'

'I wish it was just gossip but it isn't,' said Faye. 'Dad and I have cross-checked quite a few news articles and when my mum eventually picked up the phone to answer one of our many calls, she confirmed it.' She shook her head. 'Online there's video footage of my sister and the politician cosy and very much together. His wife has come forward to make a further statement and requested privacy for the rest of her family.'

'Why didn't you tell me?' Margot asked. 'I'm close by – you didn't need to cope with that news on your own.'

Faye seemed so young to be dealing with all of this. Bonnie had had a sister, older than her by seven years, and they'd got on until Mindy passed away five years ago. She couldn't imagine what it must be to have an out-of-control sibling you felt responsible for.

'To be honest I've just been working hard,' said Faye. 'At least I've been able to take my frustration out on bathroom floors and kitchen sinks.'

'You have a good work ethic,' said Bonnie. 'But Margot is right. You should turn to others for help.' The irony wasn't lost on her when she was struggling but not reaching out to anyone to tell them that she might now own the bookshop but she couldn't bear the thought of going inside ever again. 'Margot is a friend, and so am I, for that matter. You should've come to one of us.'

Faye began to smile. 'We're friends?' She was looking at Bonnie rather than Margot.

Bonnie fidgeted. Her mouth felt a little dry. 'I do believe we are, yes.'

'I'm glad,' said Faye.

'Me too,' Margot chipped in before asking Faye, 'Have you heard anything from Brad?'

'I haven't. But in one article the journalist had thought it was important to let everyone know that the politician's son was dating some socialite twelve years his junior.'

Margot groaned and Bonnie asked, 'Your fiancé – ex fiancé – is dating again?'

'It seems like it. And someone much younger, just like his dad,' said Faye.

'And how do you feel about that?' Bonnie asked. 'Not about the age gap but about Brad being with someone else.'

After a hesitation Faye answered, 'Oddly, I feel very much okay.'

Margot put an arm around her and gave her a squeeze. 'Good.'

'He doesn't sound like he was right for you,' Bonnie added for moral support.

Margot hesitated before she said to Faye, 'Is it too soon to tease you about a certain local dog owner?'

The remark at least roused a smile from Faye.

And Bonnie wanted to know more. 'Don't keep me on tenterhooks; what's this about a dog owner?'

Margot leaned forwards and conspiratorially, as if Faye wasn't even there, confided in Bonnie that Faye and Midas's owner seemed to be interested in each other whenever they crossed paths.

Bonnie approved. Theo was a lovely young man. 'He's a wonderful person, Faye. He's kind, warm-hearted. I'm surprised he's even single.' She added, 'If there's any more gossip on that front, be sure to fill me in. That's the kind of gossip I like.'

Talk briefly turned to the scandal again and Faye told them both that her dad had come to a decision. 'He's going to sell the business in Queensland.'

Bonnie took away the empty mugs and set them by the sink. 'Did the scandal drive him to give it up?'

'Actually, no. He said he's been thinking about it for a while, and with his brother needing help here and being on his own, and with Dad falling in love with Dorset all over again, he says the timing is right.' Faye shrugged. 'I think avoiding the drama back in Australia is simply the icing on the cake.'

'And you're okay if he stays here and doesn't go back to Australia?' Bonnie felt for the girl. She'd had her parents living fairly close by until she was well into her fifties; she couldn't imagine being separated from them by quite such a distance when she was Faye's age.

'It's a long way,' Margot added. 'I struggle with how far away Sebastian is sometimes.'

As Margot talked a bit more about her sons, Bonnie watched her. She looked really pretty today. It was as though the sea air was finally managing to take away the stresses of a marriage that sounded challenging and so unlike the partnership Bonnie had had with Howard and was forever grateful she'd got to experience. It was funny, on some days she saw all the positives – that she'd had a happy marriage with Howard, that Howard had reached a reasonably good age before he died, that they had retired and gone travelling. But at other times she felt the unfairness, the pain, and the overwhelming feeling that some sort of blanket was still suffocating her and stopping her from moving forwards.

Faye set her empty mug down on the table. 'I'm thinking of staying on a while longer in England myself.'

'You are?' Bonnie was all ears. 'At the caravan park?'

'Yes. Uncle Frank says I can use the caravan for as long as I like. It's got heating; I'll be fine when winter eventually comes. He has offered a room at his house if I prefer although I quite like my independence.'

Bonnie enquired, 'What about your work?'

'I can do hairdressing anywhere. I'll have to give up my place at the salon in Queensland but that's okay.' She smiled at them both. 'I never planned to come back to England but racing here to get away and to see Dad, I've discovered it's so much more than I realised. It kind of feels like I belong.'

'Well, it would be lovely to see some more of you.' When Bonnie said it, it came so naturally, talking to these women who were her friends. And then she remembered something. 'Talking of work...' She looked across at Margot. 'Did you send in your application for cabin crew?'

Margot took a deep breath as if nerves were getting the better of her. 'I did.'

Bonnie smiled. 'That's marvellous. How long till you hear back, do you think?'

'I've no idea. And let's face it, I may not hear a thing. I think these days you have to apply for hundreds of jobs to even get an interview.' She paused. 'I also had to put a home address on the application as I haven't found a proper rental yet. It was risky, but I didn't have a lot of choice.'

'I doubt they would even use the address,' Bonnie assured her. 'It's all emails and phone calls these days.'

'I don't think they would either,' said Margot. 'But putting it was just another reminder that I have left, that I've no idea what stance Perry will take in all of this, and that he could make things very difficult and unpleasant. He's out there somewhere, thinking about his next step.'

'Try not to worry too much,' Bonnie urged. The

man hadn't been violent, that was a relief, but the mind games sounded torturous. She tried to lighten the mood. 'Now, with Faye staying on in Dorset and you having applied for a job, I think that calls for an extra big slice of syrup sponge each, to celebrate.'

'I'm in!' said Margot with agreement from Faye.

Bonnie served each of them a generous piece of the sponge and between them they almost demolished two-thirds of the entire pudding.

'I can barely move,' Faye groaned afterwards. 'That was too much.'

Margot told her, 'Bonnie, that was possibly the best syrup sponge I have *ever* tasted. Howard was right.'

Faye picked up a stray crumb of sponge from her placemat and left it in her bowl. 'Have you given any more thought to un-retiring, Bonnie?'

'Un-retiring.' She turned the phrase over in her mind. 'I still think I'm too old.'

'You're sixty-six!' Margot pointed out.

How could she even begin to think about returning to her job as a district nurse? She could get out to do a food shop or nip to the bakery, but that was about it. How could she go from doing that to visiting people's homes and actually being some kind of help?

In an effort to steer them onto new ground, she took them through to the back room where it would be warmer and more comfortable.

Faye had stopped beside the bookshelves in front of the place where the urn acted as a bookend. If she'd ever noticed it before today, she'd not mentioned it.

'I haven't scattered them yet,' said Bonnie, glancing first at Faye and then Margot, who seemed to have cottoned on to what she was talking about, and came to Bonnie's side. She felt a hand on her arm when she confessed, 'I just don't feel ready.'

'No rush, Bonnie,' said Margot. 'You do it when the time is right.'

Her next words were out before she had a chance to really think about them. 'I'm considering selling the bookshop.'

Margot acted surprised, so did Faye, but Bonnie wasn't born yesterday. 'You both knew, didn't you?'

'Iris mentioned it,' said Margot.

'Do you think I'm a terrible person?'

Faye came straight to her side. 'Bonnie, no, of course not.'

'But Howard saved the shop from being closed down permanently. If it wasn't for him, then it wouldn't even exist any more.'

'He told us all about the developers,' said Faye.

'He did?'

Margot nodded. 'He used to talk about it in book club. He said they turned up frequently, upping their offer.'

They had. It hadn't worried Howard; he said they'd get the message in the end. But now Bonnie had their contact details. It was an easy way of moving on. All she'd have to do is make the call.

'The offer is considerably more than we paid for it,' said Bonnie.

'And what would you do with all the money?' Margot asked.

Shocked at the question, Bonnie realised she had no idea. 'I just don't want to have to deal with it. You know, along with everything else.'

'You could always just wait and see,' Faye suggested. 'You might change your mind about the place. You might want to keep it.'

Bonnie almost agreed that that could happen, but who was she kidding? She was about as likely to keep a bookshop on as Howard would've been to keep on an artists' studio.

'I'll make a decision eventually,' she told them, hopefully putting an end to the subject for now. It was her fault. She shouldn't have blurted it out. In fact, she wasn't sure why she had.

These women were so kind they didn't push her to talk any more and they were soon onto talking about something else.

Faye asked about some of the books she'd noticed on the bottom shelves. 'Howard has collected some beautiful old paperbacks here, Bonnie.' She'd found a few Hans Christian Andersen books, Howard's since he was a boy.

Bonnie urged Faye and Margot to go ahead and flip through 'The Emperor's New Clothes', 'The Snow Queen', an illustrated collection of twelve fairy tales. They moved on to C.S. Lewis and *The Chronicles of Narnia*, a collection, as well as some of the books as individual paperbacks.

'One of our foster children, Victor, loved those books,' Bonnie told them.

'You and Howard fostered?' Faye asked, still holding open one of the books. 'Howard never mentioned it.'

'He was very humble about it; that's why.' He had done so much for others. Even by bringing these two to her door, her husband was still looking out for her, although he wouldn't have planned any of this.

'We fostered for a while. Victor was the last child

we took in. We both got quite attached, especially Howard, and then he went back to his mother. I suppose the mother didn't want to remember the rocky past and never kept in touch with us.'

'That's a shame.' Margot slotted back the book she was holding. 'I can imagine you both were really good foster parents.'

Bonnie smiled at the compliment.

Margot moved towards the easel facing away from the room. 'May I?' she asked before she went around to take a look.

'Of course.' Bonnie had been sitting in front of the easel day after day and it was yesterday when she finally managed to start working on her painting again. Midas had been with her – apparently Faye had so much cleaning she'd be at it all day; Iris had a crazy day at the bookshop, because it was only her there; and Theo was teaching so she stepped in to be the dog-sitter, which she didn't mind at all. With Midas sitting beside her, at one point resting his chin on her knee while she worked, she'd finally felt the energy and drive to paint, return. She'd made a start on the sky and the street using colours she'd mixed into the desired shades. She was yet to add the details of the pavements with their uneven squares, the cracks, the kerb and the weeds sprouting up between slabs every now and then, or the people on the street to make the scene really come alive.

'It's brilliant,' Margot declared, all three of them standing in front of the easel to see what she'd been working on.

Bonnie's laughter filled the room. 'You don't have to lie. It's not brilliant but it's a start.'

Faye nudged Bonnie. 'And that's what brilliant.'

Faye was right Bonnie realised. To have started was a major milestone in itself. She tried not to let her voice catch when she said, 'There's still a way to go but...'

'You'll get there,' Margot finished for her.

And for the first time she started to believe that yes, perhaps she would.

22

MARGOT

Over the last week Margot and Faye had been popping in regularly to see Bonnie, either separately or together. Faye had gone through more of Howard's book collection, Bonnie had taught her how to make the syrup sponge, and Margot had dug out the pots in the back garden and those out front and planted daffodil bulbs in a couple and a variety of tulip bulbs in the others. Neither of them had mentioned selling the bookshop to the developers. The locals were on tenterhooks wondering what would happen with the shop but at the same time they held a respect for Bonnie just as they always had for Howard, and Margot got the feeling Bonnie would be left to make her own decision. They just hoped it would be the one that saved Driftwick Bay Books.

This morning Faye was busy at her cleaning job, but Margot couldn't wait to see Bonnie because she had news.

'I have an interview,' she announced the second Bonnie opened the door. It was a grey late September day, the sun had done a bunk, and you could barely see Lulworth Cove for the fog, but it didn't detract from Margot's excitement which, mixed with nerves, had her a bit all over the place.

Bonnie took her coat and hung it up while Margot removed her shoes. 'Tea and a scone for you, and you can tell me all about it.'

Over tea and a delicious scone that Cathy from the bakery had dropped round, Margot told her that she'd had an email first thing and she had to go into London for an interview tomorrow.

'I can't believe I actually got past the first hurdle – the application form. And it's more than an interview. There'll be an assessment process too.' She barely took a breath in her delivery.

'Firstly, let me say that I can completely believe you got over the first hurdle.' Bonnie spread a thick layer of raspberry jam onto one half of a scone she'd warmed briefly in the microwave. 'You have a lot to offer.'

Margot passed the cream over to Bonnie now her own scone was prepared. 'I'm not sure I can even eat this. I'm a bundle of nerves.'

'Nonsense. You must eat, then we must talk strategy, practise interview questions.'

The scone was deliciously moist but her mouth felt dry. She was all riled up. For years she hadn't applied for jobs let alone been interviewed for one. Was she veering out of her lane? Was she really anything more than a housewife and someone who supported her husband's corporate life? Perry had said to her more than once over the years that she didn't have to work, that many women would be elated to be in her position. He'd given her the guilt trip too when she'd talked about study or looking for work; he'd told her that her boys needed her. They had but only now could she see that they also needed a role model, a mum who showed them that it wasn't okay to be ignored in a marriage and treated the way Perry had treated her.

Her sons were both rooting for her too – she'd told them both in a text message earlier – but Bonnie was leaping into practical mode. She and Faye may not have managed to get her outside, at least no further than the back garden, and really back into the community of Driftwick Bay let alone the bookshop, but what she was doing right now was a part of it. She was interested in something, making steps to get involved.

With the scones eaten Bonnie was ready to make a start. With her iPad in front of her she said, 'I've found some information online. Firstly, have you researched the airline you've applied to?'

'I've done that already. Probably over-researched if I'm honest.'

'Better over-researched than under.' She pulled her glasses back down to focus on the iPad screen again. 'Right, I've found some sample questions. Ready?'

Actually, this was making Margot more relaxed, watching Bonnie so animated and invested in her success. 'You really want me to get this job, don't you?'

'Of course I do. Come on, no time to waste.'

And so over another mug of tea, plus an interruption from Iris at the bookshop who was checking whether Bonnie was happy with the hours she was putting in, Bonnie ran through umpteen questions Margot had already been churning over and over in her head, reciting the answers as she walked here today – 'Tell me about your most recent role' almost had her stumped but she'd adapted it so that despite it not being an official job, there was plenty in her answer to make her sound like she might be able to do this.

It was easy for doubt to creep in, but Bonnie's quickfire questions and treating this like an interview rather than a chat, was good for Margot. The more she went over her skills the more she realised what she'd actually taken on in her marriage. She'd always known she did a lot but had never really thought those skills might be transferable out of the home and into the work environment. She could go into an interview and talk about her hospitality experience – she had plenty of that entertaining Perry's business clients, serving food, keeping them happy. She could talk about her kind and caring nature having raised her sons. She could talk about her patience and composure in her role as a parent with plenty of examples and how similar situations might demand the same quality if she was faced with a difficult passenger.

After a two-hour practice, which at times was fun, at other times like an interrogation, Margot felt incredibly prepared. Bonnie even came up with some bizarre situations that might happen on board and asked Margot how she would deal with each. The situations had been inspired by some of the journeys she'd been on with Howard, and after Margot answered each one Bonnie confirmed how the flight attendant had dealt with each situation, like the one where a man refused to sit in his own seat because he preferred the one on the aisle, or the lady who put her feet through the armrest of the seat in front of her, or the kids tearing up and down the aisle at food service time. Margot had intended to go home and practise alone after seeing Bonnie, maybe in front of a mirror, but Bonnie had done a lot of the hard work already and Margot's confidence was on the up.

Finally it had been time to take a break from the interview scenarios and Margot wanted to see Bonnie's painting again.

'It's really starting to look like the view from the hill taking in the bookshop.' Margot admired the canvas. 'I find the painting process fascinating. It's easy to forget that the artist paints a picture in stages; it doesn't just get painted in one go. There are sketches, practice paintings, various versions before the final one.'

'I've scrapped my work many a time, believe me.

With this one I think I left it so long to start that my mind was ready as well as my hands.'

Margot wasn't quite sure what she meant by that, but it sounded like a step in the right direction.

Before Margot left Bonnie's to go home and do some more practice questions because she wouldn't be able to help herself, Bonnie pulled her into a heartfelt hug.

'Be proud of yourself.' Bonnie stepped back, her hands on Margot's upper arms. 'I don't know you well but from what you've said about your marriage, getting this far must have taken a lot of guts. And you have an interview. You're on your way to a new life.'

Margot smiled. 'It all feels a bit surreal. Every now and then what I'm doing and what I still need to do seems insurmountable and I think that I should come to my senses and go home—'

'Is that what Perry would tell you?'

'It's exactly what he would say. His voice is still in my head and I hate that.' By the look on Bonnie's face she was likely thinking that Howard's voice was still in *her* head but she didn't ever want it to leave.

'Make sure you get a good night's sleep tonight. And come here after the interview and assessment tomorrow. I'll need to hear all about it.'

* * *

The next day Margot woke ridiculously early, before the sun had had a chance to creep up over the horizon. She'd put on the black and ivory Hobbs jacket and skirt she'd brought with her to Dorset, knowing that she needed to be prepared in her quest to get work and along with some black patent shoes and tights she was smart enough beneath her coat.

She got the train from the station at Wool that would have her arriving into London a good hour before the interview and assessments, which gave her time to find the airline offices and gather herself. She almost talked herself out of it on the train, almost told herself that she wasn't going to be able to do this; she was nothing more than a housewife and mother, and the world of work had passed her by. But then she heard Perry's voice in her head backing up those thoughts and Bonnie popped into her imagination, wagging her finger at the man she'd married, telling him 'shame on you'.

The image of that made her chuckle as she walked from the station to the airline offices. When she arrived she tried to work out who else looked as nervous as she was. Or perhaps others milling around in reception weren't here for a job – maybe she was the only one at the assessment day who had turned up this early because she was so paranoid about being late.

The interview itself went better than expected. She was asked about situations that may arise and how she would react, and it was just like she and Bonnie practised. A couple of the scenarios had her stumped but all in all she thought she did well. The tests covered reading, English fluency, conflict resolutions and group activities. And Margot especially loved working with other people, as a team, the way it should be.

The day went by in a flash and before she knew it the train back to Wool was trundling along the tracks and Margot was pretty sure a smile was fused permanently on her face. She must look like a loony! But she decided that even if she didn't get the job, this day had been monumental and showed her just what she could do. She was capable of so much more than she'd ever thought possible. She could function independently out in the big wide world. And no longer would she let anyone cast doubt over that.

She got a taxi from Wool station back to her accommodation, had a shower to freshen up, and when she was dressed in jeans and her favourite soft cashmere jumper she pulled on her coat and set off for

Bonnie's place. Faye had organised to be there this evening as well, and they had all agreed that no matter how today had gone they'd be there to support her in whatever came next.

She realised she was humming as she walked down the hill and a lady walking her dog up the other way smiled at her. She felt so alive, the nip in the air signalling summer was behind them, the sky so dark she could see the stars above.

When she reached the cottage she bent down to open the little gate, and at the same moment she heard a car pull up at the kerb behind her.

And the voice that came from the open window had her halting in her tracks.

He'd found her.

'Get in the car Margot,' came the familiar voice. 'It's time to come home.'

She didn't look at him. She couldn't.

'Margot.' The engine was still running. 'Come on,' said Perry, with more than a note of impatience, 'you've had your fun. Enough is enough.'

The car engine stopped. She heard a door open and clunk shut, and she turned to face him.

'Whatever were you playing at, running away?' He came closer and closer.

She took a deep breath and determinedly told him, 'I wasn't running. I left.'

'Same thing, isn't it?' He pushed his hands into his trouser pockets. The way he was looking at her reminded her of the man he'd once been, the graduate who she'd met at the pub with the kind demeanour and ability to make her feel safe and special. 'You've made your point, Margot. And now it's time you came home.'

And there he was, no longer the graduate she'd met but the man he'd turned out to be.

He took her by surprise when he said, 'I know all about the storage unit.' She didn't have to ask how because he told her, 'A leaflet came through the letterbox, then I had a phone call from the same place asking to speak to you and it clicked.'

Had he got access? Had he moved all her things back in as if she'd never got away at all?

'How was the interview?' he asked with more than a hint of glee in his eye.

'How did you...'

'You keep notes in your phone; you saved them to the cloud.' He was likely thinking how terrible she was with technology, how that was his thing not hers, how she'd made a stupid mistake. *Silly woman, silly decision* – that's what was likely going through his mind right now.

When she said nothing he pushed on. 'So, cabin crew?'

She wanted to run, to stop the conversation in its tracks. 'It's none of your business.'

He grunted, raked a hand roughly through his hair. 'You're my wife, of course it's my bloody business.'

Her heart beat faster, but her feet stayed where they were. She could do this. She wouldn't be intimidated.

'You're important to me,' he said, way too close and invading her personal space already. But she wouldn't move, she told herself, not unless he touched her. 'If you want to see the world there's a far easier way to do that, you know. Come home, we'll plan a holiday.'

Did he really think she was doing this to make a point? Applying for a job so she could go travelling? And did he think that a holiday would fix everything just like that?

'Margot, I've always given you everything you've ever needed, haven't I?'

He had – financially. But emotionally she'd been robbed of so many things and she'd slowly let herself be ground down into a different version of the woman she'd once been.

'The boys haven't said anything,' said Perry, hands back in his pockets. He didn't have a coat on and it was chilly out. He'd always hated the cold. The heating at home had been on too high in the colder months for Margot but he was unbearable when he moaned. 'I take it you haven't told them.'

'This is between us, Perry.'

'They'll be hurt. You don't want to upset them, do you? Now get in the car and we can talk about this properly. You've had some time away, come home, and let's get on with our lives.'

She wondered then whether he'd told any of his business clients, or the neighbours. She'd put money on him having not told a soul that she'd walked out on him or even that they had separated. It wouldn't be good for his image.

'Margot... just get in the car. Please.' He spoke through gritted teeth.

'I'm not getting in the car, Perry.' And then she looked him in the eye for the first time since he'd started the confrontation. 'And I have told the boys.'

The remark knocked the wind out of him and she could see his mind adjusting to the knowledge.

'You're turning them against me.'

'I'm not.' He'd done that all by himself and it wasn't her job to point it out or her job to try and fix it. She'd been attempting to do that over the years, but he never listened. He never saw anything wrong with his behaviour or what he said to his sons and she was tired of trying to make him see reason.

When she looked at him again he was sneering. It was a particular look that he managed to hide so often that sometimes she'd wondered whether she was imagining it. But she didn't look away as she usually did. She kept her gaze fixed on him, on the whites of his eyes as he grew more frustrated.

'You're being ridiculous, you know.'

She said nothing.

And he got nastier and became sarcastic. 'Oh, you've had such a terrible life in a big house not having to work, staying at home, food on the table, all the luxuries you could ever want.'

Usually when he got like this at home she'd walk away, avoid the conflict. But she'd got this far. She had to show him that things had changed. And there was no going back.

She delivered her blow quickly and bluntly. 'I've been in touch with a solicitor. I've filed for divorce and you'll be hearing from them soon.' Her heart thumped wildly as she got it all out and waited for a reaction.

He looked up at the sky, at her, around them. And finally, he got it. He understood.

He stomped around to the other side of the car. 'Well, I hope you've got a good one; you'll need it.'

He was threatening her, but she wasn't scared. She'd never felt afraid of him. He'd just got into her head and made her feel like she would never be able to have her own life without him.

'You don't know how lucky you are!' He jabbed his finger in her direction.

She held her head up high the whole time he fixed her with a glare that usually made her crumble and admit defeat.

Yes, she knew she was lucky. She was lucky to have finally left him.

Lucky to be free.

23

FAYE

Faye set down a jug of mint sauce on the kitchen table at Bonnie's cottage. 'Wherever has Margot got to?' Her tummy grumbled at the enticing smell of the roast lamb that filled the room. 'I thought she said she'd be here by 7 p.m.'

The curtains had been left tied back and when she stepped closer to the window she spotted their friend. 'She's here!' She was about to knock on the glass to get Margot's attention, but Margot was talking to someone.

Bonnie came up behind her and both of them huddled next to the window.

'Oh, he's handsome,' said Bonnie. 'Do you think he's asking for directions?'

'Does that happen a lot?'

'Oh yes, Howard always found it fun to help people out. I didn't mind but sometimes it got a bit tedious.'

But when the car roared into life and Margot turned to face them, they saw the expression on her face and they both knew that was no lost soul in the car.

They raced to the door at the same time as the car tyres let out a screech when the man took off. Faye would put money on him being Margot's husband, Perry.

Bonnie ushered Margot inside. 'Was that him?' She'd obviously come to the same conclusion.

'He knows where I am.' In a daze Margot came inside. It was as if her legs were barely working as Bonnie led her to the table and sat her down. 'All this time I've been waiting to get another email or for him to make a move.'

'Well now he has.' Bonnie unbuttoned Margot's coat for her. 'So that's done, over with. And you're safe with us.'

Faye made a mug of tea for Margot and set it in front of her and Bonnie turned down the oven.

'The dinner,' said Margot. 'I'm ruining dinner.'

'Nobody is ruining anything,' said Bonnie firmly.

'The dinner will be fine. The potatoes are still in the oven, the lamb is covered and ready. Now tell us what happened exactly?'

Faye covered up the mint sauce as Margot recalled the confrontation with Perry, the way she stood her ground, that she told her husband she had left him and she'd been in touch with a solicitor. She was shaking and Faye encouraged her to sip the tea and by the time she'd finished it and Bonnie had begun to dish up their dinner she finally managed a small smile.

'I didn't get in the car,' Margot told them both although it sounded like she was telling herself as much as anyone else. 'I didn't go with him. Even up until today I didn't know what I'd do if...'

Faye put an arm around her shoulders and only let go when dinner was on the table and she felt Margot's body finally relax.

Dinner and conversation were exactly what they needed. Margot was in shock after her encounter but as they talked she realised this moment had been coming and now that it was out of the way, she could keep moving forwards.

Eventually they moved on from talking about Perry to chatting about Margot's interview, a topic

Faye knew would put a smile back on her friend's face despite her husband's behaviour.

Margot told them all about the people she'd met, the fun she'd had, the challenges, her nerves.

'Even if I don't get the job,' she said with a smile, 'today was a day to remember.' Margot raised her glass. They'd opened a bottle of red to share. 'To new beginnings and to new friends,' she said.

'To new beginnings and new friends,' Bonnie and Faye chorused.

'I know we're talking about brighter things,' said Margot, 'but can I just say that until today I'd never stood up to Perry like that, unless you count the time he talked about sending the boys away to boarding school. I think I got so busy raising a family and doing the right thing that I didn't see how bad he'd got until it was too late. Half the time I thought I was being ridiculous; some of the time I told myself just what he told me today: that I was lucky. And I was. He was never violent; I never wanted for anything in the financial sense. But I was lost and it took my boys leaving home for me to really see it.'

Faye had known that her distraction, the talk about the interview, would've eventually given way to more talk about Perry. Margot needed to get it all out and Faye was glad that she felt comfortable to do so in the safety of the cottage.

'You're a strong person, Margot,' Bonnie assured her as Faye cleared the plates away and dismissed Bonnie's effort to help.

The plates still in her hands before she reached the sink, Faye beamed. 'I bet it felt good to tell him no and to watch him drive away.'

'It really did. This is it. I am never going back to my marriage.' She looked at both of them, determination on her face as she removed her wedding ring and platinum engagement ring that had been on the fourth finger of her left hand for far too long already. 'I'm going to get a job,' she said firmly. 'I'm going to make my own money; I won't have to answer to anyone.' She said it with such conviction it was clear she was no longer going to put up with the life she'd had before.

And then Margot turned to Bonnie. 'Your Howard was so kind to me. He never told me to get out of my marriage, not in so many words, but somehow it was better that way. The things he said helped me see it for what it was, helped me see I could have more, that I was worth more.'

'That's my Howard.' Bonnie smiled.

Faye sat down at the table again. 'You must miss him so much.'

'Every single day.'

'I know he's missed at the bookshop,' said Margot. 'People mention him often. And we all miss him at book club,' Margot told her.

'He'd always be there,' Faye added, 'every week. He'd always have his pyjamas on apart from when you guys were travelling. He said that coming to the club was like being a part of a midnight mystery, an adventure. He said he felt like a character in an Enid Blyton book.'

Bonnie seemed to love that. 'Does the book club have anyone else like Howard?'

'There was only ever one Howard,' said Margot.

Faye told Bonnie a bit about some of the other members in the Midnight Book Club and Bonnie told them about some of the book clubs Howard had tried over the years, including the one he'd gone to every Tuesday and came home complaining they talked about whisky more than stories. And as they talked Faye exchanged a look with Margot. Bonnie was very chatty these days and she was taking more of an interest in what went on beyond her cottage. Getting her to the bookshop was going to be a challenge but she was taking small steps all the time, like the painting she hadn't been able to work on and then suddenly found she was able to start, like not inviting them in when they first knocked on her door and now forming a wonderful friendship. Bonnie was changing and every little step was a win.

'Are you going to be all right?' Bonnie asked Margot when it was time to pull on their coats and call it a night. 'You don't think Perry will be lurking near your accommodation, do you?'

Margot looked like that was exactly what she suspected. 'He doesn't like to lose at anything, but he has a job that means more to him than anything – that's why he was in a suit and why he was here in the evening; he wouldn't want to take much time off work.'

'But you *are* worried?' Bonnie pressed.

'Didn't you say you had one of those Ring doorbell things at the house in Berkshire?' Faye asked.

'We do, but it was only set up on Perry's phone, not mine.'

She didn't need to say that it would be to keep tabs on her. Faye worked that out for herself. 'Shame. That would've come in handy to know whether he'd gone back home or not.'

'I know for certain that I didn't note the address of my accommodation on my phone. The only way he knew I was in the town is because I'd made some notes about Driftwick Bay.' She explained all about the cloud, and not realising she had saved the information there rather than to her device.

'Are you absolutely sure you didn't put the accommodation address in your notes?' Bonnie said, worried.

'Yes, I checked when I was in the bathroom earlier,' she admitted a little sheepishly.

Bonnie let out a sigh of relief. 'Thank goodness for that. I was thinking I'd cooked a dodgy lamb; you were in there for quite a while.'

Margot laughed and hugged Bonnie, thanking her for her company and a delicious meal.

Faye hugged Bonnie too but had an idea for Margot. 'Why don't you come back to the caravan park with me?'

'I couldn't impose on you like that.'

'Of course you could. Plus it means I don't have to walk by myself. There's an extra bedroom. You'll feel a lot better if you're not alone tonight.'

Bonnie added, 'And I'd feel much better if you went with Faye, Margot.'

* * *

Faye had heard Margot get up during the night – the static caravan didn't have the thickest of walls either internally or externally – and she'd been sound asleep when Faye headed off for her cleaning job. By the time she got back there was a little note on the table from Margot to say that she had gone to see her solicitor again but she would meet her at Bonnie's cottage later.

Faye had some lunch and then got on her bike to cycle to Driftwick Bay. She wasn't sure, if she stayed much longer, whether she would keep using the bike. She could barely feel her fingers they were so numb with cold by the time she stopped at the cycle rack on the hill.

When something soft brushed against her arm as she bent over to do up the lock around the bicycle frame and steel post she turned to see Midas looking at her innocently, his tail wagging.

'Hey, you.' She knew full well she'd look up and see Theo too.

'Hey, to you too,' said Theo before she could say a word. 'You're putting the rest of us to shame with all your cycling up and down this hill, you know. Mum was talking about it yesterday, telling people in the bookshop. Cathy was talking about you in the bakery.'

'Now that's the sort of local gossip I actually don't mind.' And for the first time since her sister had done what Faye considered the unthinkable she didn't feel got at, she felt almost unreachable, like she'd taken a step back and the same things wouldn't get to her the way they once had. It was crazy to think that of course, but perhaps it was the magic of Dorset.

'How are things in that regard?' He had Midas sit at the kerb before they crossed over the road. 'The gossip I mean.'

They carried on their way. 'I love my sister but I'm beginning to accept that she will never change. I don't even know the full story about her getting back together with Mark, and I don't think I want to.'

'Maybe it's time to make yourself a priority,' he suggested.

She almost asked whether it was selfish to think that way, but she'd had a long talk with her dad about it and after all these years she was beginning to see that thinking of herself was only fair. In the same way Margot deserved a life away from Perry, Faye knew she needed the separation from her sister.

'I will start putting myself first,' she assured him, 'but it's still hard to do.' She stopped before they reached the bookshop, not ready to go inside yet.

'I get it. Sibling relationships are powerful. It's hard to admit when they aren't working. It's not like a friend – you'd walk away a lot easier if a friend behaved that way, wouldn't you?'

'I suppose, when you put it that way, yes. I think we put up with more when it's family.'

'So, what will happen when you're back in Australia?' He looked good today, a dark navy waterproof jacket bulky around his frame to ward off the autumnal chill, his strong hands exposed to the elements as he held Midas's lead with one and fussed the dog's head with the other.

'I'm not sure. And I don't really know when I'll go back either.'

'But you live there.' Did she detect hope in his voice? 'What about work?'

'Hairdressing is kind of mobile.' She definitely detected a smile now – just a small one that wouldn't quite give him away unless you were looking carefully. 'I can make it work here too.'

He pondered what she'd said. 'You know it gets really cold in winter here, don't you?'

'I know.' And she didn't care. 'I think it might be the right thing for me, at least for a while. I'm not sure whether it will be permanent, but I'll go with the flow.'

'Well, it will be nice to see a bit more of you.'

She wasn't sure what to say to that as they went inside the bookshop.

'Mum looks a bit frazzled,' said Theo. 'I'm just going to go and make sure she's all right.'

Faye sat down in one of the little nooks and fussed over Midas until Theo came back over.

'Is Iris okay?' she asked him.

'She's stressing. She's only had the bookshop open half the time it was operating when Howard was around. Bonnie insists it's okay – she was on the phone to her just then – but Mum doesn't want to let her down.'

'I think she's doing well to manage on her own.'

'I'll tell her you said so.' He nudged her and the touch felt electric.

'What's in the bag?' Faye asked him as he shrugged off a backpack.

'A few things for Midas. I'm off to visit my sister for a couple of days and Mum is dog-sitting. Which I feel terrible about now.' He looked over at Iris again and frowned.

'You don't want to take Midas with you?'

'I could've done but felt bad as he's needed here tomorrow. So it's a bit of a catch-22 I suppose.'

He really was incredibly kind and thoughtful. It

reminded her of the way he'd been at school especially the time he told her that her skirt was tucked into her knickers when she came out of the girls' toilets. She almost emitted a giggle at something she'd forgotten about until now.

And as Theo handed over the bag to his mum and fussed over Midas as if he was going to be gone for a month rather than a couple of days, the second part of her master plan presented itself. This was perfect. And so before Theo left she took him aside and shared her idea with him. And then she told Iris.

All she had to do now was let Margot know and it would be all systems go.

Maybe, just maybe they could get Bonnie to go back inside Driftwick Bay Books, and if they did then she might see that even though Howard had gone his legacy hadn't. The bookshop had become a part of him like the book club had become a part of Faye after her auntie died, and sometimes holding on to something so special ended up bringing more meaning to your life than you ever thought possible.

She kept everything crossed that this would work.

24

BONNIE

Faye and Margot were impressed with her painting when Bonnie showed them both. They'd been late to come over today, having taken advantage of the dry weather by doing a circular walk along Lulworth Cove beach and then up and around West Lulworth village. They'd stopped at an inn for lunch too, before heading back to their accommodations to read. Bonnie had almost wished she'd said yes to the invitation to join them on the walk or for lunch, but she'd made her excuses. She'd do it soon though, wouldn't she? Howard would be so disappointed if she didn't. And yet, her feet kept her inside her cottage, within the walls that held so much comfort. She might not have lived here all that long but it already felt like home and Howard's presence was still around her with his books and his coats and shoes, and a couple of his flat caps.

'It looks so real.' Faye marvelled at the painting. 'The hill looks as steep as it really is, the red telephone box library is there, and you've captured the bookshop perfectly. You're a real artist, Bonnie.'

'And you sound like you're writing a review for the newspaper,' said Bonnie.

'She's right,' Margot said. 'It's brilliant. I wish I was so talented.'

Maybe it was better than she thought. And the bookshop really did look exactly like it was in real life. Which made her feel even worse for what she'd done a couple of hours ago.

That morning she'd finally made a call to the developer. She'd just taken another call from Iris who was still fretting over the smallest of decisions and Bonnie felt terrible at leaving her to manage it all on her own. And given she wasn't going to work there herself to help Iris out, it seemed like the only option she had was to get going with a sale.

What she'd wanted, however, when she made the call was to merely check that the price the developer had offered Howard last time still stood. Then she was going to think about it some more. But they were persuasive; they'd steered the conversation so that before she knew it they were coming to the bookshop in the morning and would meet her or her assistant there and would certainly provide an up-to-date valuation.

That hadn't been what Bonnie wanted at all.

But she'd made the call. So this was all her fault.

Had she made a terrible, terrible mistake?

'Tell me how it went with the solicitor,' said Bonnie to Margot, eager to put the bookshop out of her mind for now. She still hadn't told Iris to expect a visitor tomorrow.

Margot let out a breath. 'The wheels are in motion. It's really happening.'

'Good.' Bonnie nodded firmly before she tidied away some of the paints she'd left on the table and a dry brush on the shelf of the easel.

She picked up the jar of water she'd rinsed off her brushes in and forgotten to empty earlier and when she looked up both women were huddled near the back door, their gazes fixed outside. 'Whatever are you two whispering about?'

Faye's head whipped round. 'Nothing. We're trying to see any of the same view from the photograph.'

Bonnie laughed as she waltzed away with the jar

of water and called over her shoulder, 'Best of luck with that when it's dark.'

When she emerged, Faye and Margot were sitting at the table and, as previously agreed, they were looking over the menu for a Chinese takeaway a few miles away.

'Have you checked they deliver?' Bonnie used kitchen towel to dry the outside of the jar she'd had paint water in.

'They deliver.' Faye and Margot were running through suggestions and they all sounded delicious. Bonnie never minded cooking, in fact she liked hosting, but a takeaway this evening would be a real treat.

Once they'd placed the order, Bonnie got some plates ready, the cutlery, and some napkins. 'I don't think I've had Chinese food in months, possibly years.'

'Hmm... spring rolls are my favourite,' said Margot.

'Crispy duck with plum sauce,' said Faye.

'Stop it, both of you, my mouth is watering.' And she was laughing. It was a sound she'd forgotten all about, and yet it was beginning to come more naturally in recent days.

When there was a knock at the door some ten minutes later Bonnie got up. 'Well, that was quick.'

And the girls must be hungry because they were lingering behind her as if ready to snatch the bags inside quickly to devour the food.

But it wasn't the takeaway at all.

'Iris... everything all right?' It didn't look like it. The woman seemed frazzled. Was this another worry about the bookshop? Or had the developer shown up already and dropped her in it for making the call?

'I'm in a bind,' said Iris, stood on the step with Midas at her side.

'Come inside,' Bonnie urged.

'I won't, but thank you. I just really need to get a move on.'

Bonnie reached a hand out to fuss Midas on the head. 'Iris, tell me what's happened.' Sometimes the woman really could take her time to get to the point. But Bonnie felt relief that if this was about the developer she probably would've called rather than visited.

'It's my mother-in-law; she isn't well and I really need to go to her. I think I'll have to stay the night to make sure she's okay, but I have Midas, and she's in a flat. She isn't allowed a dog.'

'Okay, take a breath,' said Bonnie. She'd have to get her a paper bag to breathe into in a minute if she didn't calm down. 'Where's Theo?'

'He's away. And I'm looking after Midas.' She smiled at the girls who had stepped closer to hear what was going on. 'There's more... The bookshop is locked up at the front, but there's a problem with the rear door. It won't lock. I've called a twenty-four-hour locksmith and he'll come out as soon as he can, but I can't leave it like that.'

Faye picked up her coat and pushed one arm through a sleeve, then the other. 'Leave it with us, Iris. We can migrate down to the bookshop. We'll help you.'

'We have takeaway coming,' said Bonnie desperately. She didn't want to walk down the hill. She didn't want to be stopped and asked questions, looked at like she was a widow, the word that fitted but a word she couldn't bear to say. And she definitely didn't want to go anywhere near the bookshop.

'Would you consider bringing the takeaway to the bookshop?' Iris pleaded. She really did look stressed and Bonnie didn't know what to do.

Except deep down she did. She couldn't leave the bookshop unlocked. She was the owner after all, now that Howard had gone. And what if vandals broke in? What if they made a mess of it? Destroyed the books and everything in their wake? Oh, she couldn't bear the thought of that. Right now the developers were the least of her worries because Howard would've been so upset if something like that had ever happened.

'The bookshop is my responsibility,' said Bonnie, surprising herself as the words left her mouth. 'It's not for you to worry about, Iris. You go to your mother-in-law and we will deal with the shop and the locksmith.'

Margot took Midas's lead. 'And you can leave Midas with us. What are friends for?'

Iris thanked them all, handed the keys to the shop over to Bonnie, and reminded them that there were some treats for Midas in a bag back at the shop as well as a couple of his favourite chew toys.

Iris left and Faye offered to wait for the takeaway while the others went ahead, but the takeaway arrived as they were pulling on their coats.

'We'll need plates,' said Faye and Bonnie found a few plus cutlery to put into a bag.

Bonnie was going through the motions, trying not to think about the enormity of setting foot inside the bookshop. Howard would want her to do this; he wouldn't want his bookshop put at unnecessary risk with a door that wouldn't lock. But that didn't mean it was going to be easy.

'Bonnie,' Faye urged. 'Come on, let's go.'

But she couldn't move. 'I can't.'

'You can,' said Margot. 'We're both with you.'

'No, you don't understand.' She looked at them, these kind women, these friends Howard had brought into her life. 'I called them.'

'The locksmith?' asked Faye, confused.

'No... the developer.'

Margot's face fell. 'What did you tell them?'

'They're coming to do a valuation. In the morning. It was arranged before I could say what I really wanted.'

'And what's that?' Faye asked.

'I... I don't know. I thought I'd find out if the valuation is the same. Then take it from there.' She didn't miss the look of disappointment on Margot's face, on Faye's. In the short time they'd been here they'd fallen in love with the bookshop as much as the locals had. They had, after all, known just what it meant to Howard.

'I've messed up.' She slumped down on the stool by the phone. 'What have I done?'

Margot crouched down and put her hands over Bonnie's. 'You haven't done anything wrong. We all understand how hard this is for you. Now, one step at a time, eh?'

'One step at a time,' she repeated.

Margot got back up again and picked up the bag filled with eating paraphernalia. 'Step one is to help Iris.'

'Help Iris,' Bonnie repeated. It felt like the only thing she could do.

Faye took the keys to the shop, Bonnie took Midas's lead, and they all filed out of the cottage.

Midas nudged Bonnie's hand with his head as she waited for Faye to close the gate behind them and, by her side, he escorted her down the hill into Driftwick Bay and towards the shop she hadn't set foot in since her husband died.

When they arrived at the bookshop the lighting was down low and Bonnie stayed on the pavement with Midas while Faye opened up.

She could do this. She could step over the threshold.

And now she was no longer thinking about it or worrying because Midas had taken the decision out of her hands and was leading the way.

She stepped inside and the warmth embraced her. She knew it wasn't possible, but the smell reminded her of Howard. Perhaps it was the aroma of books, a scent she'd always associated with the man she'd loved so dearly. A man she missed so much.

Margot closed the door behind them and over in

the story corner laid out the blanket Bonnie had thought to pack around the plates. Faye was sorting out the food and Bonnie, well Bonnie was taking it all in until Midas shuffled and she realised she still hadn't taken off his lead.

'Sorry, boy.' She removed it. 'There you go, you're free. But no eating the food.'

'I've got the bag of treats,' said Margot emerging from the back. She pulled one out for Midas so he had something while they sat down to their takeaway.

'I feel bad eating in here,' said Bonnie, daring to look around them as they began to enjoy their food. She hadn't thought she was hungry what with the guilt over her phone call, the dread of tomorrow.

'Let's think of ourselves as part of an adventure,' Faye suggested, 'like Howard did when he came to book club.'

'That sounds like a good idea,' Margot agreed. 'And we won't make a mess, we'll be careful.'

'He wouldn't be happy with me,' said Bonnie.

'Bonnie, let's just enjoy the food for now, shall we.' Margot's smile put her at ease and her thumping heart gave way to satiety and good conversation. Thinking of this as an adventure was exactly the right thing to do, and it was really, wasn't it? This was adventurous compared to the way Bonnie had been closing herself off to the world lately. Forget the developer for now, focus on tonight, focus on being here with these two very special women.

'Did Iris leave a number so you could call him?' Bonnie asked once they'd finished eating and cleared everything away. Neither Margot nor Faye had grilled her about selling up as they ate and for that Bonnie was grateful.

'Call who?' Margot asked, a paperback in her hand. She and Faye had both been looking at some of the titles on one of the book tables.

'The locksmith,' said Bonnie.

'Oh yes.' Faye took out her phone. 'Good point. I'll message Iris and get it.'

Margot started talking about the book she had a hold of – *Eleanor Oliphant is Completely Fine*. 'I'm reading this one at the moment.' She read the wording on the back out loud, presumably for Bonnie's benefit.

Bonnie patiently listened. It did sound like a good story. She'd have to let Margot down gently. 'I don't really fancy it.'

'We have to do something while we wait,' said Faye.

And then Margot pulled her phone from one of

her back pockets and from the other took out a small rose-gold case.

'What's in there?' Bonnie asked.

'Headphones.'

'Oh, those fancy sort. Earbuds, that's what they're called, isn't it?'

'They're brand new actually.'

'Very nice,' said Bonnie.

'Try them.'

'Whatever for?'

Margot turned her phone to face Bonnie and the same title – *Eleanor Oliphant is Completely Fine* was on the screen. 'This is the audiobook version. I've been listening to it on my walks.'

'I thought you said you were reading it.'

'I am, but audiobooks are a type of reading.' She held the case out again. 'These earbuds are new. I got them in case I lost the others, so you'll be the first to try them.'

'But you're listening to it.'

'I know which chapter I'm up to – I'll use the paperback copy. I'll buy it. I wouldn't mind having it anyway.'

'I don't know, I don't think it'll keep my interest.' And she was still getting used to simply being in the bookshop after all this time.

Margot ignored her. 'I've paired the headphones with the phone but didn't get the chance to try them out yet.'

'Paired them?'

Margot rolled her eyes. 'Would you just put them in.'

Margot was so determined that it made Bonnie realise that sitting around doing nothing but think about how Howard was no longer here any more, or how she'd alerted the developers to a potential sale, wasn't necessarily a good thing. She needed a distraction.

Bonnie pushed each earbud into her ears.

'Volume okay?' Margot asked.

'Volume is fine.' The narrator was going through the opening credits.

Margot laughed. 'You're shouting.'

Bonnie removed an earbud. 'What?'

'Just put them in, go sit in the armchair and give it twenty minutes.'

'Very well.' Bonnie was pretty sure she shouted that too given Faye's look across the room from the window where she was probably looking out for the locksmith.

Bonnie did give it twenty minutes. In fact, before she knew it, almost an hour had passed. Midas sat by her side. She fussed over him, and she got absorbed in the story as he went to sleep. The book was riveting. It wasn't long before she was fully immersed; the locksmith could've come and gone without her even realising.

She was about to take her headphones out and stop so she could go to the toilet, but she realised she didn't need to. She could keep listening.

She used the toilet out the back and when she went back into the bookshop both girls were sitting just like Howard would have done, each with a book in their laps, looking up briefly and then straight back down at the page. There was something comforting about doing this among friends. Reading was a solitary activity, but there was companionship and a connection. And even though she might never appreciate books in the same way as Howard did, with darkness surrounding the shop and the time creeping towards the midnight hour, on an adventure herself, it struck her why he'd loved the Midnight Book Club so much. It was a shared love of something and the bonds of friendship that did it.

She settled back down to listen to more of the story and when she eventually noticed Faye moving about, her watch told her that it was almost midnight.

'It's good, isn't it,' said Margot when Bonnie took out the earbuds and went over to where she was sitting.

'I'm hooked.' The book was quirky, sometimes sad, but filled with hope. 'I need to know what'll happen next.' And she'd quite forgotten how uncomfortable she'd felt first stepping inside the bookshop.

'You can get the audiobook on your iPad at home. I'll help you sort it out.'

'Thank you.' Howard would be delighted she was even interested and to have found the joy of listening to a story right here in his bookshop felt like a sign that maybe everything was going to be okay.

'Where *is* the locksmith?' Bonnie asked when she remembered the real reason they were here hadn't been to eat or to enjoy the books. She'd been quite distracted, hadn't she? 'And whatever is Faye doing?'

'It's Wednesday,' Faye called out from the story corner. She'd set up a laptop on the low table that usually had kids' books spread out on it. 'I'll put everything back as it was afterwards, don't worry.'

She caught her breath. 'You're holding the Midnight Book Club here, tonight?'

'Any second now,' said Faye.

She was about to ask more questions, suggest she

got out of the way, when suddenly a voice came from the laptop.

Bonnie peeked tentatively around the side of the screen. There was a woman there, then someone else popped up in another rectangle.

'Hello, Sarah. Hello, Joel,' said Faye.

'How many tonight?' the woman who must be Sarah asked.

'Six of us,' said Faye.

'You can sit here.' Margot ushered Bonnie to one of the three chairs they'd sat in earlier to eat.

'We have Bonnie with us tonight,' said Faye to the other attendees.

'Hello, Bonnie!' came Sarah's greeting followed by another, the man this time, and then the next person who popped up, someone called Winston. Each name was beside the person on camera.

'Hello.' Bonnie didn't want to be rude, but this was so odd, so unlike anything she'd done before.

Faye smiled brightly. 'Bonnie, tonight is a very special Midnight Book Club, because we decided that rather than focusing on a book, tonight's session is especially for you.'

It was clear from the faces on the laptop screen and Margot's expression that everyone else knew this already.

'It's wonderful to see you all!' said Faye, taking the heat off Bonnie but not for long. She rested a hand on Bonnie's shoulder. 'As you know Bonnie was the love of Howard's life.'

'Apart from books and his beloved bookshop!' Winston announced and it had a few people open-mouthed but Bonnie started to laugh.

'That is so true,' she told him, tears in her eyes.

'Your Howard was one of a kind,' said Sarah, who was quite a bit older than Bonnie. 'When I lost my husband, Howard didn't give me the usual platitudes, he gave me his phone number in case I needed to talk.'

'I'm sorry for your loss,' said Bonnie, who knew how this woman had probably felt. 'I appreciate that that's what everyone says, but I am.'

'Thank you, Bonnie.'

'Howard thought a lot of you. All of you.' She took in each of the faces, including those beside her in the bookshop now. 'He loved this book club.'

'Howard always cheered me up,' Sarah told her. 'I'm wheelchair-bound now and some days I feel so sorry for myself. I can't leave the house. Howard would make me laugh when he turned up in different pyjamas every time. I would make sure my carers put me in a top that looked like a shirt but he said it was more fun in PJs.' She laughed. 'After that I put on my best nighties for book club.'

Bonnie felt a warmth spread through her that Howard had touched these people's lives. She listened to Joel talk about Howard's passion for books, how he was quite convincing when he felt strongly that a story was important to read, how some of them had read books they never would've picked up if it hadn't been for Howard. Winston talked about how Howard had looked into local libraries in his area and sent him an email with all the information, including step-by-step instructions on how to join when he hadn't been able to do it quite as easily as he'd thought he would.

'I hear you're not much of a reader,' Winston said to Bonnie after he told her that he and Howard had the most disagreements about what made a good book than any others in the group.

Bonnie found herself responding with: 'I'm not, but this evening I started an audiobook. *Eleanor Oliphant is Completely Fine...*'

And for the next half an hour all the talk was about that book, Sarah piping up with comments about it because she'd loved it, Winston was adding it to something called a TBR pile, and Joel said it sounded like they should all tune in next week having given it a go.

Not only was she in the bookshop right now but Bonnie felt drawn in to this group in a way she'd never seen coming. And when the session came to an end and Faye closed down her laptop Bonnie wrapped her in a big hug, then the same for Margot. 'You two are wonderful human beings. Thank you from the bottom of my heart for what you did not only tonight but ever since you knocked on my door.'

'You are so very welcome,' said Margot.

'Thank you for not telling anyone about this place,' said Bonnie. 'Selling it, I mean.' She didn't miss the look of disappointment on both their faces.

'Will you come and meet the developer in the morning then?' Margot asked. She was being kind, accepting things the way they were, letting Bonnie know that this would be her decision.

'We could be here with you,' Faye offered. 'Howard always found them a bit overbearing. I think I'd feel better if we were with you.'

Margot agreed. 'Yes, definitely. Howard would want that. If only so they don't try to low-ball you.'

'I'd appreciate that, both of you, thank you.' But being here, in the bookshop, actually participating in the Midnight Book Club, made her feel closer to

Howard all over again and she knew he wouldn't want her to rush into anything. And he definitely wouldn't want to let the locals down.

She took a deep breath before she said, 'You can both help me tell them to... go to hell!' She pumped her fist in the air at the powerful words she wouldn't usually use.

'Really?' Margot leapt up. 'You mean it?'

'Wait,' said Bonnie, palms out in front of her to halt the excitement. 'I still might sell, eventually, but I've decided that if I do then it will be to someone who wants to run this as a bookshop. So tomorrow we tell the developer that it's time to stop visiting, to stop sending letters. I always feel it's better to tell someone to their face, don't you?' And already she felt more powerful that they were going to do this although she didn't want to do it without her new friends by her side.

'That sounds like a really good plan,' said Faye.

Margot told her, 'I'll get *Eleanor Oliphant* onto your iPad first thing tomorrow.'

'Oh no, you can come to my cottage and do that now. I'm going to need to listen while I lie in bed. I'll need to find out more and I shall carry on when I wake up in the morning. Unless, of course, you need to wait for the locksmith to fix the door that doesn't really need fixing.'

She enjoyed the way their mouths fell open as they prepared to leave the shop via the front entrance. Halfway through book club, she'd nipped to the downstairs bathroom again and as she did so she'd checked the back door, wondering whether to perhaps move something in front of it in case somebody came inside without them hearing. And the lock had worked perfectly. She'd known then that these girls and Iris and Theo as well as Midas had hatched this plan to get her out of the cottage and here to Driftwick Bay Books. It was another thing that convinced her she shouldn't rush into getting rid of the shop. She'd take her time, make the right decision. Because she was a part of this town; she really was.

And she couldn't have been more grateful for their subterfuge.

'No?' she asked, still amused by their guilty and flabbergasted expressions. 'Come on then, up to the cottage we go.' She took Midas on his lead and with a big smile on her face, left the bookshop to walk up the hill.

And as they did so the stars up above seemed to twinkle that little bit more.

25

SEVEN MONTHS LATER

Faye

Faye didn't mind finishing late at the salon now spring was here. The winter had been cold, long, and dark but spring in England, with its long days that promised to get even longer in the summer, was something else.

That day in October when Theo came to pick Midas up from the bookshop after his trip away, Faye had been so excited to tell him the plan to help Bonnie had worked. They'd got her down to Driftwick Bay Books, they'd got her inside the shop, and more than that, she'd stayed a while and realised that it could be a comfort rather than something to push away now that Howard had gone. She also told him about the developers and how Bonnie herself had been the one to face them the morning after they ate their takeaway in the shop.

'This bookshop is not for sale now, or ever,' Bonnie had said boldly to the developer, who was dressed in a pinstripe, slightly-too-tight suit. 'Driftwick Bay Books is a part of this town and I'm afraid you're just going to have to build your luxury condo or whatever it is, elsewhere.' And before the man could argue his case she added, 'Now, please leave my bookshop.'

Margot and Faye had at least waited for the door to close behind him before they let out a big cheer. And although Bonnie hadn't been quite ready to face customers, Faye and Margot, along with Iris a couple of days later, had run the bookshop together, Bonnie out back listening to some of the banter, the sound of customers coming in and out, this shop Howard had saved and brought back to the community.

As Faye had talked to Theo that day he'd stayed quite quiet, his gaze drifting away from her now and again, settling on Midas instead. He never usually had a problem making eye contact or chatting to her, but in that moment he was so unsure of himself she hadn't been surprised when he asked her out on a date.

Of course she'd said yes. And she'd told him that she'd had a major crush on him when they were at school, which gave him a bit of confidence that perhaps she liked him a lot now too.

Faye's dad had sold the business in Queensland and moved back to Dorset for the foreseeable future. Faye had vacated her apartment after a brief trip over to Australia during which she'd put her belongings into storage. She'd caught up with her mother and with Steph while she was there, but no longer did she find seeing either of them stressful because she'd stopped assuming responsibility for anyone's behaviour other than her own. Steph was still with Mark, but Faye hadn't asked for any details. In fact, the only thing Steph had said about him was that they were moving in together. Faye had congratulated her. She hadn't tried to advise or talk to her about what she was doing. She didn't ask about how Brad was taking it either. Brad had done her a favour because without him running away and breaking off their engagement she'd never have met Theo. Theo, the man she trusted more than any man she'd ever been with. She got the feeling they would never hurt one another and these days he was very happy to let her cut his hair.

After her visit to Australia she came back to England and almost immediately started the job at a salon in Dorchester. It was a full-time role covering a maternity leave. She wasn't sure whether it would lead to a job there eventually, but come summer when Theo had his long school holidays, she was taking him to Australia so he could see what all the fuss was about. When they were there she'd sort through her belongings in storage, see what to keep, what to toss, and for the six weeks they were out there they had a house-sit. By some sort of magic, a house-sit in Queensland near the water-sports business had come up. They'd have to look after two dogs for the duration, but Theo said it would help him to not miss Midas quite so much. And Midas would be busy anyway because Bonnie and Iris would look after him between them.

Faye was still running the Midnight Book Club each week and they'd had two new members join up: forty-year-old Zac and sixty-two-year-old Bridget. Both from the Northern Hemisphere, they'd so far turned up every week and slowly Faye was getting to know them. She couldn't see herself ever stopping the book club, no matter where she was in the world. She would always be a part of it. There had been some talk about reverting to calling it The Seaside Book Club again and perhaps changing the time but it hadn't felt right to anyone. Auntie Clare had founded the club, Howard had renamed it, and their lives had changed because of both of those things. Besides, just as Howard said it did, it felt like an adventure taking part in the book club when the sky was dark, the world was quiet, and most other people were sound asleep.

Today, after she'd met Theo on a gloriously warm and sunny May evening for a long walk with Midas, he wanted to know whether she'd be patient enough to teach him how to paddleboard so that by the time they went to Australia he wouldn't be totally inexperienced. She'd assured him that she was very patient and not a bad teacher and she couldn't wait for him to embrace a love of the water just like she did.

Following their walk, they made for Bonnie's cottage and when Bonnie opened the door she rolled her eyes as Scout, her own dog, leapt out from behind her legs and jumped up at her visitors, no matter what she said.

'He'll learn,' said Theo.

'Early days,' Faye agreed as she gave Bonnie a big hug.

Faye wondered whether Midas might think he was a role model for Scout as he trotted inside the cottage and Scout, a much smaller version of Midas, followed after him.

26

—————

MARGOT

Margot was in her compact Toyota Aygo driving from London down to Dorset. She'd finished five days on and had three days off, and she couldn't wait to get to Driftwick Bay and see Faye and Bonnie, her girls as she thought of them, even though they were all from a different generation. They were true friends, just like Trinny and Bethany had once been. She was in touch with Trinny and had visited her already, and she had plans in the summer to catch up with Bethany. She hadn't told either of them the details of her marriage, the reasons why she left Perry, but perhaps she didn't need to. Perhaps they already knew. And like true friends they might not have been in touch for a long while but they'd always been there waiting, in the background.

She hadn't got the cabin crew job she'd first applied for and she'd almost talked herself out of applying for more positions. She'd wondered whether she was doing something silly, whether she thought she was better than she actually was, but Bonnie and Faye, as well as her sons, had urged her to keep on trying. She'd got another interview elsewhere, she hadn't got that position either, and then an interview with a third airline came up and it was that company who had offered her a job. She had officially been cabin crew for the last three months. So far Margot had sent her boys postcards from Copenhagen, Stockholm, Oslo, Rome, Chicago, Tokyo. And she planned to send them many more. At some point she'd take holidays to see cities and countries in more detail but with money tight right now she'd have to make do with seeing the world via work. She was getting quite the collection of photos on her phone too and soon she'd have them put into those wonderful photo books like Bonnie and Howard had done, and add to her collection for as long as she could.

She parked outside her little cottage, the same cottage she'd stayed in when she first left Berkshire.

She'd been back to the house to collect more belongings rather than just what she'd put in the storage unit. Perry, cold during their marriage, had been the same since she'd seen him that day when he turned up in the bay, and although Margot wasn't afraid of him it was better that she didn't go to the house on her own. Faye's dad had gone with her just in case, but there had been no sign of Perry and so she'd taken what she wanted and left as quickly as she could.

Perry was in touch with his sons now and then. Both said any contact was strained, but it was down to Perry to keep a relationship with them both. It wasn't something he was entitled to any more. They were adults and if he treated them the way he had for years, he might well lose them. But that was out of her control.

The cottage was warm with spring upon them. When Margot had been house hunting last October, she'd enquired with the owner of the holiday cottage about renting it for a while longer. In fact, she'd asked for a few months and the owner had agreed on twelve, which suited Margot perfectly. Once she started work she'd been able to give the boys some of their money back and now that the divorce was going through it wouldn't be long before she could pay them back fully and find her own place to buy and put down roots.

It was a glorious evening, the sun was shining and after a thank-you text came in from Sebastian for her latest postcard and she took a quick call from Alistair, thanking her for the same, she knocked on Bonnie's door. The wisteria was in full bloom, great plumes of fragrant purple flowers bordering the front door. The planters at the front had yellow tulips in them, adding a further pop of colour from the bulbs she'd planted last year.

She could already hear laughter coming from the back garden. It was the sound of a happy home. And one that the Midnight Book Club had guided her towards.

27

BONNIE

How lovely it was to have everyone here in her garden on this beautiful day, chatting and drinking Pimm's. Scout was at her side, although not for long. She hoped with enough work and training the dog would settle down – Theo had assured her that would be the case. 'Midas gnawed all my chair legs,' he'd revealed, painting Midas as no saint when he first came home with him. 'He peed everywhere too,' he'd added. So far Scout had done both of the things Theo had warned her about but the dog was great company, always happy to see her, and Bonnie loved her to bits.

Bonnie had never regretted telling the developer who had been sniffing around the bookshop that she wouldn't be selling to him. Howard would've been proud of her.

One wintry day last December, Margot and Faye had gone with her out on a boat to scatter Howard's ashes. The cove had been in sight as the girls stood next to her and she finally said goodbye to her husband. When they'd got back to the cottage, Faye had insisted she give the syrup sponge a go and, while she was making it, Margot wanted to repay the favour and start quizzing Bonnie as if she was in an interview to return to nursing. That was when Bonnie had made a surprising admission.

'Going into the bookshop again was something I never thought I would do,' she'd told them that day. 'I thought it would be too painful. That's why I closed it, why I never wanted to see it again. But going inside with you both that night and being in the place Howard adored, as well as me finding a surprising love of audiobooks, I felt closer to him than I had since the day I lost him.'

Her admission had been laced with a lot of emotion but ever since she scattered the ashes she'd got braver. She'd started to go down the hill to Driftwick Bay Books each day and eventually she even started working alongside Iris, who was very organised and very bossy. Bonnie had settled into a pattern of going in for a few hours each day. She had Scout to consider now, but it was enough to help Iris and keep things going. And it had led her to a decision. She was going to keep working there for now, and if and when the time came to sell Driftwick Bay Books she suspected she'd have Howard's blessing if she sold it on to someone who would keep it as it was, as a bookshop in the heart of the bay.

'How was work, Bonnie?' Margot asked as she tried to get Scout to sit. If her shifts permitted, Margot was one of her dog-sitters when Bonnie was working at the bookshop. Faye and Theo helped out when they could, and Bonnie also had a professional dog-sitter on hand if nobody could be with Scout, who wasn't quite ready to take with her to Driftwick Bay Books. She'd need to be considerably older for that, Bonnie suspected.

'Busy today now we've got more tourists flocking,' she told them. She'd given Iris the okay to take on an assistant over the summer if it got too much between the pair of them, but for now Bonnie would see how it went.

She left her friends sitting in the garden talking about Margot's exotic travels while she went inside for more Pimm's. On her way back from the kitchen she paused at the painting of the couple in front of the ice-cream van, the couple so in love with their future stretched out in front of them. She thought of Howard and imagined him right here with them. After all, when you lost someone, they were never really gone, were they? They were always by your side.

The bookshelves in the cottage were still filled with Howard's books. Bonnie wasn't sure she would ever want to empty them. But what she had done was got rid of those books about grief – they weren't for her, but she'd found what was. These days she was having fun going through Howard's books and when she came across the titles he'd rambled on about the most, she'd order them as an audiobook. Sometimes she'd groan out loud that the book wasn't anything like Howard had said. She'd disagree with him as if he was right there with her. She had quite the collection of titles on her iPad now, plus she was on to her second pair of headphones – the nice large kind that sat over her head and didn't come with the risk of falling out all the time – and what she loved was how she could multitask when she was listening to a story. She was a long way off doing that on a dog walk though. Right now, Scout needed her full attention. It was all part of the training, and Bonnie was enjoying it. She had purpose again. She had Scout to love, and gone were the days she hid away from the rest of the world.

When Scout came to her side and sat for once, she patted her head. 'Howard would've loved you,' she whispered to her furry friend.

She went outside again to pour more Pimm's for her guests and join in the conversation about book club. Even though she wasn't a full-fledged member she went every now and then. The Midnight Book Club still happened every week. The membership had grown, and no matter whether Faye had work the next day or not, she always ran it. Because people needed it, not just for the books, but for each other.

After all, it had worked for Howard. And it had worked for her.

* * *

MORE FROM HELEN ROLFE

Another book from Helen Rolfe, *I'll Be Home for Christmas*, is available to order now here: https://mybook.to/HomeChristmasBackAd

ABOUT THE AUTHOR

Helen Rolfe is the author of many bestselling contemporary women's fiction titles, set in different locations from the Cotswolds to New York. She lives in Hertfordshire with her husband and children.

Download your exclusive bonus content from Helen Rolfe here:

Visit Helen's website: www.helenjrolfe.com

Follow Helen on social media here:

instagram.com/helen_j_rolfe

facebook.com/helenrolfeauthor

tiktok.com/@helenrolfebooks

ALSO BY HELEN ROLFE

Heritage Cove Series

Coming Home to Heritage Cove

Christmas at the Little Waffle Shack

Winter at Mistletoe Gate Farm

Summer at the Twist and Turn Bakery

Finding Happiness at Heritage View

Christmas Nights at the Star and Lantern

New York Ever After Series

Snowflakes and Mistletoe at the Inglenook Inn

Christmas at the Little Knitting Box

Wedding Bells on Madison Avenue

Christmas Miracles at the Little Log Cabin

Moonlight and Mistletoe at the Christmas Wedding

Christmas Promises at the Garland Street Markets

Family Secrets at the Inglenook Inn

Little Woodville Cottage Series

Christmas at Snowdrop Cottage

Summer at Forget-Me-Not Cottage

The Skylarks Series

Welcome to Whistlestop River

Written in the Stars

Something in the Air

Standalone Novels

The Year That Changed Us

The Best Days of Our Lives

So This is Christmas

The Sweet Life Café

The Seaside Book Club

I'll Be Home for Christmas

Boldwood

Boldwood Books is an award-winning fiction publishing company seeking out the best stories from around the world.

Find out more at www.boldwoodbooks.com

Join our reader community for brilliant books, competitions and offers!

Follow us
@BoldwoodBooks
@TheBoldBookClub

Sign up to our weekly deals newsletter

https://bit.ly/BoldwoodBNewsletter